The waiter had described Susan Wright as "average" looking

She wasn't. "Damned pretty" was more accurate.

"Can I help you?" she asked.

He walked over to the desk. "Whitaker Lewis. We talked briefly at the restaurant last night."

"Yes, I remember." She cocked her head and smiled, changing from "damned pretty" to "beautiful."

"Look, I apologize for barging in like this, but I have a confession to make. I asked the waiter about you. He said you're no longer married."

That statement seemed to fluster her. "No, my husband died several years ago. Why?"

"I was wondering—would you like to take a walk? I haven't had much of a chance to look around the town. Seeing it with a beautiful woman would be better than seeing it on my own."

She blushed. "Are you asking me out on a date, Mr. Lewis?"

"Trying to, Mrs. Wright, but apparently not doing a very good job of it."

"I appreciate the compliment and the invitation, but I don't really know you. I don't go out with men I don't know."

ABOUT THE AUTHOR

Fay Robinson lives in Alabama, where she enjoys gardening and playing with her Jack Russell terrier, Dex. Her first Superromance novel, *A Man Like Mac*, won the 2001 RITA® Award—the most prestigious award in romance publishing—for best first novel. Watch for her next book, *Christmas on Snowbird Mountain*, in November of this year.

You can e-mail Fay at fayrobinson@mindspring.com or write her at P.O. Box 240, Waverly, AL 36879-0240. She invites you to visit her Web site at http://www.fayrobinson.com or to check out the Friends and Links section at http://www.eHarlequin.com.

Books by Fay Robinson

HARLEQUIN SUPERROMANCE

911—A MAN LIKE MAC
961—COMING HOME TO YOU
1012—MR. AND MRS. WRONG

The Notorious Mrs. Wright

Fay Robinson

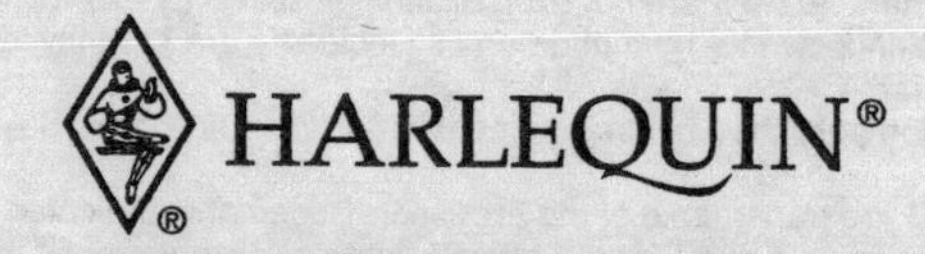

TORONTO • NEW YORK • LONDON
AMSTERDAM • PARIS • SYDNEY • HAMBURG
STOCKHOLM • ATHENS • TOKYO • MILAN • MADRID
PRAGUE • WARSAW • BUDAPEST • AUCKLAND

ISBN 0-373-71068-2

THE NOTORIOUS MRS. WRIGHT

This edition published by arrangement with Harlequin Books S.A.

Visit us at www.eHarlequin.com

Printed in U.S.A.

Dedication

For my mother, who was fearless.

And for my husband, Jackie,
who chauffeurs, supports and rarely complains.

Acknowledgment

My deepest appreciation to:
Steve Rose and other officials and residents of the
City of St. Augustine, Florida, for their help and hospitality;
Ms. Pat Barrett of the Renaissance Cleveland Hotel
in Cleveland, Ohio, for helping me visualize the hotel
and main entrance as they were in 1979; Dave Manelski,
the Cleveland guide at About.com for his childhood
recollections of the historic Public Square area at
Christmastime; and Ms. Morgan Acker, lately of Hong Kong,
for her help with Spanish translations.
Any errors are mine and not theirs.

Dear Reader,

The Notorious Mrs. Wright, the story of former con artist Emma Webster, was great fun to write. First, I had the chance to bring back Emma's unusual family from my last book, *Mr. and Mrs. Wrong*. Her brother, Jack, sister-in-law, Lucky, and father, Ray, are some of my favorite characters. Second, I was able to incorporate my love of great food, movies and archaeology into this plot.

On the following pages you'll find romance, intrigue, drama and also a bit of comedy as two mismatched people fall in love. This story is about illusion, but also about the heroine looking beneath the facade she has created to understand who she really is. Love and happiness with handsome investigator Whitaker Lewis await Emma if she can forgive herself—and the thieving father who caused her to run away from home at fifteen.

The setting for *The Notorious Mrs. Wright* is St. Augustine, Florida, the oldest city of continuous residence in the United States and one of the most romantic places on earth. Having visited there a couple of times in the past ten years, I felt it was a fabulous place for Emma to set up her restaurant and display her remarkable talents with costumes and makeup.

I hope you enjoy learning what happened to Jack Cahill's (aka J. T. Webster's) big sister from my earlier book.

Sincerely,

Fay Robinson

PROLOGUE

Cleveland, Ohio
December, 1979

I DIDN'T FEEL RIGHT doing it, but Ray said I had to if me and J.T. wanted to eat anytime soon. Ray was broke—again. All he had in his pocket was a couple of tens and some change. And he still owed last month's rent on the rat hole we called an apartment.

"Please, Emma?" he asked, saying a couple hundred would be enough for groceries and to have the phone turned back on. "One pocket sting. Somethin' to hold us over till I score big."

Slouched next to me on the back seat of the beat-up Chevy, my kid brother let out a low snort and mumbled, "When pigs grow wings," pretty much what I was thinking but was too chicken to say out loud. Like me, J.T.'s tired of all the bull. Ray's been promising to pull a major scam as long as the two of us can remember, boasting he'll get rich and find us a decent place to live, even quit thieving for good.

I gave up on "rich" years ago. These days I'd settle for just owning clothes that haven't been worn by somebody else.

"C'mon, Princess," Ray coaxed. "Ain't nobody better than you at makin' a drop."

He smiled his thousand-watt smile, then reached back to pat me on the knee, a fatherly pat I guess you'd call it, but Ray Webster's never been much of a father to me so I try not to think of him that way. Maybe once he could win me over with his syrupy talk. No more. I'm fifteen going on fifty, too old to fool.

Besides, I hate it when he calls me *Princess*. He only does that when he wants something.

Disgusted, I turned to the window where my breath fogged a circle on the cold glass and kept me from seeing out. I didn't care. Nothing outside to see anyway except sad old buildings and dirty snow piled up on the curb.

We'd parked on Frankfort at the edge of the warehouse district, a place I wouldn't be caught dead in after dark and don't like visiting even in daylight. The area's not any crappier than our neighborhood, but the old-lady disguise I had on made me an easy target for muggers.

That's called *irony,* I think, but my grades in school suck, so I'm not sure.

The outfit is an old-timey dress, a coat with a fake fur collar and a hat with a big brim that sorta tilts back and has a short veil that dips across one side of my forehead. Pretty cool. The clothes came straight off the rack at the Salvation Army, but they're classy, elegant even. I don't look like I've stepped out of a mansion on Millionaire's Row, but you wouldn't think I was a bag lady, either.

I'd slipped the dress on over my sweatshirt and rolled-up jeans, then stuffed the middle with more clothes to round me out and give me a saggy top.

Gloves cover my hands and forearms. Dark stockings hide my legs.

Since I needed wrinkles, I'd made a life mask out of foam latex to put over my face and neck. That part's always a drag, two hours of baking, painting and gluing, but when I'm done—wow! There's a gray wig over my dark hair. Artificial teeth force my mouth into a slight pucker. With the glasses and a walking cane, I look like somebody's sweet, plump granny.

I call my lady *Mrs. Abercrombie.* She's my favorite character, but I have others as good: a Puerto Rican woman in her forties, a twenty-something dancer, a fat maid with an attitude. The psychic and fortune-teller I do would fool anybody.

Pretending is fun. Anything's better than being me. The bad part is ripping people off. And knowing I'm helping Ray, of course. I'd rather poke pencils in my eye than do that.

"Emma, Emma, Emma," he said with an exaggerated sigh. He shook his head. "What's got into you lately, girl? Ain't like you to be so contrary."

"I just don't want to do it, Ray. Please, can't we go home? I'm freezing to death." Twenty-seven degrees, and the heap of rust that had brought us downtown didn't have a heater. "Why can't you lift some wallets instead?"

"Now, Em, you know this works better. Put a hand in a man's pocket and even if you get away with it, he's goin' to the cops. Scam him, though, and he'll keep his mouth shut. He'll figure it's his own fault for bein' stupid."

"Get Vinnie to play my part."

"We need Vinnie to take the call. J.T. here can't do it. He's too little."

J.T.'s twelve and already near big as Ray, but I knew what Ray meant. We needed a man's *voice* to pull this off because of the supposed call to Cowell and Hubbard jewelry store a few blocks east on Euclid Avenue. A kid talking on the other end of the phone wouldn't work.

Ray had asked his friend and sometime-partner Vinnie DeShazo to be that voice. We'd spent most of the day at Vinnie's apartment, where I'd put on my granny clothes and made my mask.

His wife, Estelle, is the one who taught me about latex appliances and junk like that. She has a job in a funeral home making smashed-up dead people look right again. Creepy job, but the makeup works great for disguises. She lets me have all the free samples she gets from the salesmen, too, so usually I don't have to fork out any money.

We'd dropped Vinnie off at a public phone before parking so he could wait for my call. He'd play the *boss* of the swindle.

A cap, a boss and a catch. Three people. That's what Ray likes to use. As the cap, Ray'd find the victim and set him up for the sting. Vinnie as the boss—or in this case the voice—would make everything seem legit. Then, I'd make the catch. But in short cons like this, the cap can also play the catch. I told Ray that's what he should do, and to leave me out of it.

"Now, Emma, I've taught you better than that. Who's a mark more likely to trust, a strange man or a kindly grandma?"

"A grandma."

"That's right. Besides, I don't have your touch. I might get caught again. You wouldn't want that, now would you?"

Maybe I would, but I didn't say it. The only times I could remember being happy were the months Ray'd been in jail.

"We could pawn something," I suggested, desperate.

"Can't. Ain't got nothin' left to pawn or fence. I've hit rock bottom, Princess. That's the truth. And you know today's the fifteenth."

Yeah, I knew. Keel Motor Company paid its salespeople on the fifteenth and the thirtieth. Mama would expect Ray to come home with money from his check and some kind of Christmas bonus. Only…Ray hadn't worked for Keel in almost two years.

I closed my eyes and tried to send myself somewhere warm and safe, where I didn't have to decide between hurting my mama and breaking the law. I was almost there. A log fire burning in a cozy house…my toes stretched out toward the hearth…

A rumbly noise yanked me back to the cold car. J.T.'s stomach growled loud enough to wake the dead. We both giggled, not that it was funny but laughing helps sometimes when you're stuck in hell.

He was hungry. Cripes, *I* was hungry! At least during the week we got a free lunch at school, but this was Saturday afternoon and all we had at home was a dented can of peas and a box of raisins. Knowing Ray, he'd throw them together and call it dinner.

I sagged against the door, unsure of what to do. If I helped Ray, at least me and J.T. would get a decent meal out of him for once.

But I'd hate myself, too. I always did.

Then again, I had to think of Mama, suffering in that tiny basement apartment with its peeling paint and leaking pipes. We shared the floor with the building's ancient furnace and the coal pile. The heat went up. The dust came down.

If I could scam more cash than Ray needed to buy groceries and pay the worst of the bills, Mama might give in and get some medicine for the hurting in her chest.

J.T. slipped his hand in mine and gave it a little squeeze, his way of letting me know he understood the fight going on inside me and whatever I decided was fine with him. My brother can be a jerk sometimes, but mostly he's pretty great.

"Okay, I'll pull the stupid drop," I told Ray with a hard look. I forced him to give one of his tens and swear to use the other to feed J.T. at the restaurant.

"Twenty minutes after we go in, you come," he reminded me as we got out of the car and headed south on foot. "I need time to pick us one." A mark, he meant. Some traveler in an expensive suit or an out-of-town businessman we could fleece for whatever money and jewelry he had on him.

As we walked, we left behind most of the run-down buildings. Two blocks over, we came to Public Square and found it packed with people—mamas and daddies shopping or who'd brought their kids to see the Christmas decorations. Higbee's and May's department stores had tried to outdo each other with wreaths and bows and lights. Red, green and blue bulbs even glowed from the leafless branches of the trees.

"Look!" J.T. said, pointing. He ran about laughing, taking in all the sights. A fake gingerbread house stood in one part of the square. In another was a manger scene. Music spilled out every time a door was opened.

For a few seconds I let myself believe we were a family and that Ray had brought us to see the animated figures in Higbee's windows. Stupid. But I couldn't help it. Those Christmas carols fried my brain, I guess.

I stopped and gazed at the fragrance rings on display at a boutique. Big and gaudy, they had a fake "jewel" that opened, and inside they held a soft wax perfume you could rub with your finger and dab on. All the girls at school had one. I thought they were about the neatest things I'd ever seen.

"Pretty," Ray said, coming up beside me.

"Pretty *hokey,*" I said, as if I wouldn't wear something like that in a million years.

Lesson Number One in Emma Webster's Book of Survival: never let Ray know what you like or don't like. If he knows you, he can hurt you. That's why the Emma he sees isn't real. She's a character, like all the others I've created.

Ray handed over a small sack, one of the props I'd need, and I stuck it into a pocket I'd sewn into the inside of my coat. He'd chosen to play the game at The French Connection, a restaurant inside a ritzy hotel called Stouffer's Inn on the Square. Ahead of us, the hotel rose up like a sideways *E* and seemed to disappear into the clouds.

"You remember the number where Vinnie's at?" Ray asked me. I nodded. "Don't let the mark get too good a look at the real number on the receipt or we're sunk."

"I won't." I've pulled this at least ten times, although never here. The scam's a basic pigeon drop, but my disguise gives it an Emma Webster twist.

In my head I rehearse what I have to do. After I sit down in the restaurant, I wait until no waiters are around, then slip the sack out of my coat and pretend to find it where it might've been overlooked for a few days by the cleaning staff—pushed down in the seat cushion of the booth, behind a plant or trapped by a table leg...something that fits the layout and feels right. That part I play by ear.

Inside is a box wrapped in fancy paper and a sales receipt for a $15,000 bracelet from Cowell and Hubbard. Funny that nobody ever wants to open the box and see what's *really* inside, but Ray says that's why they deserve to get bilked. Eight hundred years this swindle's been around, and dumb smucks still fall for it every day.

Then I show the box and the receipt to Ray and the mark and ask them what to do. Ray pooh-poohs telling the restaurant manager, if that's what the mark suggests. Call the jewelry store first, he says. Report the package found.

I ask for a phone to be brought to my table. I pretend to call the store and identify myself as Mrs. Wilbur Abercrombie. What I do instead is dial Vinnie.

When I say I've found the bracelet, I'm supposedly told the owner has authorized a $1,000 reward for its return. Being an old lady, I get shaky at hearing that. I hand the receiver to the mark to get the information. Vinnie repeats the stuff about the reward. The store will pay it when the bracelet's returned, Vinnie tells him.

I do a real acting job here. I fan my face and pat my heart. Such a large amount, I say. Oh, my! Since

I have arthritis in my hip and can't walk too well, would one of them return the bracelet? I'll split the reward with him.

Ray quickly says *he* will.

But, I point out, I'm trusting a stranger with an expensive piece of jewelry, and I've given *my* name to the store owner. If the bracelet should disappear, wouldn't I be in trouble?

As a show of good faith, Ray offers to give me his wallet to hold while he's gone. He takes it out and opens it, then fakes embarrassment. He's low on cash, he explains. The wife's taken his money and credit cards and gone shopping. He doesn't even have his driver's license on him. He left it in his hotel room.

The mark always jumps in at this point and offers to return the bracelet, seeing his chance to make a quick $500 and cut Ray out of the deal. Ray congratulates us on our good fortune and splits. He does that because being alone with me makes the mark feel okay about leaving his goodies behind. No old lady is going to rip him off, right?

The mark hands over *his* wallet for me to hold. He leaves with the package. In the fifteen or twenty minutes it takes him to walk to the store and realize he's been scammed, we're all long gone in the other direction—with his dough.

Bait, hook, reel in. Disappear clean. That's how it works. At least it does when Ray takes time to plan the sting properly and scout out the right mark.

This day, though, I felt uneasy. Quick stings with random victims were risky.

"This is it for me," I told Ray as we came to the hotel. "I'm not helping you again. You've got to give up griftin'."

"Straight life and me don't get along too good."

"I know, but you've got to try."

"I will, Princess. Honest. When I hit it big I'll retire and..."

He went on and on about everything he planned to get me when that happened—nice clothes, a big house, my own car. I stopped listening. I wanted so much to say what was in my heart, to admit I was ashamed to be his daughter. But I couldn't.

I hate Ray. I mean it. I really do hate him. The problem is...I love him a little bit, too. And that makes me not want to hurt him, even with words.

"Let's just do this," I said, cutting him off.

We rounded up my reluctant brother and they left me outside the hotel. As planned, I waited twenty minutes, then hobbled into the lobby on my cane. Wonder replaced my uneasiness. I had to clamp my mouth shut before my false teeth fell out. I'd never seen such a place—marble walls trimmed in gold... curtains the color of wine...arches shooting up two full stories.

A grand staircase led to a huge fountain. Around it people sat on overstuffed couches listening to a man playing a piano and a woman a harp. A sign read that high tea would be served at four. I didn't know what that was exactly, but it sounded elegant.

I took a hard left down the hall to the restaurant. A guy with a fancy suit and an even fancier accent led me across carpet that was so thick we didn't make noise when we walked. He asked me where I'd like to sit.

"Over there would be lovely," I answered, pointing to a spot near Ray and J.T. Ray drank coffee and talked with a bald man at a nearby table while J.T.

wolfed down a sandwich. With a scratch of his chin, Ray let me know Baldy was my target.

A waiter wearing white gloves helped me sit. I took off my coat and placed it next to me, then nodded to Ray and the mark. "Good afternoon."

"Good afternoon," they both said.

Opening the menu, the part of me that's most like Ray came out, skipping the meat and the vegetables and everything practical and going straight for the desserts. I ordered a cup of tea and something called crème brûlée—warm custard with a browned spun-sugar glaze and raspberries. The waiter served it in a delicate china dish with a silver spoon. Heaven.

At that moment, surrounded by those pretty things, I was as happy as I'd ever been. I felt…I don't know. I can't say *important,* because that's not it. But maybe, for once, I felt not *worthless.*

I could have stayed there forever but, of course, I was only halfway through eating when Ray signaled me to hurry up. Cursing silently, I put down my spoon and made the drop. Baldy took the bait. I set the hook and reeled him in. When Ray and J.T. left me alone with him, I got his goodies: six hundred in cash and two credit cards.

But then, everything fell apart. Baldy got suspicious. Or maybe he wasn't so dumb. He had a friend with him, he said, another engineer in town for a convention. Why didn't he call the room and have his friend come down and keep me company while he returned the bracelet? I smiled and said the only thing I could— "A grand idea."

Baldy called Friend. Friend came down and Baldy whispered something to him I couldn't hear. Baldy paid his bill and left with the package. I figured…

fifteen minutes. That's all the time I had to get away, and Baldy had probably told Friend not to let me out of his sight.

I laid my ten on top of my lunch bill, where the waiter would find it. Skipping out on the ticket and having the management after me wouldn't be very smart right now. I told Friend I needed to be excused. "Ladies' room," I said. As expected, he popped to his feet to escort me. I acted flattered. "What a sweet boy you are."

The bathrooms, I remembered, were between the restaurant and the lobby. I held on to Friend's arm with one hand and my cane with the other. Slowly I hobbled down the corridor with him. Coming in, the walk had seemed short. Now it felt five miles long. The minutes ticked by. Sweat trickled down between my breasts.

Once inside the bathroom, my problems weren't over. Two women stood at the mirror. Calmly I went into a stall and pretended to do my business. I waited and waited. I didn't have much time left. Baldy would be getting to the store any minute. *Leave!* I wanted to scream at the chattering women.

Finally I heard the door open and the women go out. Racing, I ripped everything off, down to the shoes and my own jeans and sweatshirt. The gloves I kept on for the time being, so I wouldn't leave fingerprints on anything in the cleanup.

I pocketed the teeth. I didn't know if the cops could tell a person's identity from spit, but I wasn't taking any chances. Hurriedly I put the wallet with the credit cards in the right pocket of my jeans, along with four hundred of the cash. The other two hundred went into the left pocket.

But what should I do with all the clothes? The pile before me seemed huge. No way could I wear them or hide everything on me.

Stay calm, Emma. Use your brain.

If Friend and Baldy decided to squeal, I didn't want to leave behind any evidence. But I might have to. I looked around, then up. And smiled in relief.

A minute later I strolled out the door. I'd gone in an old woman. I came out teenager. Friend barely noticed me.

With my heart beating a million miles an hour, I left the hotel and ran all the way to the car. By then I was a wreck, shaking not only from cold but from fear. J.T. wrapped me in his coat.

"Where are your granny clothes?" Ray asked.

"In the ladies' bathroom." I explained how I'd almost been caught. "I pushed up a tile and hid them in the drop ceiling."

"Smart girl. But did you get the money?"

"Yes, I got your stupid money!" I took out the wallet and slapped it into his hand. "Didn't you hear me? I almost got caught!"

"So next time we'll be more careful."

Next time? Something inside me broke then. I saw the truth, the real truth, not the one I'd made myself believe for the past few years. Ray wouldn't change. He *couldn't* change. He was a con artist and a thief and he'd never be anything more. If I stayed with him, that's all I'd ever be, too.

We picked up Vinnie. Him and Ray used the credit cards to get all the available cash off the accounts. Ray was happy. We hadn't made his *big score,* but after Vinnie's cut, he had a little over a thousand dollars. I figured that would last him...two weeks, tops.

Maybe less. He'd play cards with his "business associates" and buy them too many drinks. He'd blow it, like always, on stupid stuff we could do without.

Sure enough, he told J.T. on the way home that he'd get him the dog he'd been wanting and also the hockey equipment. He promised us a television. Did I want a pair of leather boots like the ones Estelle had on that morning?

Food was nowhere on his list. Neither was rent. Or paying the overdue utility bills. Or money for medicine.

He tried to talk to me, but I was so disappointed I couldn't stand to look at him. I stared silently out the window, remembering what had happened to me that day. In only one hour, I'd had the best experience of my life, and also the worst. I'd never forget either.

The pain stayed with me. I couldn't shake it. Two nights later, after everybody had gone to sleep, I pulled out wigs and clothes from behind the loose wallboards in the bathroom. The masks that went with the disguises were hidden there, too, along with nearly three hundred in cash that had taken me two years to save. I'd known this day would come eventually, and I'd prepared for it in secret.

I felt guilty about having squirreled away the money, but it was my stake. Without it, I had no chance at freedom.

The letter I left for Mama on the kitchen table said I was sorry about having to leave. I *was* sorry. Grace Webster raised me as best she could. I wasn't running away from her, but from my life. I prayed she'd understand that.

Inside the letter I stuck the two hundred dollars I'd

held back from the scam. *My baby-sitting money,* I lied. *Use it to go to the doctor.*

Writing the other note, the one for J.T., was harder. It tore out my guts. *I had to do this. Please forgive me. And always remember who loves you best.*

Stuffing some clothes into a suitcase, I slipped out of the apartment dressed as a male college student. The series of rides I hitched took me as far as Missouri by the next day. There, I used the second disguise to erase my trail again, becoming a forty-year-old woman.

I bought a bus ticket and headed someplace warm and safe. And, God forgive me the most for this last part…

I never looked back.

CHAPTER ONE

St Augustine, Florida
Present Day…

MARILYN MONROE SASHAYED into the restaurant's dining room, causing Whitaker Lewis to almost swallow his tongue.

She was, of course, only a talented imposter, but if Whit had to swear she wasn't the original, he couldn't do it. The face—perfect, right down to the beauty mark. The body—hotter than a two-dollar pistol.

She'd poured herself into the dress. Must have. The glittering flesh-colored number showed off every hill and valley, and man, oh, man what a landscape! Every male over the age of twelve, including himself, had gone slack jawed.

As if a vacuum had sucked out all the air in the place, conversation stopped. Meals were forgotten. Tips lay unclaimed.

In the sexy baby-doll voice that was the real Marilyn's trademark, her look-alike began to coo "Happy Birthday" to a red-faced but clearly enthralled man a few tables away. A server in a 1950s suit with slicked-back hair and a Clark Gable mustache brought out a cake. Another, dressed as Lawrence of Arabia, set out dessert plates.

"Happy Birthday, Mr. President of GXA Electronics..." She let out a sultry sigh and it raced straight down Whit's nerve endings to his groin. "Happy Birthday to you."

The crowd exploded with applause. Marilyn threw kisses in response. She stayed a moment to talk with the man and his companions, then wound her way through the tables to speak briefly to some of the other customers. Finally, after Whit felt he'd waited an eternity, she reached him.

"Hi, honey," she purred, still in character. "Enjoying your dinner?"

"Very much."

"I'm so glad." Her mouth moved in that pouty way Marilyn's had. Thousands of tiny beads on her dress sparkled, creating waves of light that made her skin seem to shimmer. "You've eaten here before, haven't you? I rarely forget a handsome face."

"I've been in the last couple of nights."

"I thought so. Local or tourist?"

"Tourist." He pulled the name of a state out of the air. "Michigan's my home. I'm here for a few days' vacation."

"That's nice. Would you like a little something sweet to finish your meal? Besides me, I mean."

He chuckled. "What do you recommend?"

"A sinful, hard-glazed custard we call the Blonde Bombshell. Eating it is the *second*-best experience in the world." She winked. "If you know what I mean."

"Yes, ma'am, I do. Is it your recipe?"

"Oh, honey, I don't cook. I tried once but the spaghetti kept falling through the grill." When he threw back his head and laughed, she playfully tweaked his chin. "You're very cute. You come back and visit again before you go home, okay, Michigan?"

"I'll do that."

As she sauntered off, he enjoyed the pleasing sway of her backside for a moment, then searched her right arm. A red, puckered scar at her elbow marred her otherwise perfect flesh. Last night, Cleopatra had had the scar. The night before, Dorothy from *The Wizard of Oz*.

Reconciling the voluptuous fair-skinned sex goddess with the dark Egyptian beauty and the innocent Kansas teenager was hard, but Whit couldn't deny the evidence. The same woman had played all three characters. And she hadn't simply dressed up those other nights. She'd played *Elizabeth Taylor* playing Cleopatra. She'd played *Judy Garland* playing Dorothy.

Illusions. The name fit the place well. From the outside, the tall Spanish-style building with its red-tiled roof, stucco walls and curved archways looked like a hundred others in the nation's oldest city. Inside, though, history merged with elegance and a touch of whimsy. While the integrity of the historic structure seemed to have been retained, movie posters decorated the back wall. Along each side, display cases held original costumes and props from Academy Award–winning pictures like *Platoon* and *West Side Story*.

Every employee portrayed a movie, music or television star or a star's character. The Flying Nun, complete with habit, had shown him to his table. Mad Max in black leather had taken his order. Marilyn, though... She'd gone beyond simply putting on a costume. She'd somehow become the character. *Sensational* was the only word to describe her.

Whit finished his fish and ordered the dessert Marilyn had recommended.

"How was it?" his waiter asked when he'd scraped every last drop of custard from the dish.

"Excellent. So was the flounder."

"The head chef is Spanish and is known throughout Europe. We were lucky to get him."

"He's very talented."

"We think so. Anything else I can bring you? More iced tea? Wine? We also have a variety of coffees."

"Just the check."

"Your meal's on the house, sir. Compliments of the owner. She said to say you're the first person in weeks to laugh at one of her stupid jokes, and she thanks you."

Whit stopped in the act of reaching for his billfold. A knot the size of a baseball formed in his middle.

"The woman dressed as Marilyn Monroe is the owner?"

"Yes, sir. Susan Wright. She's fabulous, isn't she?"

"Terrific." Whit smiled and nodded, but inside he was cursing his own stupidity.

What an idiot he was. For three days he'd been trying to get a look at the elusive Susan Roberts Wright. Tonight she'd been standing right in front of him and he hadn't even known it.

He went ahead and pulled his billfold from his shorts, took out a single bill and handed it to the young man. "At least I can give you the tip."

The kid's eyes bulged at the amount. "Sir, do realize that's a fifty and not a five?"

"Keep it. A young guy like you can always use a little extra spending money, can't he?"

"Sure can, sir. Thanks." The kid quickly slipped the money into his pocket.

Whit motioned for him to bend down so he could speak and not be overheard by the other customers.

"Maybe you can help me out with something."

"I'll try."

"When might I see your boss *not* in costume? One guy to another, I'd like to know what she looks like in real life."

"I gotcha. Our male customers ask that a lot when she plays Marilyn. Cleopatra, too."

"I'll bet they do. When can I catch a glimpse?"

"Well, during the day. Early afternoon. She lives upstairs, so even when she's not working the floor she's around here somewhere, usually in the office."

"Dressed in street clothes?"

"Yes, sir. She only puts on a costume for the dinner crowd, six to eleven."

"Describe her, so I'll know who to look for."

"Oh, five-four, short dark hair. Average size. Average appearance."

"Short hair as in...like a man? Above the ears? What?"

"Like—" he glanced around and then nodded toward a woman in a red blouse three tables down "—that lady's over there. Short but feminine. She wears it hooked behind her ears. And she's about the size of that lady, too."

"I take it, then, she isn't really built like Marilyn Monroe."

He chuckled. "No, sir, that must be padding she puts on. When she's herself, she doesn't seem that, uh..."

"Curvy?"

"Exactly."

"How old would you guess she is? Mid-forties?"

"Mmm, younger. Her son helps out around here sometimes and he's maybe sixteen or seventeen. I guess she'd have to be at least mid-thirties, but I wouldn't imagine she's much over that."

"Married, huh? Just my luck." Whit frowned and tried to act like a disappointed suitor.

"Oh, her husband's dead, I think."

"Recently?"

"No, I heard Tom say once that he never knew his father, so I assume Mr. Wright must've died when Tom was small or before he was born."

"Are they natives of Saint Augustine?"

"That I don't know. We opened a little over six months ago. Before that, I'm not sure if Mrs. Wright and her son were living here or somewhere else. Now, Ms. Townsend—she was born here, although I believe she somehow knew Mrs. Wright before."

"And Ms. Townsend is?"

"The catering manager."

"And her first name is?"

"Abby."

"Thanks, son, you've been a big help." More help than the young man realized. The lady needed to warn her employees about giving out personal information to customers.

Whit knew the answers to most of the questions he'd just asked, but it helped to hear what Susan Wright was telling others.

A sleight-of-hand artist was about to perform in the courtyard. A placard on the table said the restaurant offered entertainment Friday and Saturday nights and supplied catering for weddings and parties off-site and on-site in private rooms. Coming in, Whit had ambled through the gift shop off the lobby where coffees, teas, wines and the house cookbook and salad dressing were for sale.

The dining room was packed tonight, as it had been the other times he'd been in. Business seemed to be thriving.

He decided to skip the show and head over to his room to follow up on the couple of new pieces of information he'd just learned. He glanced around before leaving, but Susan Wright seemed to have disappeared.

Tomorrow he'd try to get a better look at her. Maybe then, after two months of following dead-end leads, crisscrossing the country and driving himself insane, he could finally start wrapping up this case and get his life back to normal.

OUTSIDE, THE HOT JULY AIR rushed to envelop Whit and brought a fine sheen of sweat to his skin. He inhaled the scent of the pink tropical flowers growing near the restaurant's porch. Across the palm-lined boulevard, a barrier island blocked his view of the Atlantic Ocean, but the Intracoastal Waterway and the bay it ran through seemed to have turned to silver in the fading light. He decided to walk back to the motel along the wide concrete seawall.

The town, he'd discovered during the past two nights, didn't wind down at dark. Although the colorful street ''trains'' that shuttled visitors to attractions ceased at six o'clock, there were plenty of horse-drawn carriages. People milled about, browsing in shop windows or taking walking tours of haunted houses. Music and laughter poured from the bars and restaurants.

His motel was only two blocks away. Inside his room, he sat on the bed and checked his messages. He returned a call to his Pittsburgh office, knowing that even if his assistant wasn't in, someone probably would be.

Cliff Hodges, one of his investigators and a good friend, picked up.

"Cliff, I didn't expect you to answer. What are you still doing there at eight on a Friday night?"

"Working. What are you still doing in Florida?"

"Working."

"Then I'd say we both need to reevaluate our social lives, old buddy."

"I have no social life."

"I've noticed that about you."

"Is Deborah still there? She left a message saying an Allen Morrow was looking for me, but I don't know who that is."

"She's long gone, but I was here when she took the call, and I talked to Morrow briefly. He identified himself as an assistant district attorney from Los Angeles County. Says he's met you before and kept your business card."

"I don't remember him. Did he say what he wants?"

"He needs us to locate a missing witness in a case he's prosecuting. His in-house staff hasn't come up with anything. He left his private number and wants a call back as soon as possible."

"Hand him off to Cordell in the West Coast office, and let him handle it."

"I tried. I told him you were out of town, but he

still wants you to call him. He's insistent. Apparently he's prosecuting the murder of a cop, and he's afraid his star witness might not turn up to testify. He needs a little hand-holding from the boss."

"Too bad he didn't call last week when I was out there working on this case." Whit checked the time. Just after five o'clock in California. "Okay, give me the number. But in the morning, fill in Cordell so he can take over. And ask Deborah to run the usual checks on Morrow to make sure he is who he says he is."

"Will do. When are you coming back?"

"I don't know. I'm following up on a few things and they may or may not pan out."

"Are you still on the same case?"

"Afraid so."

"Pro bono, right?"

"Right. The client's a friend of Wes Campbell's at the Pittsburgh PD. As a favor to Wes, I said I'd dig around and see what I could turn up on the guy's runaway sister, never dreaming I'd still be doing legwork two months later."

"Must be a bugger to keep you tied up so long."

"It's a cold case."

"How long has she been gone?"

"Twenty-three years."

"Jeez, Whit, that's not cold, that's frozen."

"Yeah, the time gap's not making it any easier to find her, that's for sure. The case is fascinating, though. I can't remember when I've worked on one that frustrated or excited me as much. I'm having to resort to some old-fashioned investigative techniques to get what I need. The computer's been pretty helpful, but it hasn't helped me as much as the face-to-face interviews."

"What do you have so far?"

"I've traced her whereabouts in the early 1980s to Los Angeles and Hollywood, where she was living on the streets for a few years and calling herself by various names, but then her trail suddenly ended again. I've found no public record anywhere of her after that under her real name or any alias she's used. No social security activity, no driver's license, nothing."

"Sounds like she's dead. Could be she ended up an unidentified Jane Doe."

"That's what I figured at first, but I've come to believe she's just good at covering her tracks. Maybe as good as anyone I've come across."

"She must be good if *you* can't find her." He chuckled. "So somebody's finally outfoxed the master, huh? If you ever do find her, maybe you need to give her a job training our investigators in the Witness Location division."

"Don't laugh. That's not a bad idea. She's already taught me a few things. Every time I think I'm close to figuring out what she's done to hide, I have to do a one-eighty and backtrack."

"But you think now you've got a good lead on her?"

"More like a hunch. I think I know what she did. My gut tells me I may even have found her, but I don't have proof, just some scraps of information that are adding up."

"Your hunches are usually solid."

"Yeah, and I believe I'm solid this time, but I'm a long way from where I need to be to take it to the client. I think she's calling herself Susan Roberts Wright, the widow of William Wright. Someone's been moving from state to state under that identity for the past several years, but I can't find any marriage certificate or death certificate for the supposedly deceased husband, and the widow's age and description change as often as her hairstyle."

"Can the client ID?"

"That's what I'm hoping. I've been checking local records the past few days and trying to work myself into a position to get photos I can show him."

"Have you set up surveillance?"

"Yeah, but the lady apparently doesn't have any more of a social life than you and me. I haven't been able to catch her outside of the restaurant she owns. She hasn't even used her car in three days."

"What about her home?"

"She lives above the business and has a separate entrance in the rear. I've backed off from watching that. I can't do it without being pegged as a prowler."

"So what *are* you doing?"

"Playing tourist. I decided I might have better luck getting close to her if I walked in the front door and ordered dinner like everyone else."

"Sounds as if you've got a handle on it."

Whit snorted. "I sat two feet from this woman tonight and we carried on a conversation, yet I still can't tell you exactly what she looks like."

"Huh? I don't understand?"

"Long story. I'll explain when I get back."

"Okay, buddy. Let me know if you need help. I'm available."

"Thanks, Cliff."

He hung up and called Allen Morrow in California,

talking briefly to the man about his criminal case and reassuring him that the San Pedro office of Lewis Investigations could locate his witness.

After a shower, he unlocked his laptop computer and opened his file on Emma Webster. The blasted woman had begun to occupy his thoughts day and night, and he didn't like it. He had other cases he was working on, cases that could benefit from the time and attention he was giving Emma, but they didn't interest him at all.

She had aroused his curiosity. And tonight—if the woman he'd talked to was indeed Emma—she had aroused much more. He'd gotten worked up over a body made of foam rubber. Damn, that galled him.

Well, it served him right. He knew better than to let his emotions cloud his perspective, especially over a woman with her background.

She'd been a criminal and maybe still was, and Whit didn't like criminals. He'd spent most of his life catching them, or at least locating them. He'd been a special agent with the FBI for ten years before opening his own national firm seven years ago.

He had offices in four states and a hundred and fifty top-notch investigators, all experts in a particular field: corporate security, encryption, terrorism, insurance fraud, witness location. His personal specialty was finding people. And he was very good at it. Usually.

This case baffled him. He could understand why Emma had run away as a child, but most runaways didn't bother to stay hidden after adulthood. Many actually attempted to reconcile with their estranged parents and find their siblings.

Emma had been close to her brother. She had to

expect that one day he would seek her out. So why was she still running? And from whom?

He clicked on the photo he'd scanned of her, and brought it up on the screen. The quality of this shot was poor, and in it she was only twelve, but there weren't any others, not even from school. She had dark hair and sad, dark eyes. The facial resemblance to her brother had been strong back then, and still should be.

When he'd started this investigation, Whit had used a software program developed for the bureau to age Emma's features by twenty-six years, to see what she might look like now at thirty-eight. He brought up that altered photo.

Beside it, he opened the most recent driver's license photo of the woman calling herself Susan Wright, maiden name Susan Roberts. She wore glasses in this one, so he couldn't tell much about the eyes. "Hazel" was the color listed, rather than brown.

The facial bone structure seemed similar to the first photo. The hair was long here, though, not short as in the aged photo of Emma or as Susan Wright supposedly wore her hair now. But it occurred to him that she could be wearing a wig. And the nose… different somehow. Longer. Maybe a bit wider. She didn't look forty-five, as her license said.

He brought up a third photo he'd acquired only yesterday by courier. This one, a black-and-white, was from the 1973 yearbook of Marsville High School in Virginia, where the real Susan Roberts had been a sixteen-year-old student at the time. He used the software to colorize it and age the photo twenty-nine years, to her current age of forty-five. He replaced the long hair with short and gave her brown eyes.

Two bits of information stood out in his mind as important: One, Emma Webster and Susan Roberts had both been runaways. Two, the woman calling herself Susan Roberts Wright had named her son John Thomas, the same first and middle names as Emma Webster's brother. Coincidence? Maybe, but he didn't think so.

Emma had been proficient with disguise, just like the Susan Wright he'd talked to earlier tonight.

The software allowed him to analyze the three photos using a sixty-five-point system of comparison. He did that, but the results were inconclusive.

He leaned back in the chair, put his hands behind his head and studied the different faces. Sometimes experience was more valuable than technology.

His gut was speaking again. What it said disturbed him. The "widow" Wright might or might not be Emma Webster, but she clearly *wasn't* the real Susan Roberts. So what had happened to Susan? And more importantly...did the woman impersonating Susan have anything to do with her disappearance?

CHAPTER TWO

"SUSAN! DIDN'T YOU HEAR me calling?"

Emma jumped. As always, a fraction of a second passed before she associated herself with the name. She closed the textbook and casually slid it under the ledgers on her desk, hoping her action hadn't called attention to it.

She'd tried all morning to study, but one problem after another had broken her concentration—late linen, a smoking motor on the ice machine, two kitchen assistants who'd shown up late. Saturday was always the worst day of the week.

But she couldn't complain. She adored this place. After years of waiting tables and washing dishes in every cheap dive from California to Maine, after years of scraping by from paycheck to paycheck, she was living her dream.

She owned this restaurant. She had money in the bank. The respectability she'd craved all her life was within her grasp.

And soon—she hoped—she could fulfill another dream, that of receiving her high school diploma. *And* before Tom, who'd be a senior when he started back in the fall. She'd worked in secret for several months to prepare for the equivalency exam.

"What's wrong now, Abby?" She'd asked not to be disturbed for a couple of hours.

Abby stood in the office doorway with her hands on her hips and a look of panic on her face. "Houdini's loose in the kitchen."

Emma sighed. Not again. She was going to strangle that stupid bird. "Please tell me he hasn't gotten into any food preparation areas."

"No, he flew right into the storage room, but that crazy Spaniard you hired is threatening to fricassee him for lunch."

"Great. Exactly what I need today."

"Really, Susan, he's impossible."

"Who, the parrot or the chef?"

"Both. At the moment, I'm not sure which one of them is crazier. The bird's squawking insults, and Santiago's waving a very large knife. Did Tom teach the bird Spanish? If he wasn't so gorgeous, I'd say boot his butt out the door."

"Who? Houdini?"

"No, silly. Santiago."

Emma often felt she was missing something in conversations with Abby. Like…understanding.

She walked to the wall and punched the button on the intercom to her apartment. "Tom? You still up there?"

"Yeah, Mom. Just walking out the back door to go to work."

"I need your help for a second. Houdini's gotten out of the aviary and made his way down here somehow."

"Ah, sh—"

"Watch your language, young man."

"Sorry. Be right there."

Emma went with Abby through the kitchen to the storage room and found chaos. Santiago Chaves, their young, brilliant but sometimes volatile chef, cursed and waved a meat cleaver at the gray parrot running nervously back and forth along the top of a shelf filled with sacks of flour.

Twenty or so kitchen assistants crowded the door, but were wise enough to stay out of Santiago's reach.

"*¡Basta ya!* I will wring your skinny neck! I will chop you into pieces and serve you with garlic sauce."

"Call the cops!" Houdini said, and flew to the top of a shelf across the room. "*¡Como quieras!*"

"I'll make your day," Santiago vowed, grabbing hold of the support and trying to shake the bird down. "I will make this your *last* day. *¡Madre del amor de dios! ¡Este es un manicomio!*"

Emma rushed forward. "Tom's on his way to catch him, Santiago. Please, put down the knife before you accidentally hurt yourself or someone else."

"Susan, you said this would not happen again. You promised Santiago."

"I know, and I'm very sorry. We've been keeping the upper door on the stairway closed. He must have come down on the dumbwaiter."

"Yes, and last week it was that…that giant lizard riding up and down."

Oh, great. She hadn't known about that. "Tom's iguana was down here?"

"Yes. Santiago open door to get dirty dishes, and is hissed at. Heart nearly stop."

"I'm sorry. He probably got a little scared. Rambo's usually very gentle."

"But I do not like this...Rambo. And that one—" he pointed the cleaver at the bird "—I hate. He is menace. Santiago cook him like squab, *¿no?* Stuff him with bread crumbs and almonds."

Houdini did his imitation of a police emergency siren, then bullets firing. "Hold it, scumbag," he said. "*¡Policía!*"

"*¡Maldición!*" Santiago cursed. "Do you hear? He mocks me."

"He isn't mocking you," Emma explained, gently taking the weapon from his hand. She slipped it behind her back to Abby. "Houdini mimics sounds and phrases he hears, and it doesn't matter what language they're in. He gets lonely when we're not home, so Tom leaves the TV or the radio on for him. He's hooked on police dramas this month. Last month it was old comedies."

"Birds and lizards do not belong in kitchen."

"I agree."

"Birds inside are...how you say...*un presagio malo.* Bad omen."

"I promise Tom will fix both cages this weekend so the bird and the lizard can't bother you again. All right? Am I forgiven?"

"Hmph! Must give thought."

Houdini shrieked an ear-splitting "Dial nine-one-one" and Emma was tempted to get the cleaver back from Abby and use it on the bird herself.

Thankfully, Tom came in and relieved her of the need. He climbed the shelf, spoke a few calming words and Houdini immediately hopped onto his hand.

"I'm really sorry, Santiago," Tom said when he was back on the floor. "There's a board propped against the door of the cage and a rock holding it in place, but I guess he knocked it loose or found another way out."

"It is all right, Tom. Santiago was not so very upset."

Behind Emma, Abby let out a strangled cough of disbelief. "I'd hate to see him when he *is* upset," she whispered in Emma's ear.

Emma tried to keep a straight face. She turned her head and gave Abby a warning look.

Turning back to Santiago, she made a peace offering. "We can lock the dumbwaiter, if that would help. I don't mind cooking for Tom. You're sweet to send up dinner, but I can take care of it."

Santiago glanced at Tom. Emma thought she saw something pass between them, some private message she wasn't privy to.

"No, no, Susan. Santiago does not mind making plate for Tom when he asks. Tom is good boy."

"Are you sure? He can always come down here to eat. Or I can cook for him."

"No, is okay. Tom promise to keep bird in cage. Santiago fix dinner and send upstairs when Tom want."

"Thank you. That's very sweet of you."

The crisis over, Santiago and his helpers returned to work. Abby, Emma and Tom walked through the kitchen to the hallway.

"You've got to make sure both Houdini and

Rambo stay upstairs,'' Emma warned her son. ''Or we'll have to give them away. Understand?''

''But Mom—''

''No buts. It's unsanitary for Houdini to even be on this floor, much less near the kitchen.'' She began to stroke the bird's breast, but jerked back her finger when he tried to nip it.

''I'll make sure they don't get out again.''

''I'm going to hold you to that.'' She reached up and lovingly mussed his hair. He'd shot up like a weed this summer and had gotten so handsome. ''Go on. Your boss will be wondering what happened to you. And be sure to close the upstairs door.''

''Don't forget I'm going to Tony's after work and staying over there tonight.''

''Will his parents be home?''

He rolled his eyes. ''Yes, his parents will be home.''

''Okay, but if you go out, curfew is still midnight.''

''Ah, Mom, nobody my age comes in at midnight! Aunt Abby, tell her, will ya?''

Abby held up her hands. ''Sorry, Tom. I'm staying out of this one.''

''Be back at the Parkers' on time,'' Emma told him. ''I'm trusting you.''

''Oh, okay,'' he grumbled with the kind of long, exaggerated sigh that only a teenager can make. ''Are you gonna let me take scuba lessons with Mr. Parker? You promised to think about it.''

''I don't know, Tom. We'll talk this week.''

''I'll pay for them myself.''

''We'll see.''

''Mr. Parker's got extra equipment and stuff. I

wouldn't have to buy any. And he's giving me a great discount."

"I said, we'll see. Now scoot or you'll be late."

Tom started up the back stairs still grumbling.

Houdini squawked. "This is a .44 Magnum, the most powerful handgun in the world."

"Yeah, yeah," Tom told him.

Abby laughed, and Emma couldn't help chuckling, too. She leaned into the stairwell. "And Tom," she called out. "Before you leave, make sure the TV is set on cartoons or PBS. I don't think Houdini needs to watch any more Clint Eastwood movies."

BACK IN HER OFFICE, Emma fixed herself a cup of hot tea and one for Abby, then plopped down in her chair again.

"That menagerie is going to be the death of me. If I'd been smart, I'd have given them away when we moved in here. You know how important this place is to me. Every one of our inspections has been perfect, and I want to keep it that way. No parrots in the kitchen."

"Even fricasseed and stuffed?"

Emma laughed. "Especially not that."

"Tom would be upset if you gave them away."

"I know. Maybe it won't come to that."

She'd threatened almost daily to find other homes for the animals, but she'd have a difficult time following through. Tom cared about them. They'd been a bequest to him from Marie Marshall upon her death eighteen months ago. Marie was the same woman who'd earlier given Emma her collection of movie costumes and props.

Emma had kept the collection in storage for several years, thinking Marie would change her mind and want it back. But then Marie had died brutally. She'd surprised a burglar in her Hollywood home and been slashed repeatedly with a knife.

Emma saw no reason to hang on to the items after Marie's death. She looked into the value of movie memorabilia and found, to her astonishment, she owned a gold mine.

The most valuable costumes she had put up for auction. She used the money to finance the restaurant and create a trust fund for Tom's education. Those remaining were displayed in the dining room and stored on the third floor. The staff wore imitations rather than the real thing.

Without that generous gift, Emma would still be waitressing, working for tips and soaking her aching feet every night. She felt an obligation to take care of the pets Marie and her late husband Bert had loved. But living with a smart-mouthed bird and a three-foot iguana was beginning to try her patience.

"I see Tom's still got his heart set on being a navy diver," Abby said, sitting on a corner of the desk. "I thought he'd outgrow that."

"Me, too."

"Has he said anything else about enlisting?"

"Yes, but I told him he'd have to do it over my dead body."

"Susan, honey, you can't blame him for wanting to be like his father."

"I don't, but he's got the opportunity now to go to college and make a life for himself that's far more desirable than the one I've given him. I refuse to let him throw that away over an idealized image of a man he never met."

"You act as if he's had a terrible life, but you've done okay by him."

"I could've given him more."

"How? By working three jobs a day instead of two?"

"By providing a more stable home. I counted it up the other night, Abby, and in seventeen years we've lived in nine different places. I was doing the best I could at the time, searching for better jobs and better pay, but it was hard on Tom to keep starting over in new schools."

"He hasn't suffered from it. He has perfect grades. He's never been in any trouble. Tom's a great kid."

Emma smiled, proud of her son's accomplishments. Tom was the one thing she'd done right in her life. "I know he's a great kid, but sometimes he zeros in on something and won't turn it loose."

"Like his mother."

"I admit it."

"Have you talked about this with him?"

"I've made it clear that he can't, under any circumstances, drop out of high school. I want him to get a college degree, too, maybe even go on to graduate school or medical school. He knows I won't give him my permission to join the navy."

"Honey, when he turns eighteen in two months he won't need your permission."

"I know." She'd suffered many a sleepless night over that horrifying fact.

Payback for her sins. That was it. The older Tom got, the more he wanted to know about his father and to be like him. And Emma perched precariously atop a powder keg of past lies, waiting for it to explode.

His father hadn't been in the navy. He hadn't died during a training dive, as her son and everyone else believed. William Wright was only a fake name on Tom's birth certificate and a couple of fake photographs over the mantel. He didn't exist.

"Well," Abby said, standing. "I need to go check the setups for the Scott rehearsal dinner. Oh, before I do...what happened last night? I'm dying to know."

"We had a good crowd again. I had multiple compliments on the sleight-of-hand artist, so I'm going to talk to him about performing at least a couple of weekends a month."

"Oh, knucklehead, I don't care about that! Tell me about the cute guy. Did he come in again? Did you find out anything about him? Was he wearing a wedding ring?"

"Who?" Emma asked, playing coy.

"Don't tease me. You know who I'm talking about. Blue eyes and a fine set of shoulders. The one you've been sighing over all week."

"I was *not* sighing over him."

"Aha, so you do know who I'm talking about."

"Mmm, I might vaguely remember a fine set of shoulders."

She remembered them, all right. And the beautiful eyes. He'd had a nice smile, too, with a dimple on the left side of his mouth that showed when he laughed.

"Did you talk to him?" Abby asked.

"For a few minutes. I told him my spaghetti joke, and he thought it was funny."

"Lord have mercy. Rope and tie that one before he gets away."

"He's from Michigan. Vacation."

"Oh, no!"

"He's probably already on his way home."

"Well, bummer. The good ones are always tourists."

WHIT TIMED HIS ARRIVAL to avoid the busy lunch hour. He didn't wait to be announced. While the hostess seated customers, he wandered down the hall past the gift shop and the rest rooms to where he assumed the offices would be.

He carried a camera, just in case Susan Wright went for his idea. And if she didn't, the miniature camera concealed in the sunglasses sticking out of his shirt pocket would do.

The woman sat alone at a desk in the last office on the right, head bent over a book. She read under her breath.

"If Mary buys three cans of beets on sale at five for a dollar, and Fred buys four cans of beets for twenty cents each but has a coupon for ten cents, which one got the better deal?" She snorted. "Well that's easy. Neither. Nobody in their right mind eats beets."

Whit chuckled. She looked up…and blushed.

The waiter had described Susan as "average" looking. She wasn't. "Damned pretty" was more accurate. He'd also been wrong about the bodysuit and padded parts. Her parts were fine just the way they were.

"Can I help you?" she asked, closing the book.

"Susan Wright?"

"Yes." She stood.

He walked over to the desk. "Whitaker Lewis. We talked briefly last night. You were kind enough to buy my dinner."

"Yes, I remember."

"I wanted to thank you, and to say how much I enjoyed your performance as Marilyn. Your Cleopatra and Dorothy were great, too."

She cocked her head and smiled, changing from "damned pretty" to "beautiful."

"How did you...?"

"The scar on your elbow gave you away."

"Ah." She rubbed it. "You're very observant."

"And you're very talented."

"Thank you."

"Look, I apologize for barging in like this. I hope I'm not interrupting anything important." He glanced down at the book title: *Algebra With An Introduction To Trigonometry.*

She bent and put the textbook in a drawer. "No, you're not."

"I have a confession to make. I asked my waiter about you last night. He said you're no longer married."

That statement seemed to fluster her. "No, my husband died several years ago. Why?"

"I was wondering—would you like to take a walk? I haven't had much of a chance to look around the town since I've been here. Seeing it with a beautiful woman would be better than seeing it on my own."

She blushed more deeply. Her face was now the color of the beets she found so disgusting.

"Are you asking me out on a date, Mr. Lewis?"

"Trying to, Mrs. Wright, but apparently not doing a very good job of it."

"I appreciate the compliment and the invitation, but I don't really know you. I don't go out with men I don't know."

"I promise I'm a nice man."

"I'm sure you are."

"My only major vice is being spoiled rotten all my life by three older sisters."

She smiled at that. "I wouldn't call that a vice, but rather a lovely way to grow up."

"Do you have siblings?"

"No, unfortunately, I was an only child."

"There were times I'd have given anything to be an only child. Now I realize how fortunate I am."

"Yes, you are."

"If I can't interest you in a walk, how about a very public cruise around the bay?"

She hesitated, and for a moment he thought she might say yes. But then she shook her head.

Whit scratched his jaw. God, he was rusty at this. Okay, the lady wasn't interested. He obviously hadn't made much of an impression on her last night or today. He should take his photos, excuse himself and be done with it. But to his chagrin, he found he didn't want to.

He was about to try again when someone came in.

"Oh, Susan, I forgot—"

Whit turned. The woman stopped short. She had wild red hair and more freckles than he'd ever seen on one person.

"Well, hi there." She grinned widely and extended

her hand. Whit shook it. ''Abby Townsend. I'm a friend of Susan's.''

''Whitaker Lewis.''

''Michigan, right?''

He raised an eyebrow in surprise and glanced at Susan Wright. She wouldn't meet his gaze. ''Yes, Lansing.''

''What type of business are you in, Mr. Lewis?''

''Insurance.''

''And is there a Mrs. Lewis?''

''Abby!'' Susan sighed with exasperation. ''I'm sorry, Mr. Lewis. I'm sure you didn't come here to be interrogated.''

''That's okay. I don't mind, especially if it'll make you feel more comfortable about me.'' He turned back to Abby to explain. ''I've been trying to convince Mrs. Wright to join me on a short boat ride around the bay this afternoon, but she said no.''

''Oh, Susan, why not go?'' Abby asked. ''It sounds like such fun. You were telling me only the other day how you hadn't taken time to enjoy any of the city's historic attractions. Here's your chance.''

''I don't remember saying that.''

''Of course you did.'' Abby winked at Whit.

Susan pointed at the door. ''Abby—out.''

Abby wiggled her fingers at Whit and mouthed ''good luck'' before making her exit.

Whit took his sunglasses out of his pocket and acted as if he planned to put them on. He aimed as best he could and snapped a series of photos by pushing a small button on the right earpiece.

He figured this would be his only chance. Susan

Wright didn't appear to be giving in. But her next comment surprised him.

"*Is* there a Mrs. Lewis?" she asked, charmingly biting her bottom lip. "I don't go out with married men."

Whit smiled. Damn, she was attractive! Spending the afternoon with her wouldn't be a hardship at all, even if it was part of the job.

"The only Mrs. Lewis in my life has been happily married to my father for the past forty-five years," he told her honestly.

"Promise?"

"Promise. I wouldn't lie to you."

He felt the slightest tinge of remorse about that last part. If it turned out she wasn't Emma, she'd never know that some of what he'd told her today was a lie. But if she *was* Emma, she'd find out the truth soon enough. Like her, he was a fraud.

CHAPTER THREE

EMMA FLEW UP THE STAIRS to change out of her slacks and into something more casual. Her heart pounded. Nervousness churned inside her stomach.

Like a football player who'd just scored a touchdown, she did a little bowlegged dance in front of the full-length mirror in her dressing room, then laughed out loud at her own craziness. She couldn't remember the last time she'd felt so light hearted, so excited about anything.

Dating hadn't been part of her life. She couldn't even remember a time lately when she'd been affected by a man, had felt a raw, physical awareness of one as she did with Whitaker Lewis. Even being in the same room with him had made her restless and achy, reminded her that she hadn't had sex in...well, too long.

Nothing could come of this afternoon, but she wanted to go through with it nonetheless. For once, although it was only for a few hours, she longed to be a normal woman and pretend she really was "beautiful" like he'd said. Only one other man had ever called her that, and he'd been a liar.

She was lonely. Admitting it was easy. What harm was there in spending a few hours with someone to erase that loneliness temporarily, even if he was a stranger? None that she could see.

Feeling comfortable with him—that *wasn't* so easy. Behind the protection of a disguise she could be sexy with men and say whatever was on her mind. Not so when she was herself, especially when she was attracted to someone.

She sucked in a breath and fortified her resolve.

"You can do this," she told her image in the mirror.

Now, if she could only believe it.

Hastily she shed her dressy slacks and blouse. She pulled on a pair of white shorts and slipped into a matching top and tennis shoes. Her cell phone went into her pocket in case the restaurant needed to get in touch with her.

Excitement made her want to squeal like a teenager, but thirty-eight-year-old women didn't squeal, especially thirty-eight-year-old women pretending to be forty-five.

Oh, God, would her age matter to him? When she was twenty and about to give birth to an illegitimate child, borrowing the identity of her twenty-seven-year-old friend had seemed practical. She'd wanted to appear more mature. The ruse had helped keep Tom safe. But now she hated that people thought she was older.

She pushed away her silly insecurities. Whitaker Lewis was taking her on a boat ride, nothing more. Worrying about what he might or might not think of her was ridiculous.

He waited in her office. When Emma walked in, he repeated how glad he was that she'd decided to come. He also took a covert look at her legs and appeared to like what he saw. Her opinion of him went up another two hundred percent.

"Ready, Mr. Lewis?"

"Only if you call me Whit."

"All right...Whit." The nickname fit him. "I'm Susan."

The marina was half a block away, just past the bridge to the island. The boat held about fifty people on two decks. Whit gave her the choice of where to sit, so she chose a table on the upper deck, where they could see better. Once on the water, there'd be a breeze to keep them cool.

Rumblings of thunder told her they could expect the usual afternoon shower, but for now the clouds were to the west and not over them.

The chairs quickly filled with parents and children. The engine started, the boat backed out of the slip and they were on their way.

"Have you taken this trip before?" he asked her.

"No, and I really have been wanting to. I don't know much firsthand about the city, only what I've read or been told."

"Where did you move from?"

"Mmm...Nevada."

"Is that where you were born?"

Emma hesitated. Years of hiding out had made her wary of strangers, but the wariness was as much habit as necessity. She had no reason to worry about Patrick finding her now. He'd died years ago. And thankfully, he'd never discovered she'd had a child.

Legal ramifications existed, of course, if anyone realized she wasn't Susan, but in eighteen years no one had come looking for the dead friend whose identity Emma had borrowed. And from what Susan had told her, no one had cared enough *to* look for her.

Like Emma, Susan had run away from an impossible situation at home. But unlike Emma, she'd been unable to resist the lure of drugs and prostitution. She'd died of an overdose.

Emma's foremost concern was Tom. She wasn't sure what he might do if he learned she'd taken over someone's life. He must also never learn about his father. He'd never forgive her for the lies.

"I'm sorry," Whit said in the extending silence. "Am I being too nosy? I'd like to get to know you better, but I don't want to pry into your private life."

"No, it's okay. I'm not used to anyone being interested enough to ask, is all."

"I find that hard to believe. You're very attractive."

"Thank you."

She liked the way he was looking at her, as if he wanted to gobble her up, but it also made her very, very nervous. How to handle being gobbled wasn't within her area of expertise.

He was a toucher, too, and that heightened her sexual awareness of him, and her awareness of her own body. Climbing the steps, he'd put a steadying grip on her elbow. Crossing the busy street, he'd held her hand. She'd never known that elbows and hands could be erogenous zones.

Each contact had sent an electrical current racing through her nervous system. Right now that current pulsed between her legs.

Lord! She tried to redirect her focus away from

what his nearness was doing to her, but the pull—female to male—overpowered logical thought.

What had he asked? Oh, about her birthplace.

"I'm, uh, from Virginia originally, but I've lived different places over the years."

"And how did you wind up in Saint Augustine?"

"Abby's responsible for that. We worked together as waitresses a few years ago in a horrible place. The management was crooked. The food was awful. Only two good things came out of that job—becoming friends with Abby and hearing her talk about her hometown. I fell in love with the city sight unseen."

"So you moved here?"

"Not right away. The opportunity to own my own place only came open for me last year. I wanted to locate somewhere with a moderate climate and thriving tourist trade, but I also wanted a safe, family-oriented community for my son, and preferably something near the ocean, since he loves the water. So, I thought…here's your chance to live in the town of your dreams. I called Abby and asked if she'd like to help me run a business."

"She's your partner?"

"Legally, no, but we're inching toward that. For now she oversees the catering and she's fabulous at it. She works with the local bridal consultants and party planners to give customers an event they'll remember all their lives—costumes, props, scenery, the works. You pick a theme and we can do it. We can dress the staff, dress the customer, dress the guests. We use live centerpieces instead of ice sculptures, too, which is unique."

"Like what?"

"Oh...models dressed as mermaids reclining on a half shell in the middle of a seafood buffet—that sort of thing. No one else around here goes to that extreme."

"So these aren't specific characters like you do in the restaurant?"

"Some are. Some aren't. It depends on what the customer requests. People love themed parties, especially brides. We can whip up anything, given enough time. I have a whole third floor packed with props and costumes."

"What are some of the weddings you've done?"

"Well, we haven't done too many yet because we only opened six months ago and weddings take a lot of advance planning, but we've done several mystery parties. Those are great fun." She thought about what else. "Oh, and we did a *Gone With The Wind* anniversary celebration for an older couple. The hosts dressed as Scarlett and Rhett, and we had a replica of the front porch of Tara. They gave an elegant ball with an orchestra and period dancing and all the guests came in costumes."

"Not exactly my kind of party."

"Too cutesy?"

"Yeah. No offense."

"None taken. My son said the same thing, that it sounded like a 'chick party' to him." They both laughed. "But that's usual for this kind of event. The woman plans it and the man goes along with it because he loves her."

"Makes sense."

"The guests did have fun at that one, though. We got a lot of referrals from it."

"What kooky ones have you done?"

"Mmm, in October a couple plans to be married in one of the local haunted houses. They want me to dress them as Herman and Lily Munster."

He grimaced. "That's way too weird for me."

"Me, too. It doesn't fit in with the elegant atmosphere I maintain for the restaurant, but for private parties I try to be more flexible. Besides, it should be fun getting them ready. I haven't done monsters before. We get a lot of calls for parties with ghost themes, since the city is known for its haunted buildings, but monsters aren't my specialty."

"Can you do it?"

"Oh, sure. No problem."

"Where did you learn your craft?"

"The costumes and makeup?"

"Yes. Where did you study that?"

"I've picked up things here and there. I haven't been to any kind of school, if that's what you mean."

"You're really good for someone who's not trained."

She shrugged. "I suppose it's all that experience playing dress-up as a child." She realized her unintended pun and almost choked.

"What about your family?" he asked. "Are they still in Virginia?"

"My stepfather, yes. He raised me after my mother died."

"You're close?"

"Not much anymore. I visit him a couple of times a year."

They passed a sandbar where big, brown pelicans sunned themselves.

"Oh, look!" she called out. "How pretty."

The boat was fully under way now, and the captain had begun his monologue. The star-shaped Spanish fort, or castillo, on the left bank had once helped protect the town from invaders. Whit took photos of the birds and then the fort, moving from one side rail to the other for a better view.

Emma watched, as entertained by him as by the trip. He seemed to find everything interesting and asked a million questions.

She was having fun. She'd started to worry about the storm, though. Lightning zigzagged over the town. The rain fell in a wide, blue sheet in the distance, but was much closer than before.

They made a circle of the bay, then went up toward the island's lighthouse, painted like a barber pole and topped with a red housing. Whit pointed his camera at the structure. "Great lighthouse."

"Isn't it? Abby and I have done a few parties there."

"Wish we were closer so I could see it better."

"You have to be on foot to get right up to it. There's a little park around it."

"Too bad the boat doesn't go nearer to shore. The scenery here's pretty, though." With the viewfinder still to his eye, he turned the camera toward her and snapped a photo. "Very, very pretty."

"Why did you do that?"

In rapid succession, he took several more shots.

Exasperated, she held her hands in front of her face. "Whit, would you stop it, please?"

"Okay, sorry." He put down the camera. "I only

wanted to show the men in Michigan what they're missing."

"I'm sure they have women in Michigan."

"Not like you."

She rolled her eyes at his outrageousness. "Are you flirting with me?"

Before he could answer, thunder boomed overhead. Rain began to pelt them as if a heavenly hand had opened a faucet. Everyone on the top deck squealed and scrambled for the cover of the lower one.

"Come on," he called out, ushering her down the narrow metal steps. They were among the last people to exit, and all the seats were taken. People crowded between the tables. Whit and Emma could barely get inside.

"Here," Whit said, pulling her against the back wall. He shifted his hanging camera to his side to keep it from digging into her. His muscular arm came to rest above her head.

Very conscious of his impressive chest, Emma felt intoxicated. The man's body was made of steel. He smelled good, too. Fresh, like the rain. Little droplets still clung to his long eyelashes. Goodness! Even soggy he looked great.

Bending down, he whispered playfully, "The answer is yes."

"Yes?"

"Yes, I'm flirting with you."

"Oh." She stifled a grin. "I'm glad we cleared that up."

"Me, too."

"By the way," she whispered back, feeling very

at ease with this man and a bit playful herself. "Your...um...crotch is vibrating."

"That's my phone. It's letting me know I have a message."

"Ah, and here I thought you were just excited about being close to me."

He chuckled low. "Well, that, too."

EVERY WORD THAT CAME OUT of her mouth was probably a lie, but it was such a pretty mouth that Whit had almost convinced himself not to care.

His first priority was to his client, getting what he needed to prove the lady either was or wasn't Emma Webster, but he found himself forgetting that when he looked at her. She had eyes the color of fine aged whiskey and a perfect little body that, at the moment, was so close he could feel the wrinkles on her shirt.

He wasn't sure who was emanating all the heat—him or her—but they were in danger of setting the boat on fire.

Needing a distraction, he got his phone out of his pocket and punched in an encrypted password. The call a moment ago had come from his assistant, Deborah. The message on the small display said: *Morrow is hinky.*

Ah, hell. *Hinky* was Deborah's slang for fishy. Apparently something about Allen Morrow of California hadn't checked out.

He dialed Deborah's cell phone. "It's me," he told her when she answered.

"Can you talk?"

"Having a wonderful time. Thanks for asking."

She chuckled. "Apparently not. Why don't I give you the highlights?"

"That'll do."

"I talked to one of my contacts in the D.A.'s office in Los Angeles and she's never heard of an Allen Morrow or an upcoming case involving a cop killing. He's bogus. The phone number where you reached to him last night is a nonworking one this morning. I had someone check out the location. Vacant office. A guy rented it for a week and paid cash. This joker went to a lot of trouble to talk to you, Whit. Any idea why?"

"I'm thinking."

The firm had its share of phony calls every month—convicts posing as legitimate clients, stalkers trying to locate victims in hiding, nuts wanting information for one reason or another. More than once he'd had people try to hire him to track down the home address of a movie star or musician. They were convinced the star would become as enamored of them as they were of the star....

Whit always had his staff investigate their respective clients before they agreed to take a case. While it was impossible to be completely certain about anyone through a cursory background check, his prerequisites for acceptance were simple: clients had to be reasonably sane, able to afford the hourly fee of four hundred dollars, not desirous of causing damage to another's life and they had to be telling the truth.

He personally had three cases going at the moment in addition to this one—two witness traces for a defense attorney and a missing heir for a multimillion dollar estate. Morrow had obviously been hoping to get information on one of those. But which one? And what info?

The last one most likely, because it carried a two-hundred-and-fifty-thousand-dollar finder's fee. Morrow could be another P.I. trying to beat him out of the money.

Whit couldn't think of anything he'd told him, though. In fact, Morrow had done most of the talking; he'd offered information instead of soliciting it. He'd been polite, open, professional. Nothing the man had said or wanted had raised the "hinky radar," as Deborah called it.

"At the moment, I don't have a clue," he told her.

"Goldblum case, do you think?"

"That's the most probable, but I don't want to make assumptions and miss anything."

"Then let me follow up and see what else I can find out."

"Sounds like a plan. Thanks, Deborah."

He signed off and returned the phone to his pocket.

"Problems?" Susan asked.

"No, nothing major. The office manager needing advice on some claims."

"Ah, I thought maybe it was one of your sisters missing you."

"I've only been gone a few days."

"I'd miss you after a few days." She turned red. "If I was your *sister* I'd miss you. If I was close to you and I was your sister and you went away for a week. Oh, you know what I mean."

He chuckled. She was even lovelier when she got flustered.

She moved to get more comfortable in the cramped

space, and he groaned inwardly as damp fabric slid against damp fabric. Lord! he deserved a medal for good behavior. He'd had a hell of a time keeping his hands to himself today.

"The rain seems to be easing up," he pointed out.

She craned her neck to peer out beyond the couple next to them. "Yes, it does. At least it won't be so hot now. Oh, look, we're coming up to the marina. Darn it, I guess the ride's almost over."

Thank God. He couldn't take much more of this.

Someone bumped him from behind, pushing him even closer to her. She put her hand against his chest to keep from getting crushed. He looped his free arm around her back.

If they'd been in private and horizontal rather than in public and vertical, he'd be in big trouble right about now. Only sheer will kept his lower body from reacting to the intimate contact.

Oh, hell, he was going to do something crazy. He felt the question rising in his throat. Even though he didn't want to ask it, he couldn't seem to stop himself.

"How about when we dock we ride out to the lighthouse or to the beach?"

Damn, now he'd gone and done it. He wanted to kick himself.

Her eyes lit up. "Really?"

"We can have dinner later and you can check out your competition. We could even see a movie after, or go on one of those ghost tours."

"That sounds wonderful, but I've never taken a whole night off before."

"Then you're due one. They can get along without you for a little longer, can't they?"

Whit was walking a fine line. Spending more time with her meant additional opportunities to get information. But it also meant increasing difficulty in retaining his objectivity, already on shaky ground. But a few more hours together probably wouldn't hurt… maybe.

"Come on," he coaxed. "At least help me shop for presents for my nieces and nephews. Otherwise my sisters will be mad and they won't spoil me anymore. You don't want that on your conscience, do you?"

"Of course not."

"Then come with me. And let me take you out to dinner. We'll have a night on the town. Whatever you want to do."

"All right, but I'll need to call in and leave word for the manager. Do you think we'll be back by midnight?"

"What happens at midnight? Do you lose a slipper and turn into Rodney Dangerfield?"

"Maybe," she said with a giggle.

Lord, it was a sweet sound.

"Late date?" he asked.

That really got her tickled. "Yes, fifteen of them. But they don't have to wait until the stroke of twelve to turn back into mice, unfortunately."

"Huh?"

"Never mind. I'm being silly. But I really do need to be back by then to make sure everything's properly closed up."

"Scout's honor, I'll have you home whenever you want."

"We're you ever a Boy Scout?"

"Not even close."

CHAPTER FOUR

TOM WRIGHT loaded the microfilm reader with a roll carrying the April 17, 1984, edition of the *Los Angeles Times* and fumbled around trying to figure out how to work the machine. He didn't like hiding what he was up to from his mom or lying about his whereabouts, but she got so freaked out when he asked questions about his dad that he'd decided he'd get his answers another way.

As he'd told her, the bike rental shop *had* wanted him to come in today and work four hours. But then he'd read an article in the newspaper about this place, a Family History Center they called it, where you could find out about your relatives. He'd asked his boss for the day off and told his friend Tony Parker what he was doing, in case he was late getting to Tony's and his mom called.

Tom fiddled with the knobs. If he could figure this out, he might actually find something.

He asked one of the workers for help. She showed him how to fast-forward, focus on the pages and move them up and down. The name index didn't list William Wright, but Tom hoped to find a news story on his father's accident. The worker suggested he look ahead two weeks in case the navy had delayed reporting it.

He found nothing, not even an obituary.

"Are you certain the date of death is right?" the woman asked.

"Yes, ma'am. My mom gave it to me years ago, but I wrote it down."

"Do you know what your father's date of birth was or his social security number? A middle initial would be good, too."

"No, ma'am, I don't, but I might be able to get them."

"That would help. Meanwhile, I know of a couple of databases we can check and some online sources. Let's see what we can find."

An hour later, they still hadn't come up with anything. Tom's disappointment grew.

"That's odd," the lady said. "I would've thought we'd at least find newspaper articles. Well, here's what we'll do." She went and got a booklet and handed it to him. "In here you'll find instructions for requesting your dad's military records. Those may or may not have the details you want about his death, but they should give you something. One little tidbit often leads to another. Try to fill out as many of the spaces on the form as you can and indicate you want information under the Freedom of Information Act."

"How much will that cost?"

"The search is free, but they'll charge you a fee per page for photocopying. They'll notify you of how much it is before they send the records, though."

"How long will all this take?"

"Honestly, it can take months."

"Months?" He slumped in the chair.

"I know that's discouraging, but they get several million requests every year."

Tom nodded. Whatever it took, he'd do it.

"Meanwhile, I suggest you talk with your mom and surviving members of your family to see what news clippings and documents they already have. That's the best place to start with a genealogy project. What about your grandparents, your dad's parents? Are they still alive?"

"No, ma'am. At least I don't think so."

"Did your dad have brothers or sisters?"

"Not that I know of. My mom's never talked too much about her people or my dad's. She told me once that her and my dad got married real young and their families didn't like it too much. They stopped talking to each other. I never met my grandparents. I don't even know their names."

"That's too bad. But much of this information is readily available if you know where to look."

Tom perked up. "Really? Tell me how."

EMMA WOULD REMEMBER this afternoon as close to perfect. After the boat ride, Whit retrieved his rental car from his motel and took her out to Anastasia Island. He made her climb all one hundred and ten of the circular steps of the lighthouse, and then coerced another tourist into taking a photograph of them together at the top.

After, they visited the public pier, since he said fishing was one of his favorite pastimes. They sat on the concrete seawall and talked. She asked if he'd been out on one of the charter boats yet.

"A few days ago."

"Which one?"

"Uh...*The Blue*...something or other."

"You don't remember?"

"Not off the top of my head."

"I don't know of one with blue in its name."

"I could be wrong."

A couple of hours later, they drove back to the mainland and parked behind the restaurant, then strolled Saint George's pedestrian walkway, shopping for gifts for his seven nieces and nephews.

Ignoring her pleas not to, he picked a hibiscus flower to put behind her ear and bought silly matching T-shirts with cartoon fish on them that read I'm Hooked on Saint Augustine. He insisted they both had to put them on over their clothes and have another photo taken.

After dark he fed her ribs and took her on a carriage ride through downtown. The slow clop-clop of the horse's hooves on the street as they rode along was as soothing as soft music.

"You've asked about me," she said, "and now it's my turn. You've told me hardly anything about yourself."

"Not much to tell. I was born in Lansing. I work with my dad in the office. My sisters live nearby so weekends tend to be a family affair with all of us getting together at my parents' house. I like to play golf and watch football."

"And fish."

"Yeah, and fish. I inherited that gene from my dad."

"Tell me about your mom. What's she like?"

"She's great. She sells real estate, loves antiques

and asks me at least once a day when I'm going to do my part to add to her pool of grandchildren."

"You've never been married?"

"No, and I can't say I've ever even been serious about a woman. I work long hours, and it's hard to sustain a relationship. What about you? Why haven't you remarried?"

"I never met anyone I liked well enough to spend my life with. And I have a son to consider. His welfare and happiness always come first with me."

"He's a lucky kid."

She smiled. "I'm the lucky one. Being both mother and father has been hard at times, but having a child has been the best part of my life."

"Can I ask how your husband died?"

"His unit was training off the coast of California at night. The navy said his equipment must have malfunctioned, because he didn't make the rendezvous. They never found his body."

"Damn, that's rough." He smoothly put one arm around her shoulder and reached over with the other to take her hand, entwining his fingers with hers. Emma didn't mind.

"How old was your son when his father died?"

"Tom wasn't born yet. I'd only just found out I was pregnant."

"I'm sorry."

"It was a long time ago."

"Tell me about your son. How old is he and what's he like?"

"He's talented, smart, handsome and inquisitive, but I guess all mothers think that about their children. For a seventeen-year-old, he's also remarkably self-sufficient. I guess he's had to be, with me working nights most of his life. Thankfully, I don't have to worry about leaving him alone anymore, now that we live above the restaurant."

"His name is Tom? Isn't that what you said?"

"Yes, John Thomas. He'll be a senior in high school this year."

"So you named him for his father?"

The question confused her for a moment. Memories of her little brother nearly closed up her throat. She wondered if J.T. thought of her as often as she thought of him.

"No, my husband's name was William. I named Tom for…well, a little boy I cared very much for as a child."

"A relative?"

"No, a friend."

"Where's Tom tonight? Will he worry about you not being at work?"

"No, he's with his friend Tony Parker. I'm sure they're off somewhere attempting to woo women. That seems to be their primary mission this summer."

He chuckled. "I remember those years well. Wooing women was always my goal on a Saturday night."

"How old are you, Whit?"

"Thirty-six."

Oh, dear. He was even two years younger than her real age.

The carriage finished its loop and dropped them off at eleven-thirty on the bay front across from Illusions. Whit walked her around back, where the double doors were still open and the light barely illuminated the small parking area for staff. The restaurant had closed at eleven but, from inside, the clash of dishes and voices signaled that everyone was still cleaning up.

She stuck her head in to let them know she was back, and then moved out of the light for some privacy.

"I had a great time today, Whit."

"Same here."

"Would you like to come by for lunch tomorrow? My treat. Or drop by in the afternoon and we'll walk up to that store I told you about that has all the unusual china. They have some lovely things that would make good gifts for your sisters and mother."

"I can't, Susan. My plane leaves early in the morning. My vacation is over."

She tried not to look as devastated as she felt. "Oh, I didn't realize."

"Yeah, I need to get back to work on Monday."

"I'm sorry we didn't have more time to get to know each other."

"I wish I'd introduced myself when I first arrived so we could have spent the week together."

"Me, too." She folded her arms across her chest, suddenly feeling chilly, although the temperature had to be seventy-five. "So...this is goodbye, then."

"I'd offer to keep in touch, but I don't want to make promises I might break. I don't know when, or if, I'll ever get down this way again."

"I understand. And you're right. With you way up there and me down here, it doesn't make sense to plan anything."

"The day was great, though."

"Yes. Yes, it was."

"Thanks for showing me around."

"No need to thank me. It was my pleasure."

They stood quietly for a moment facing each other, Emma not knowing what the proper etiquette was for saying goodbye when you didn't want to say goodbye. Every hormone in her body screamed at her to take him to her bed, complications be damned, but sex had never been something she could do without involving her heart.

Sadly, though, with time to get to know this man, the involvement of her heart could have been a real possibility. She sensed it. And that was the only thing she'd regret about this day.

"I should go," he told her, but he didn't.

"And I should go in," she countered, but couldn't make herself.

He stepped forward. She leaned into him. The kiss that followed was even more than she'd imagined it could be—mindless, erotic, wet…perfect.

Afterward, he held her without speaking, just held on tight, as if he didn't want to let her go. He wrapped his arms around her and stood there with his face against her hair, lightly rubbing her back with one hand. His heart beat in staccato, matching hers.

His simple act touched something deep inside her.

"Tom won't be home tonight," she said, no longer caring about propriety, or what was right or wrong.

He'd stiffened at her question. Now he asked, "Was that a statement or an invitation?"

She swallowed hard. "It's whatever you want it to be."

WHIT NEVER GOT THE CHANCE to make a decision. He caught movement in the shadows under the stairs and his instincts and years of training kicked in. He shoved the woman behind him and made a grab for the lurking figure, catching hold of a scruffy man in a military jacket. Who in his right mind wore a heavy jacket in the middle of summer?

He hauled the man into the light. God, he was dirty. He seemed to be bundled up for a snow storm—extra shirts, a cap. His gray beard reached nearly to his waist. He reeked of sweat.

"Whit, don't!" Susan yelled. "Don't hurt him." Suddenly she was between them, protecting the man. "Brownie's a friend."

"He was spying on us."

"No, he wasn't." She made Whit let go of the man. "Brownie, darn it, I've told you not to do that," she scolded, straightening his clothes. "What were you doing under there? You know better."

"Roast duck's the special tonight night, isn't it?" he asked, licking his lips. "Didn't want to miss out. I came early."

"Well, don't be skulking about. It scares people."

"I'm sorry."

"No harm done. Whit, this is Mr. McCormick Brown, known to us around here as Brownie. Brownie, say hello to Mr. Lewis."

"Mr. Lewis," he said politely, and held out a grimy hand.

Whit imagined all the places that hand might have been and didn't want to touch it, but Susan's face silently implored him not to hurt her "friend's" feelings.

He shook it. "Mr. Brown. A pleasure."

The smile Susan gave him was worth getting a few bacteria.

"You a cop?" the old guy asked.

"No, I'm an insurance agent."

"You move like a cop."

Whit didn't respond. Silence, in this instance, was probably the best defense. He looked over at Susan, whose head was cocked as if in thought.

"Can I speak to you a moment?" he asked. "Privately."

"Of course." She turned back to the vagrant. "Sit down on the steps and I'll bring you a plate in a moment."

"Roast duck?"

"Yes, Brownie. Roast duck and a big piece of pie."

Whit walked inside with her to the kitchen and they both washed their hands. "He's homeless?" Whit asked, pulling out a paper towel.

"Yes."

"How often do you feed him?"

"Every night. Throwing away leftover food is wasteful when someone's hungry. We have a few regulars who come by at closing."

"Your *dates* you mentioned earlier?"

"Yes, my little mice. Only they'll never be turned into carriage horses by the swish of a fairy godmother's magic wand."

"Is the food really left over?"

She wrinkled her pert nose. "Well..."

"I thought as much."

"The staff has orders always to fix fifteen to twenty extra plates and set them aside. We pretend the food's left over and that we'll throw it away if it's not eaten. These people have so little dignity left, Whit. We let them believe they're doing us a favor by taking the meals."

"You're inviting trouble having that kind of element hanging around your back door."

"They're *people,* not elements. They've had a streak of bad luck and need someone to be nice to them."

"Admirable on your part, but still, I don't like it."

"You don't have to—it's none of your business."

He tightened his jaw. She was right. He was overstepping his boundaries here. "I'm sorry. It's just that I'm concerned about your safety, Susan."

Her face softened. "I appreciate that, but your concern isn't warranted." She pulled over a serving cart and started stacking it with foil-wrapped plates left on the counter. "Just because a man is homeless doesn't automatically make him a threat."

"No, but a high percentage of the homeless have emotional and mental problems. Many are drug users."

"I'm aware of that. But you don't need to worry. If nothing else, I know how to take care of myself."

He acknowledged to himself that was true. She probably knew a great deal about street people, too, since Emma had been one and she probably *was* Emma.

Had she once lived like McCormick Brown, wearing all her worldly possessions on her back, filthy, reeking of perspiration?

Whit couldn't imagine it. His research into that area of her life had produced sketchy results, but he couldn't visualize her sleeping in an alley and begging for food.

He helped her load a dispenser of iced tea and paper cups onto the cart, then push it outside. She gave a plate and a drink to Brownie. Within a few minutes, other bodies began to emerge from the shadows, first one and then a couple more, until a group of men and women crowded the entrance.

"Here you go, Mr. Ford," Susan said, handing him one of the dinners. "That's a little hot, so don't burn yourself. Hello, Mrs. Maguire. Good to see you. Why Mr. Kinset, how nice to see you back. I missed you last night. Which would you prefer, steak or roast duckling?"

By twelve-thirty, her "mice" had eaten their fill and gone. The staff finished cleaning up and departed, too, leaving them alone.

They stood at the door.

"Well," she said, "here we are again, back at goodbye."

"I'll wait to leave until you've locked up."

His words made his intentions clear: he wasn't going upstairs with her.

She nodded slowly, regret in her expression.

Despite it, Whit vowed not to get close. Touching her, kissing her, had almost done him in. To be on the safe side, he stuck his hands in his pockets and stayed some distance away.

"Bye, Whit. Have a good trip home."

Her voice was so sad, he wavered for a second. Then resolve kicked in.

"Bye, Susan."

He didn't linger, but hightailed it straight for his

car. Susan hadn't gone inside. Instead, she stood and watched him.

He backed out, stopping to put the car in forward gear, and briefly threw up his hand. She lifted hers in response, then went inside and closed the door.

If her friend Brownie hadn't interrupted them before, would he have accepted her invitation and made love to her? The question haunted him as he drove away. He didn't know the answer.

CHAPTER FIVE

SUNDAY MORNING Whit returned his rental car at the Saint John's County Airport. As a precaution against anyone tracing his flight, he bought a ticket in the name of Riley Cantor on a small commuter plane bound for Atlanta.

False identities weren't necessary often. He used them only when the safety or the whereabouts of his client could become an issue. This was one of those instances.

Once in the air, Whit expected his stress to melt away as it often did when he flew, but it stayed with him this morning in the tightness of his shoulders and in the dull headache between his eyes.

He hadn't slept well. A restlessness had plagued him when he'd gotten back to the motel, and had refused to turn him loose. Restlessness, hell. *Arousal* was a better word for the excruciating condition he'd suffered all night.

At dawn, he'd risen and tried to work it out with a long run followed by an ice-cold shower, but neither had done the trick. The cause of his distress—Susan…Emma. With one kiss, she'd managed to inject herself into his blood and leave his body aching for her.

An emotional attraction existed, too, and it was

even more disturbing to him than the physical one. She was bright and funny. He liked her. And he didn't want to. Having feelings of any kind for her was a complication he couldn't afford in his life or with this case, especially today, when the welfare of others had to be foremost in his thoughts.

His destination by a circuitous route was Potock, a little town along the Black Warrior River in the northwest area of Alabama. His client lived there with his newspaper photographer wife and their nineteen-month-old daughter.

That client, J.T. Webster, had legally changed his name years ago to Jack Cahill. He'd been a thief and burglar from the time he could walk, assisting his father, Ray Webster, a career criminal.

Jack's hellish existence had worsened at twelve when his sister Emma ran away. Two years later Ray was arrested for burglary and went to prison again as a repeat offender. Jack was left with the responsibility for his ailing mother. By the time he was sixteen, Jack's mother was dead from emphysema, and he was on his own.

With a background like that, he easily could have ended up incarcerated like his old man. Instead, he'd become a Pittsburgh, then an Alabama cop, working his way up the ranks. Now he was a captain, head of the investigative division of Potock's police department. Whit found that pretty extraordinary considering Jack's childhood.

Although Whit and Jack had lived in Pittsburgh at the same time, Whit hadn't known him when he was with the force. But they had a mutual friend, Jack's former supervisor, Major Wes Campbell. Wes had been the one who'd asked Whit to find Jack's sister.

Initially Whit had agreed only as a favor to Wes. Once he'd met Jack, though, he'd quickly grown to like him and his quirky little wife Erin. "Lucky" her family called her.

The Cahills were nice people. Whit hoped the news he brought them today would be welcome.

FROM ATLANTA, Whit used a different identity to lease a puddle jumper to fly himself the rest of the way to Potock. When the plane touched down at the small rural airport, Jack was waiting.

"Hey, Whit," Jack said warmly. "Good to see you again."

"Good to see you, too." They shook hands. "How's the family? Are you keeping Lucky out of trouble?"

"As best I can, but it's a full-time job."

"I'll bet."

Jack's wife had a knack for being in the wrong place at the wrong time and for stumbling over dead bodies. Twenty-one in the past fifteen years, to be exact. Whit was sure Jack was pulling his leg about that until he'd looked up the newspaper articles and confirmed it.

Two years ago, she'd almost become a victim herself, along with her unborn child, when she'd gotten tangled up in a double murder investigation. She'd been shot, and for the second time in her life, nearly drowned in the river. Somehow, she'd survived, and her uncanny intuition had helped Jack solve the two murders—bodies number nineteen and twenty.

Jack put a lot of stock in Lucky's intuition and therefore Whit did, too. He was curious to know what she'd recommend—whether Jack should attempt to see Emma or not.

Whit and Jack walked to Jack's Blazer, stowed Whit's bags in the rear and got in. "Lucky insists you stay at the house with us instead of going to a motel," Jack told him. "You can take the downstairs bedroom again, if that's okay."

"That's fine. I appreciate it."

"How come all the secrecy with the flight?"

"Only being cautious."

"I was surprised to see you exit that cockpit. I didn't know you were a pilot."

"Yeah, I got my license when I was nineteen, but I've been hopelessly hooked on flying most of my life."

The blame for his obsession, he told Jack, fell on the shoulders of his grandmother, who was a pilot like her late father. When Whit was twelve, she'd taken him aloft and let him pilot the plane by himself. A big mistake. He'd pestered her every weekend after that to give him lessons.

He loved to fly. When he'd chosen a career as an FBI agent rather than as a commercial or military pilot, his decision had been a surprise to everyone in his family, just as it had been a surprise when he'd suddenly left the bureau to become a private investigator.

But he'd made the right decision both times. Flying, in his case, wasn't a good fit as a career. He thought of it as fun, not work. And he'd been stifled by the bureaucracy of the FBI. Having his own company and running things his own way was better, even if he occasionally had to do things he didn't like.

"So," Jack said, his anxiety apparent. "You have good news for me?"

"I do."

"Thank God. You were so cryptic on the phone, I've been driving myself nuts wondering what to think."

"Sorry. I felt it was best to wait until we could talk in person and I could let you look at some photographs. I'm pretty sure I've found Emma, but I'll be honest with you, Jack, the news isn't all good. We have complications. And we need to discuss the ramifications before you decide where you want to go with this."

Jack blew out a nervous breath. "What kind of complications?"

Whit gave him an abbreviated version during the ride to the house. Later, after eating a light lunch Lucky had prepared, she put the baby down for a nap and the three of them sat on the deck overlooking the river, the couple's old dog at Jack's feet. Whit repeated the story he'd told Jack on the drive in, but with more detail.

Before he'd left that morning, he'd taken his photos to be developed at a one-hour processor. Now he arranged them on the table in front of them.

"What do you think?" Whit asked Jack. "Is it her?"

"I don't know. Dammit! I can't tell. I was only a kid when Emma left home. I think there's a resemblance to my late mother, but I'm not sure if it really exists or if I'm seeing what I want to see."

Lucky picked up the photo of Whit and ''Susan'' in their matching T-shirts and studied it. Her gaze met Whit's. Under her scrutiny, he shifted in his chair like a naughty child.

He wondered what she was thinking. He didn't have to wait long to find out.

''You two look as snug as two worms in an ear of corn,'' she drawled in her thick Southern accent. ''Even Jack and I don't own spiffy matching outfits like this.''

''The tourist charade was necessary to get the photographs,'' Whit explained, finding his mouth suddenly dry. ''I didn't like lying to her, but sometimes subterfuge is necessary in my line of work.''

''Uh-huh. Was it a hardship to put your arm around her waist like that?'' she asked, amused.

Jack jabbed her in the ribs with his elbow. ''Lucky, don't tease the man. He was doing a job.''

''I was only asking a question—trying to understand the situation. Whit doesn't mind, do you, Whit?''

''No, I don't mind.''

''What's she like? You obviously had a good time.''

''She's interesting. Funny. Creative. I enjoyed spending the day with her.''

''And *her* with *you,* I'd bet. You're not exactly butt ugly.''

''That's a compliment, Whit,'' Jack explained.

''Uh...thanks.''

Lucky looked at the photo again. ''I don't imagine this woman, regardless of who she is, would be too thrilled to find out her handsome sightseeing buddy was really a P.I. hired to get information."

Boy, she'd read his mind.

"Probably not," Whit told her.

"So how do we handle that? If she *is* Emma, do we mention to her, at some point, that you were the private investigator we hired? Or do we keep your name to ourselves and never let her know the truth?"

"That depends on what decisions you make here today. You need to do whatever is best for you and Jack. I'll go along with it."

"You're likely to be put between a rock and a hard place."

"That won't be anything new."

THE WAIL OF A CHILD made all three adults turn toward the patio door. Even the dog got up to have a look through the glass.

"Uh-oh," Jack said. "Sounds like Her Highness doesn't want to sleep today."

Lucky pushed back her chair and stood. "You two go ahead. I'll check on her."

After she went inside, Whit continued his story, explaining to Jack how he'd conducted the investigation.

"The woman you and Emma knew as a child, the old friend of your father's, Estelle DeShazo—"

"Vinnie's wife. She worked for a mortuary."

Whit nodded. "She provided good information. She thought Emma might've headed for Hollywood to try and get a job as a makeup artist or costumer for a movie studio. That bit of information put me in touch with some of the people Emma hung around with."

"Are you sure it was Emma? I searched there."

"Reasonably sure. But I had to track down hundreds of false leads before I came up with anything I could use."

"No wonder the two P.I.s I hired before you had no luck. Hell, I looked for her myself for nearly three years and didn't come up with a thing."

"I'm not surprised. She's sharp. A real chameleon. Finding her took a lot of old-fashioned legwork. I literally had to get out and pound the pavement."

"For which I'm eternally grateful. If you'd only let me pay you—"

"No—" Whit held up his hand to stop him. "We're not arguing about money again. This one's on me, Jack. Besides," he added, grinning, "you can't afford me."

Jack chuckled. "Damn, that's for sure. Four hundred an hour plus expenses? I'll never see that kind of salary in my lifetime. But I have a bit left in savings."

"No, I'm not letting you use up your savings. One day you can do me a favor in return, and we'll call it even."

"You name it, buddy. Anytime."

Jack looked through some of Whit's material while Whit outlined the various leads he'd followed and how Emma's inability to find work had affected her choices.

"I had that photograph you gave me," Whit said, "and showed it at the costume and prop businesses, homeless shelters and other places where kids who lived on the street back then hung out and panhandled. Naturally, too many years have passed for people to remember. But I did find an old priest whose church still runs a food kitchen where she often ate and sometimes worked for a few dollars. He was very helpful."

The door slid open. Lucky came out, carrying her daughter on her hip. Cute kid. Short curly hair like her mother. She favored Jack in the face, though. Lucky had her dressed in bright yellow shorts and a top with ducks.

"She refuses to sleep," Lucky said. "She knows we're out here and she can't stand not being in the middle of the action."

"Too much like her mother," Jack told Whit with a wink.

Whit tickled the toddler's midriff. "Hey, Gracie. Remember me?"

She smiled at him, not seeming to care that he was a stranger, but when he offered to hold her, she got shy and let it be known she preferred to go to her daddy.

With the baby settled contentedly in Jack's lap, Lucky sat down again. "What did I miss?" she asked.

"Emma lived on the street," Jack explained, clearly affected by this new piece of information. "She had to beg for money and eat at soup kitchens."

Lucky rubbed his back in comfort. "That was a long time ago. You can't let it upset you." She turned to Whit. "You don't think she was into anything really bad, do you? I mean like prostitution."

"No, I haven't seen any evidence of that. Police never charged her with solicitation or any other crime.

I think when she failed to get a job, she was left with the problem of simply surviving. She fell back on what she knew and was good at."

"Running cons," Jack said.

"Right. But my evidence suggests she gave them up when her son was born, or at least shortly after. She's seemingly lived a straight life for the past seventeen years."

"Only doing it as *someone else.*"

"Yes."

"And why is that if she's living straight?"

"I don't know, Jack, and it worries me. She has no reason that I can see to be using another name."

"What about the boy's father?" Jack asked. "Where is he? *Who* is he?"

"He's an unknown factor we should be cautious about. I never found a trace of him. He's listed on the boy's birth certificate as William Wright, and she tells people that's his name and that he died in a military accident. But he never existed."

"Maybe her son's the reason she's still using the name," Lucky pointed out. "Once she started calling herself Susan and had given her child the last name Wright, she couldn't go back to being Emma Webster."

"I believe that's part of it," Whit said, nodding, "but not the whole story. She's moved from place to place over the years and deliberately tried to cover her tracks. In her driver's license photos it looks as if she altered her appearance each time. She gave varying stories about her background whenever she applied for employment. People only do that when trouble is after them or they're trying to leave behind something unpleasant."

Lucky agreed that sounded like a reasonable conclusion.

"Here's what I found out," Whit said. "She never used the name Emma at all. She called herself Jennifer Hart for a while, then April Dancer and later Rachel Stanton."

Jack made a noise.

"What?" Whit asked. "Do those names mean something to you?"

"Maybe. Be right back." Jack handed the baby to Lucky, went inside and returned to the deck with his notebook computer. "Lucky, what's the address of that Web site you were looking at the other night with all the movies? The one with the searchable database."

Whit watched as Jack typed in the Web address Lucky gave him, and then did a search on a name.

"Well, I'll be damned," Jack said. "I thought those names sounded familiar. When Emma and I played as kids, we'd pretend to be other people, mostly characters from TV and movies. We'd create these long stories and act them out, sometimes going on for months at a time. I got hooked on John Wayne. That's why I chose Cahill when I changed my name. It's a Wayne character. Emma loved Stefanie Powers. Look here."

Jack showed Whit the list of Powers's characters. She'd played Rachel Stanton in a 1971 TV movie called *Sweet, Sweet Rachel.* In the 1966 show *The Girl From U.N.C.L.E.* her character was called April

Dancer. She'd been Jennifer Hart in the series *Hart To Hart* with Robert Wagner.

"That clinches it for me," Whit said. "Combine that with the other evidence we have, particularly what she named her boy, and I'm convinced Susan is Emma. But the only way to be certain or to know why she's still living under this false identity is to confront her."

"So, let's confront her," Lucky said. "Surely when she sees Jack and knows he's her brother she'll be thrilled."

Whit and Jack looked at each other.

"What?" Lucky asked them, not understanding why their faces were grim.

"That's a problem," Jack answered.

"How so?"

"Because identifying ourselves to her leaves *us* exposed to whatever danger she's running from."

"And don't forget," Whit added, "she's involved somehow in the disappearance of the real Susan Roberts."

"Oh." Lucky frowned. "I hadn't thought of that. You don't think she actually...disposed...of Susan, do you?"

"No, I don't think so," Whit told her. At least he hoped to hell she hadn't. "I'd be very surprised if she was a killer. She doesn't fit the profile of a violent person."

He told them how she fed homeless people every night after closing the restaurant and that she seemed devoted to her son.

"That's so sweet," Lucky said. "I like her already."

Whit cautioned her not to let that sway her opinion.

"Until we know more, we can't rule out any possibility. For your safety, we assume the worst scenario. Understood?"

They both nodded.

"So what do we do?" Lucky asked. "Jack, if you walk away from your sister now...I know you. You'll regret it for the rest of your life."

"I may have to walk away, sweetheart. I won't risk you and Grace for anything."

"But you've searched for Emma for so long."

"You and the baby are my first responsibility."

"But we don't know there really *is* any danger until we approach her and talk to her."

Whit interrupted the exchange by making an offer. "Let me go to her on your behalf and express your interest in reestablishing contact. I'll be your buffer."

Jack shook his head. "I don't know, Whit. We've inconvenienced you enough."

"You haven't inconvenienced me."

"Couldn't we simply get our attorney to forward a letter or call her? Not that I don't want you to do it—I just feel bad asking you to work on this case another day. You've done so much already."

"You *could* have a letter forwarded, but I'd feel better if I handled it personally. It makes more sense. I can eliminate the risk to you two while I look a little deeper. I'll make it clear that you have concerns about why she's using this false identity. Maybe she'll confide in me. If she doesn't...you drop it. You never have to see her."

"Sounds good to me, but..." He turned to Lucky. "What do you think?"

"I think...that I'm glad I'm not poor Emma. Despite our good intentions, we're about to pull the rug out from under her."

Jack sighed. "You just said two minutes ago that I should do this. If you'd rather I didn't, I won't."

"No, you should go ahead. Definitely. If I was Emma, I'd want to see my brother again, no matter what I'd gotten myself tangled up in."

"Should Whit be the one to talk to her? Yes or no?"

She looked at Whit, and the question showed in her expression. Did he *want* to see Emma again?

He nodded.

"Yes," she told Jack. "Whit should be the one to talk to her. I trust him. I know he'll do the right thing for you. And if Emma *is* in trouble, maybe Whit can help her."

"Okay, then it's settled. Whit, do what you think is best."

"Good. I'll fly back tomorrow with any items you want me to give her—a letter...photographs. You decide how much you want her to know about yourselves. I'll keep your real names and location a secret until we understand the situation a little more."

"A videotape would be good," Lucky suggested. "It would be more personal than still shots."

"Great idea. You can put that together tonight."

A car pulled into the gravel parking area in the back and a handsome older man got out. He walked toward the deck.

"And here comes our final problem," Whit told them. "It may be the most difficult one to resolve."

Jack's father ascended the stairs. Released from prison two years ago due to overcrowding, Ray Webster had tracked down his son and eventually reconciled with him. Webster now wanted a similar second chance with his daughter.

But would Emma be as forgiving as Jack? Whit didn't think so. And that was going to make this reunion a whole lot harder to pull off.

RAY SIPPED HIS LEMONADE and listened while the Lewis fella gabbed about *the problem*—meaning him—and what they were gonna do about it. Nobody asked for his opinion, and Ray didn't offer it. He'd already made up his mind. He didn't care what they said. When the time was right, he'd see Emma, with or without their permission.

Oh, he didn't expect she'd be too happy to see him, but neither had J.T. when Ray first looked him up, and that had turned out okay. Him and the boy got along real good these days. And Lucky…well, he thought a lot of that little gal. She treated him like family.

"I think we need to consider Ray's feelings in this, too," she said right about then, and Ray smiled to himself. Leave it to Sweet Pea to look out for his interests.

The three of them argued a bit more. Ray let them. He drank himself another glass of lemonade and entertained the baby by pretending to pull M&M's out of her ears.

Time in prison had taught him patience. He'd waited twenty-three years to see Emma again, and he could wait a little longer. Let them work out *the problem* any way they saw fit. But nobody was keeping him away from his girl. Or from the grandson he'd never met.

CHAPTER SIX

ON THE PRETENSE of washing them, Emma systematically ran her hand over the glass in the windows of the largest banquet room, feeling for a ridge that would indicate a pane had been removed and put back in. She checked the locks and sills to see if any had been tampered with and looked at the sensors for loose wires.

Her security system was top of the line, custom-made to her specifications, yet last night someone had managed to bypass the zone that covered the restaurant. But how? She'd found no noticeable place of entry.

The crime didn't make sense. Nothing seemed to be missing. She knew the burglar had searched the office, because she was meticulous about the location of her papers, both on her desk and in the safe, and some had been slightly askew this morning. A paperweight had also been moved from where she'd left it last night when she'd locked up.

He'd slipped in and out almost without her knowing, which told her he was a professional.

But why a pro with the skill of this guy would be interested in her place was a mystery. True, some of the costumes and props in the display cases were valued at several thousand dollars each, but he hadn't touched them.

Besides, that was chump change for an elite thief. He'd never waste his skill or reputation on anything so inexpensive. He'd go after jewelry, paintings and other art objects. Nothing less than a couple hundred thousand was worth the effort.

The whole thing puzzled her and made her nervous. Being the victim instead of the perpetrator was an unsettling experience.

Thank God he hadn't tried to come up the interior stairs. While her apartment and the storage floor above it were both covered by separate zones of the system and had dead bolt locks on the doors, the thought of some man being *right there,* inside the building, unnerved her.

Lots of nights she didn't lock those stairwell doors. And both she and Tom were bad about pausing the zones for the stairs and restaurant and wandering down to the kitchen in their pajamas for a late snack.

"Need a hand?"

The masculine voice made her jerk. She whirled, striking out as she did, but he grabbed her wrist before she connected.

"Whoa. It's me."

"Whit? God! Don't sneak up on me like that. You almost gave me a heart attack."

"Sorry. Abby said it was okay if I came on back."

"I thought you left yesterday. What are you doing here?"

"Change of plans. Hey, you're shaking. Did I scare you that badly?"

"No, I'm okay." She pulled away and tried to compose herself.

"You don't look okay. Is something wrong?"

"I'm fine. You gave me a fright, is all."

The weirdest feeling hit her, that maybe Whit was responsible for the break-in. He was the only stranger who'd been lurking about the past few days. He'd also fumbled the name of the fishing boat he'd supposedly chartered, which was odd.

What was it Brownie had said? That Whit "moved like a cop." But professional thieves knew how to take care of themselves, too. They could disable a person in less than ten seconds using only their hands. At least that had been Emma's experience.

No, the idea was crazy. She refused to believe he'd been attentive only to get information so he could rob her. But, then again, how ironic would *that* be? Probably every victim she'd ever conned had told him or herself the same thing.

God, she hated being so suspicious. She longed to throw her arms around his neck and show him how wonderful it was to see him again. He looked good enough to eat in a pair of khaki slacks and a pale blue polo shirt, his skin lightly tanned from their day spent in the sun. His...maleness...dominated the room. She found it overpowering and wildly alluring.

He carried a large brown envelope, but he didn't offer it to her. Photos of their time together? She hoped so. A memento would be nice.

"Did you take a few more days of vacation?" she asked.

"Something like that." He smiled but it didn't

reach his eyes. "Can you take a break? I need to talk to you."

"All right, but could you help me put out these ferns first? Abby wants to use them as part of the centerpiece for the buffet table at tonight's party. And I need to make a quick check of the costumes for the servers."

"Sure, no problem." He looked around with interest at the props she and Abby had already put in place, his gaze settling on the six-foot-tall trees of papier-mâché, chicken wire, cloth and paint.

"What's this going to be?"

"A forest for a birthday party. The little girl has a favorite book about an elf queen, and we're recreating the setting and characters."

"Everything looks great."

"I hope so. We're charging the parents a small fortune, but we've also invested a lot in the decorations."

"Are those boulders real?"

"Fake. Unless you touch them, though, you can't tell the difference. Those and the canvas backdrops of vegetation and sky are really Aztec, from an old Chuck Norris–Lou Gossett movie, but no one will know that. See that blue plastic? Air piped underneath will make it undulate and look like a rippling pond."

"Very clever."

"I think so. The throne is the centerpiece for the table and will seat the queen. The servers will be dressed as gnomes and trolls."

"My nieces would love this."

They moved the palms and arranged them at the base of the throne, and then she led the way to the back of the banquet rooms, where they kept the costumes and had dressing rooms for the staff.

The long corridor contained numbered clothes racks and shelves along each side. Male costumes went on the left, female on the right. Each server had a number that corresponded to his or her specific costume and accessories.

Emma made a quick check of each piece according to the list on her clipboard, but she had trouble reading the one for the woman playing the elf queen. She pushed the intercom to reach Abby in the office.

"Abby, what's Cathy Carter's number? I can't tell if this is a thirteen or an eighteen on your sheet."

"Thirteen. But we have a major problem. Cathy called a minute ago and said she won't be able to make it. Sick child."

"Oh, no!"

"Can you take her place? You fit the costume."

"Can't one of the servers do it? Mimi's about the right size."

"I need everyone. You know how short-staffed we are. And Mimi's not scheduled to work tonight."

"Ask her to come in."

"I did that twice last week. I've been telling you we need to hire more help."

"I know, and I've scheduled interviews for the next two days, but for tonight, call the agency and see if they have a model they can send over."

"And blow my budget on this party? No way. Too expensive. Please, Susan? All you have to do is sit there and look elflike. You already do anyway, with your short hair and the way your nose turns up at the end."

"My nose doesn't turn up."

Next to her, Whit coughed, amused by her indignation.

"Do I hear the handsome Whitaker Lewis chuckling in the background?" Abby asked. "I sent him back there a while ago to see you."

"Yes, he's standing right here listening to you make fun of my face, thank you very much."

"Hey, Whit," Abby called out.

"Hey, Abby."

"Doesn't her nose turn up?"

"A bit," he said, chuckling again, "but it's really cute."

SHE WAS A hundred-thirty-pound dynamo. Whit watched as she directed the delivery of the fresh flowers, gave her seal of approval to the appetizers, checked linens and barked out orders for the arrangement of tables—all at the same time.

"I'm sorry," she told him, finally stopping. "That took longer than I expected." She glanced at her watch. "I have a couple of hours before I have to start dressing for the party. We can talk. My office?"

"Not private enough. Could we go up to your apartment? That is, if your son's not there."

She hesitated, as if afraid to let him into her home. Her reaction seemed odd, given her invitation on Saturday night.

"If that makes you uncomfortable—"

"No," she said quickly, "I think that's exactly what we need to do, go to my apartment. Let me show you around. In fact, I'm going to take you on a tour of the entire building and let you look at everything in my collection. We'll even go up to the third floor where I have the rest of my costumes and memorabilia stored."

He found her offer strange, but what the hell. If it meant getting her someplace private, then he'd play along.

"Sure, okay."

"Good. You've already seen the display cases in the dining room. Most everything of value is in there."

She showed him up the steep stairs to the second floor, and it was hell watching the movement of her jean-clad rear. The pants had a quarter-sized hole worn in the right side, and red fabric showed beneath the fringed edges. Red panties? Had to be. Her top was blue and stopped right below the waistline.

Red silk?

He pushed the image from his mind and concentrated on putting one foot in front of the other.

They reached the second-floor landing, where she unlocked her door. Her apartment was interesting, big rooms with high ceilings. The low drone of a television somewhere was the only sound.

"Nice place," he said.

"It suits my needs for the time being. As soon as I can afford it, I plan to buy a house for me and Tom. That's something we've never had."

"But won't he be leaving home pretty soon?"

She frowned. "No law says he has to rush off when he graduates from high school. He might live at home while he's going to college."

The subject was obviously a touchy one. He dropped it. "How many square feet is this place?"

"Each floor has about seven thousand."

He whistled.

A second whistle—not his—rent the air. "Stop right there!" a voice said. Whit crouched into a fighting stance but didn't see anybody. "Hands against the wall."

Susan doubled over with laughter. "That's Houdini, my son's bird. Tom must have left his bedroom door open, and Houdini can hear us."

Another whistle turned into a series and became identifiable as the theme song from the *Law and Order* TV show.

"Damn!" Whit straightened, and his heart finally returned to normal. "How does he do that? He sounds like a real person."

"Unfortunately, he thinks he *is* a person. He can mimic anything. And he's become a cop show addict. We've been trying to wean him, but it's not working."

She introduced Whit to the bird and let him look around the apartment, reciting a weird monologue as she went about the value of various objects. She showed him her son's room, her bedroom and her personal dressing room.

Even though he'd grown up with three sisters, he'd never seen so many wigs, shoes, dresses and junk jewelry in one place. She had four different "heads" that looked exactly like her and they all had fake skin attached.

A dressmaker's dummy wore a harem costume. Nearby was a wig with a long blond ponytail.

"My clothes from last night," she said. "Barbara Eden as the genie in that old show, *I Dream of Jean-*

nie. But the costume's a copy, not the original,'' she added hastily. ''Not worth anything. I no longer own many originals, and no valuable ones, except what's downstairs in the cases.''

He imagined her in the see-through pants, bra and short-cut jacket and unintentionally verbalized his reaction with a grunt.

''What?''

''Nothing.''

''You started to say something.''

''I, uh...was going to ask about the heads. Is that how you make yourself look different?''

''Yes, they're molded replicas of my face made out of alginate. Dental stone. It's like what the dentist uses when he makes impressions of teeth. The skin is liquid latex. That goes on the head to make a mask that fits me perfectly so it looks natural and not fake. Then I bake and paint it to resemble whatever character I'm portraying.''

''Sounds complicated.''

''Not too much if you've been doing it a while. The process can be time-consuming, though. Two hours for the simple ones. Four or more for the others. I always make several at one time to stay ahead. And I play recurring characters to simplify things.''

Next, they climbed the stairs to the third floor, one gigantic room without walls, but packed from floor to ceiling with more costumes and every kind of object he could imagine. And many he couldn't.

''Wow!'' He followed behind as she walked a trail through the boxes and racks, pointing out items of significance or movies they'd been used in.

''Sometimes I come up here and spend hours trying

on different things for the fun of it,'' she admitted. She pulled out a pirate's hat and put it on him, then swapped it for a World War II army helmet. ''What did you like to play as a little boy?''

''Oh, cowboys and comic book heroes. Superman, Batman, the Green Hornet. The usual stuff. But most of all, I wanted to grow up and be Bruce Lee.''

''I have a ton of martial arts things, mostly ninja. Let's look.''

They spent more than an hour going through wardrobe cabinets and racks and pulling out things to try on. The props were great—swords, nunchucks, fake throwing stars. Whit felt like a kid again.

Finally she sank down cross-legged on the carpet and motioned for him to take a seat on a box. ''Sorry, I get carried away.''

''How do you keep up with all this stuff?''

''Everything's been catalogued and labeled. See here?'' She showed him a tag on one of the garments; typed on it was a collection name and a series of numbers. ''It might not look like it, but everything has a place. Every item has a number that corresponds to a master list, which tells what it is and what movie or set it came from. And while I haven't taken every piece out and looked at it, I'm very familiar with the list. I pretty much know everything that's up here.''

''I see.''

''And none of it's worth much. I'll show you the list, if you like.''

There she went talking weird again. ''I don't need to see the list.''

''Suit yourself.''

''But I do need to talk to you about something.''

"Okay, shoot."

"I have a confession." He ran a hand through his short-cropped hair. He hadn't expected this to be so hard.

She sighed heavily. "I already know you're not an insurance agent from Michigan, if that's the confession you're getting ready to make. The whole tourist thing was a scam to get information out of me."

"What gave me away?"

"You made a few small mistakes."

He nodded. He knew he had. "So, you know why I'm here?"

"Yes." Her expression was glum. "I'm surprised you're admitting it, though. I figured you'd just do the job and run, and I'd never know who you really were."

"I didn't want it that way. I wanted to explain."

"Well, gee thanks," she said sarcastically. "That makes everything okay."

"Look, whether you believe it or not, I am sorry for the deception. And you're wrong if you believe the whole thing was a scam. I enjoyed every minute I spent with you."

"But a job's a job, and the client comes first, right?"

He tightened his jaw. "Yes."

"Well, you can go back and tell your client that he's out of luck."

"You don't mean that."

"I most certainly do. As you've seen here today, I don't have anything for you to steal."

"For me to—?" Whit was sure he'd heard her correctly; he just didn't believe what he was hearing.

"I swear that everything I own is tied up in this business and the rest is in an irrevocable trust for my son. You can look through all the boxes and closets in the building if it will satisfy your curiosity, but you wasted your time breaking in here last night."

"Breaking in? What the hell are you talking about? I didn't break in here last night!"

His own confusion was reflected in her face. "But, I thought..." She jumped to her feet. "Wait a minute. You're *not* a thief?"

"A thief? Hell, no. I'm a private investigator."

EMMA TEETERED between being overjoyed that he wasn't her thief and terrified that he might really be a P.I. like he said. She demanded he show her identification.

He took out a business card, wrote something on the back and handed it to her. She read the front to herself. *Whitaker Lewis. Lewis Investigations, Pittsburgh. Licensed in Pennsylvania, New York, Florida, Texas, Oklahoma and California.*

"This is the oldest scam on earth," she told him, not impressed. "People print up phony business cards all the time. If I call this number, who's going to answer? Some bimbo you've hired to pretend to be your secretary?"

"Dial directory assistance and get the number for Lewis Investigations yourself. Then call it. My assistant's name is Deborah. She's waiting to hear from you."

Emma walked to the wall phone by the door and did as he said. The Deborah person confirmed the owner of the company was a Whitaker Lewis.

"Describe him," Emma asked.

"Six-two, one-eighty, blue eyes, dark hair cut real short. Built like a brick wall."

"Distinguishing marks?"

"A scar on his right shoulder. Horseshoe shaped. One of his sisters bit him when they were children."

She ordered Whit to show her the scar. He undid a few top buttons and pulled open his shirt. The mark *did* look like a bite.

"Put him on," the Deborah woman said, "and I'll confirm he's my boss."

She handed him the phone. "Hey, Deborah. Yeah, she's not very trusting, but she has reason. Thanks for the help. Yeah, I will." He hung up. "Satisfied?"

To be positively sure, Emma asked him for his driver's license. The description and photo matched.

Damn! A thief she could handle. But a P.I. might be a whole lot more trouble.

Who'd sent him? One of the people she'd scammed? But that had been years ago. Surely no one was looking for her after all this time. She reminded herself to stay cool and not to admit anything.

"Okay, you're a private investigator. What do you want?"

"Before I tell you that, we should talk about this thief you thought I was."

"That's none of your business."

"I'm making it my business."

"You can't just decide it's going to be your business."

"Sure I can. Now, tell me what happened. What did he take? What did the police say?"

"Read my lips...*none of your business.*"

"I can help you."

"Help me? Why on earth would I want anything you had to offer?"

"You didn't call the police, did you? You couldn't take the chance they might start looking into your background."

"I think it's time you left."

"I warned you your mice were trouble."

"Get out."

She ushered him out the door, reset the burglar alarm and started down the stairs.

"Don't you at least want to know who my client is?"

"No."

"I'm not going away. I'll keep coming back again and again until you talk to me."

She stopped and turned, almost bumping into him. "Okay, if it'll get rid of you, I'll play. Who is your client?"

"We need privacy."

She threw up her arms in frustration. He could be the most irritating man.

"All right. My apartment. You have five minutes." She showed him back inside her place, where he took a seat on the couch. Emma sat in the chair across from him.

"Well?" she asked. "The clock is ticking."

"Your brother hired me, Emma. He's been looking for you for several years."

Emma. He'd called her Emma.

Although her insides had turned to liquid, she refused to allow herself to show any reaction. Whit had lied to her before about his identity. He could be lying now. On the heels of last night's break-in, she wasn't inclined to take anything or anyone at face value.

When she was certain she could speak, she fell into character.

"I don't know what you expect me to say. You've made a mistake. I don't have a brother. I told you, I'm an only child."

"Who visits her stepfather twice a year?"

"Yes."

"Pretty hard to do when he's been dead since 1996."

She didn't blink. "You've gotten your facts confused. My stepfather is alive and well in Virginia."

"*Susan Roberts's* stepfather once lived in Virginia."

"I *am* Susan Roberts."

"No. You're Emmaline Jeanette Webster, born May 1, 1964 in Paxton, Louisiana, the eldest child of Grace and Ray Webster. They nicknamed you Emma. Three years later, on March 10, 1967, your parents had a second child, John Thomas, born in Biloxi, Mississippi. You always called him J.T. Your family moved around because your father was a con artist and a thief. He taught you and J.T. to follow in his footsteps. Should I go on?"

"Please do. I'm finding this all very fascinating."

"At fifteen, while living in Cleveland, Ohio, you ran away. You drifted for a while, and then wound up in Hollywood and Los Angeles, California, where you lived on the streets. At nineteen, you became pregnant. At twenty, you gave birth to a son, named after the brother you'd left behind. You took over the identity of Susan Roberts and you've been living as her for the past twenty-three years."

He paused.

"And?" Emma asked. "Well, do go on. I'm a thief, a runaway and a homeless person. I'm dying to know what comes next."

"Your brother asked me to give you this." He put the package on the coffee table between them. "Inside is a videotape, a letter and photographs. They should answer some of your questions. I've rented a small bungalow over on the island. The address and phone number are on the back of my business card. Contact me when you're finished watching the tape and we'll talk again. If you can't reach me there, my cell phone number is on the bottom."

Tears wanted to fall, but Emma wouldn't let them. God! Could he really represent J.T.? She wanted so badly to believe, to rip open the package and see what was inside, but she didn't trust him. Most of the information he'd spouted was public record. The rest… he was fishing. He couldn't really know, could he? She'd been too careful.

He was a lousy, lying bastard who'd jerked her around and played with her emotions. At the moment, her inclination was not to believe him.

She leaned forward, picked up the envelope and tossed it back at him.

"I'm not interested in whatever scam you're trying to pull. You breeze into my life, romance me to get information for some strange reason, and now you have to nerve to hand me a bogus videotape. If I was this Emma person, and I'm not, why on earth would I believe anything you had to say?"

"Because I'm telling the truth."

"Oh, now you're telling the truth. Fancy that, after all the lies you've told."

"I'm sorry about the deception before. I didn't mean to hurt you."

"Hurt me? Don't flatter yourself. You were an entertaining diversion, is all." She got up and showed him to the door. "I want you out of my building."

He walked into the hallway but didn't leave. "Don't hold anything I did against your brother. He loves you. He wants very much to talk to you, to be part of your life again."

"I told you, I don't have a brother."

"Emma."

"Don't call me that!"

"Whatever trouble you're hiding from, I can help. Trust me."

She started to tell him where he could stick his trust when the exterior door across the corridor opened and Tom walked in. He looked at her and then Whit with curiosity. Emma silently cursed. Her chest still heaved with indignation, and she knew her face must be red.

"Hey," Tom said. "What's up?"

Emma plastered on a fake smile. "I should ask you that. You're home from work early."

"The weather got bad. Nobody was renting bicycles and scooters, so we closed."

"I see." Tom's gaze cut to Whit. "Oh, Tom, this is Mr. Lewis. He's…a friend. I was showing him some of the costumes upstairs. Whit, this is my son, Tom."

Whit nodded. "Tom."

"Mr. Lewis," Tom said, and then turned to Emma.

"Okay if Tony comes over tonight? We wanted to rent some movies."

"That's fine, but be sure and keep the doors locked inside and out." She didn't dare look at Whit when she added, "A couple of businesses on the block have reported break-ins lately."

"No kidding?"

"No kidding," she lied. "You and Tony both need to be very careful going in and out after dark."

"Okay, I'll tell him. Nice to meet you, Mr. Lewis."

"You, too, Tom."

When Tom left, Emma let out the breath she'd been holding. She checked to make sure the apartment door was tightly closed so Tom couldn't hear them.

"Nice kid," Whit said.

"Weren't you about to leave?"

"Yeah, I guess I was. But before I do… Your brother figured you'd need proof that he's the one looking for you. He told me to tell you he still has the note you left him the night you disappeared. He wants to know if you still 'love him best.'"

Emma gasped in shock. "Oh, God!" He really *did* represent J.T.

Whit put the package with the videotape in her hands. This time, she didn't try to give it back.

He walked to the outside door. Before he opened it, he turned to face her. "Oh, and for the record, when I kissed you…it wasn't part of the damn job."

CHAPTER SEVEN

BECAUSE TOM WAS HOME the rest of the night, Emma didn't have a chance to watch the video until the next morning, but in the past fifteen hours she'd read the letter and looked at the photographs a thousand times. And cried herself sick.

She pulled a tissue from the box on her bedside table and blew her nose. She couldn't believe it. The man in the photo was her brother. He looked exactly like Ray at the same age, had that same hint of mischief in his dark eyes. J.T. had grown into a tall, handsome man.

She'd missed him more than she'd even realized. For twenty-plus years she'd wondered what had become of him, and worried that her leaving had ruined his life.

He wrote that he was happy, that he had a beautiful wife and daughter.

All that's missing is seeing you again, he said.

Emma drew up her knees, rested her head on them and sobbed uncontrollably, not knowing how to survive the heartache. His words brought her joy—and intense sorrow.

She wanted to see him again, but then what? Continued contact meant telling her child that everything he knew, everything he believed about his life, was a lie. She didn't want to have to choose between her son's happiness and her brother's.

Confessing also exposed her to possible legal action or criminal investigation. She'd bought this building and paid for her equipment without bank financing, but she'd signed Susan's name to the sale papers. And although she'd dutifully paid her taxes over the years, she'd done that in Susan's name, too.

The police, the government, might see fit to prosecute her for falsifying documents. Identity theft and fraud weren't laughing matters. She doubted the government would find it funny that she'd stolen and used a social security number.

She was in a mess! And so much had happened with her family since she'd run away....

She reread the part of the letter about her mother—dead within four years of Emma's leaving home—and that brought more tears. She hadn't realized her mother was that sick.

What a terrible thing she'd done by walking out. At the time, her life had seemed intolerable, and she'd been desperate to change it. Running away had seemed like the only option.

But poor J.T. The hell he must have gone through without their mother as a cushion between him and Ray. Emma had never meant for him to suffer because of her.

Ray had been caught and sent to prison, which wasn't a surprise, but thirty-five years! Good Lord! J.T. had been sixteen; he didn't say much about his own life after that. Who'd taken care of him? Where had he lived? He'd still been a kid! And they'd had no other family that she knew of.

His explanation was vague. And neither the envelope nor the letter contained an address or telephone number to indicate where he was living. Whit said the video would explain more.

Still in her short nightgown, she took the tape into Tom's room, since the VCR was hooked to his TV. Houdini was watching *Hawaii Five-O* again, although Emma had told Tom not to let him. Rambo was out of his cage, sunning himself on a window ledge.

"Damn!"

"Damn!" Houdini repeated.

She picked up the big iguana and looked him in the face. "You're not supposed to be running around loose, you ugly brute."

"Book 'em, Danno," Houdini squawked.

She put Rambo back in the large fenced enclosure they'd erected for him in one corner. Now she needed to decide what to do about the bird with the big mouth.

She didn't want him listening to the video, for fear he'd mimic phrasing, but she didn't want to touch him, either. He didn't like her for some reason. He always tried to take a bite out of her hand.

His home was a floor-to-ceiling indoor aviary, part of which Tom had inherited with the pets. On the porch that ran across the front side of the second story, her clever son had built a second, smaller cage, so that Houdini could be outside in warm weather.

A hatch, rigged by Tom through the unscreened bottom of the window, allowed the bird to move between cages by himself without being handled. When the air got too brisk, they simply closed him inside.

The weather was nasty today, rainy, but the temperature was pleasant enough that Houdini could enjoy a few hours outside.

Emma went to the refrigerator for grapes, his favorite food. Putting on a robe, she slipped out onto the porch through the double doors in the kitchen. With the treat, she lured Houdini into the outer cage and lowered the hatch lever while he was preoccupied with eating.

Back inside Tom's bedroom, she pushed the tape into the VCR and sat down on the bed.

J.T. appeared immediately in what looked like a den or family room. He bent forward on the couch, the way men do when they watch an exciting football play, elbows resting on his knees, hands clasped between them. The camera seemed steady. Emma guessed it had been mounted on a tripod.

"Emma," he said. "Sissy. Do you remember how much you hated it when I called you that?" She smiled through her tears. "You used to grab me by the nose and threaten to twist it off."

He paused, obviously nervous. He leaned back, moving out of focus, and a female voice off camera gently reminded him not to move around.

"Sorry," he said. Emma didn't know if he was talking to her or to the woman. "This really sucks, having to talk to you like this. I hate it. I want to see you in person. I want to hear your voice and see your beautiful face again."

"Oh, J.T."

"Honey, I've missed you so much, and I don't blame you for leaving. I swear I don't. I know things were bad. Who understands that better than me? But the past is over and done with. It's behind both of us.''

He went on to encourage her to confide in Whit, and to let Whit know what he, J.T., could do to help her.

''I don't know why you're posing as this Susan woman, but whatever the reason, it doesn't matter. Regardless of what your circumstances are, you're my sister and I'll stick by you.''

He talked about their childhood and reminded her that it wasn't all bad. He was right; it hadn't been. But for Emma, the hurt tended to overshadow the good times.

''I want you to meet my wife and little girl,'' he said. A slender woman came and sat down beside him. Their love for each other was apparent in the way she leaned into him, the way he immediately reached for her hand.

The woman smiled. She had a natural, earthy look that was very attractive. ''Hello, Emma. I hope I get the chance to meet you and your son.''

''And this,'' J.T. said, ''is the boss of the family.'' He motioned and softly called ''Gracie, come to Daddy,'' and a little girl toddled over. He picked her up and set her on his knee. ''Her name is Grace Emma, for Mama and you.''

Emma's tears came so fast, she no longer bothered to wipe them away.

''One last thing,'' J.T. said, his expression turning sad. ''About Mama. I won't lie and tell you she didn't take your leaving hard. She did. Having your own child, I'm sure you understand what it means to be a parent and to love a child above anything else.''

"Yes," Emma cried to his image, as if he could hear.

"Mama loved you. Unconditionally. And she forgave you for running away. When they caught Ray and sent him to prison, she finally learned the truth. Later, when she was dying..."

He got choked up and had to pause. His wife lightly rubbed his back. She whispered words of comfort.

Finally he composed himself and was able to go on. "Mama made me promise on her deathbed that I'd find you. She wanted you to know...she was sorry."

WHIT WAS ON THE PHONE in the bedroom of the beach bungalow he'd rented when he heard the knock.

"Just a minute," he called out.

He told Cliff to let him know when he'd arrived, then walked to the front door and opened it. A bedraggled Emma stood there, her jeans and shirt rain-soaked from the storm that had been pounding for the past twenty-four hours and her face showing more misery than he'd ever seen.

"Emma?"

"My mother died," she said, as if it had just happened. "She was sick."

"I know. I'm sorry. That must have been hard for you to hear after all these years."

Her eyes seemed glazed. She acted shell-shocked, oblivious to where she was or the fact that it was raining.

"Ray, my father, went to prison. Twenty-five years. Then he escaped and they added another ten."

"Your brother told me."

"J.T. was left with no one to take care of him. My fault."

"It wasn't your fault."

"Yes, it was. He was alone. I wasn't there to help him."

"You're drenched. Did you walk over here?" The restaurant had to be more than a mile away.

She nodded.

"Come inside."

He pulled her in and led her to the bathroom, where he grabbed a towel from the rack and rubbed it over her head and face.

She'd been crying. Her eyes were bloodshot and the end of her nose was bright red, as if she'd blown it too many times.

He knew she'd been up all night because he had, too. He'd sat in his rental car and watched the restaurant in case her burglar came back, and he'd seen her shadow through her bedroom window. She'd paced until daylight.

"What am I going to do about Tom?" she asked, her voice pitiful. "He won't understand."

The abrupt change in subject didn't surprise him. She'd experienced more than one major shock. She wasn't thinking clearly.

"What won't Tom understand? Why you lied about his father?"

"Yes. And he'll be ashamed to have a mother who was once a thief." A shiver ran down her from head to toe.

"Hold on." He went and turned off the air conditioning, then came back with one of the dress shirts he'd packed but hadn't needed. He handed it to her, his desire to protect her outweighing his need for information. "Take a hot shower and put this on before you get sick."

She looked down at her clothes. "I'm wet."

"Yes, sweetheart, you are. You're dripping all over the place. We need to get you warm and dry."

"I can't wear your clothes."

"Yes, you can. Go on. You can't sit around in those."

"All right." She closed the door.

"I'm going to make us some coffee," he said. "Do you want cream and sugar?"

"Yes, please."

"Hand me your wet clothes and I'll hang them in front of the oven to dry."

After a minute, the door opened slightly and an arm stretched out holding her wadded jeans and a sleeveless white cotton shirt.

"Didn't you have on underwear?" he said, taking them.

"Sort of."

"What does 'sort of' mean?"

"You promise you won't laugh?"

"No."

"You're not a nice man."

"I'm a very nice man. What's wrong with your underwear?"

"I was upset yesterday after you left, and I forgot to wash clothes. I didn't have any clean underwear, so this morning I borrowed a pair of Tom's boxers."

"Give them to me. I'll try not to laugh."

The door opened a little wider, and again the hand

came out, this time with a very feminine lacy bra and a pair of not-so-feminine boxers. Like the woman, even her underwear was a contradiction. Whit didn't laugh, but he couldn't help feeling amused.

SHE FINISHED before he did. When he returned to the bedroom with the coffee, she was curled up against the headboard of his bed, the spread pulled to her waist. The sleeves of his shirt hung down way below her hands, making her look ridiculous—and irresistible.

"That was fast," he said, sitting down facing her. He set her cup on the nightstand within her reach. Taking one arm and then the other, he rolled the sleeves to her wrists. "Feeling better?"

"No, I feel lousy," she said, but she seemed better, no longer dazed.

"What will help?"

"Turning back the clock to 1979 and letting me live the last twenty-three years over again."

"I wish I could do that for you, Emma." Her hands were still shaking, either from the chill she'd sustained or from nerves, so he helped her hold the cup while she took a sip. "You *are* Emma Webster, aren't you? I need to establish that before we go any further."

"You already know I am. From that monologue you gave me yesterday, apparently you know everything about me, every dirty little secret I have."

"Not every one, but if I'm going to help you, I need you to tell me the truth from here on out."

"Help me what?"

"Help you reconnect with your family. Help you

figure out who's trying to break into your building. Help you resolve whatever trouble you've been running from."

"I understand the first two, but not the last. I'm not running from any trouble, at least not anymore."

"Then why the false identity? And where's the real Susan Roberts?"

She hesitated.

"Trust me, Emma."

Tears welled up in her eyes. "I want to."

"I'm not here to hurt you or cause problems with your son. I'm trying to reunite you and your brother. If you'll trust me and be honest, I'm hoping we can work all this out so everyone's happy."

"You won't tell who I am?"

"I can't promise anything until I've heard your story. But I'll give you my word that if you've done anything wrong, I'll use whatever resources I have to help you."

"My past is going to come out, isn't it?"

"I don't know. Maybe. Maybe not. At this point, I don't see why anyone has to know outside of your family. But let's take this one step at a time. First, you have to trust me."

She sighed, resigned. "I don't have much choice about that."

"Second, you have to explain how you came to be Susan. Can you tell me about her?"

"She..." With the back of her hand, she wiped her eyes. "Susan's dead. She's been dead a long time."

"Were you responsible in any way?"

"No! Of course not. She and I were friends, if you

can call it that. She worked the street where I hung out in L.A. We got to know each other. I liked her."

"Was she a prostitute?"

"Yes. She sold her body to buy heroin."

"Go on. You and Susan became friends."

"Sometimes she'd let me crash at her place, or she'd give me a few bucks for food. Emotionally she was messed up from years of sexual abuse by her stepfather, but she had a good heart. She was a sweet person."

"How did she die?"

"An overdose. Probably a suicide, but I've never known for sure. She was always unhappy. She believed what had happened to her as a child was somehow her fault."

"So when she died, you took her identity?"

"Not immediately, but eventually I did. She had two things I desperately needed to escape the street."

Whit had already guessed what those were. A valid social security number and a family who didn't care enough to search for her. He asked if he was correct.

"Yes," she confirmed. "She always said her stepfather probably cheered when she ran off."

"That may be true. I went through the missing person reports. Her school counselor reported her as having run away, but her stepfather didn't bother to call police."

"Thank God for me he didn't. I never had to worry about him showing up and blowing my cover."

"What name was she using?"

"Candy Kane, and that confused the police when she died."

Whit scribbled it on the pad by the phone.

"But back in Virginia," Emma continued, "before she left home, she'd had a job after school. She'd kept her social security card and she had a valid California driver's license in her real name. She kept them hidden in a plastic bag in the toilet tank where she stored her drugs. I broke in after the police took away the body and I stole them. Once I had possession of the card and the license, it was easy to get other identification in her name. I held on to everything until I was ready to use it."

He nodded to himself. It made sense. And her story could be checked out within a couple of hours, which was good. Susan's disappearance had concerned him the most.

"Who were you afraid of?" he asked. "What happened that made you decide to become Susan?"

She winced. "Do you have to know *everything?*"

"Emma, somebody's taken an interest in you, in your restaurant, and we have to figure out who it is. Who were you running from when you stole Susan's identity?"

"Tom's father."

"Who is he?"

"*That* I won't tell you. It isn't relevant."

"Okay, we'll skip it for now. At least tell me why you felt you had to hide from him."

"Because..." She closed her eyes briefly, the pain of her memories seemingly too great to bear. "God, I was incredibly naive. When I ran away, I thought I was escaping hell, but I didn't know what hell really was until I was broke, homeless and uneducated. I had no identity, no references. I couldn't even get a job washing dishes. I was scared and hungry."

"So you resorted to conning."

"I hated it. That was the very reason I'd run away from Ray. But it was the only skill I had, and the other options were prostitution or pornography. Occasionally, I'd make a few dollars working. A lady who owned a diner would let me help clean up some nights for food or cash, and a couple who supplied costumes and props for movies let me help sort and repair inventory, but mostly I got by from picking pockets and working small street cons."

"And the man? How did you meet him?"

"He came into the diner one day. He was sophisticated, rich, well-spoken, everything I longed to be. He was twenty years older, and had this really sexy British accent. I was too young and stupid to understand that evil comes in the nicest packages."

What she'd said about the accent teased Whit's memory, but he wasn't sure why. He made a mental note to check through his files.

"Did you love him?" he asked.

"I thought I did. But I was nineteen years old, and I confused love with gratitude. All I understood was that he seemed to care about me, and I needed that kind of attention right then. He set me up in a small apartment. He fed me, clothed me, bought me nice things. I'd never had anything nice before. Looking back, I realize I was an oddity to him, a pet. And I was no better than Susan. She sold her body to numerous men for money. I gave mine to one man for the same thing. The only smart move I made—and I say a prayer of thanks every day—was that I never told him my real name or about Susan. He knew me by another name."

"Rachel Stanton."

"Yes, how...?" She grimaced. "Are you always this good?"

"Probably not. But I was determined to find out the truth, no matter what it took."

"Why?"

"Partly because I like your brother a lot. And I've never had a case I couldn't resolve, one way or another. I didn't want yours to be the first."

"Wonderful. You've ruined my life because of pride."

"Is that how you feel? That your life is ruined?"

"What else would you call it? What am I supposed to do about all this, about J.T. and Tom? If I admit I have a brother and I resume a relationship with him, I have to tell Tom the truth about who I am. There's no getting around that. And I also worry about the kind of trouble I could be in if people find out I'm not Susan."

"Do you *want* to see your brother?"

"Of course I do. I love him. But I'm not sure if I *can* see him. I worry about the consequences."

"Okay, we'll get back to that and your other questions later. First, go on with your story. This man you met knew you as Rachel."

"Yes, and I was happy for a while, although lonely. He lived in London but worked as an interpreter for a cargo-shipping company with offices all over the world, including Los Angeles. Naturally he traveled a great deal. He only got to the States about once every three months. He always left me plenty of money to spend. But that wasn't the same as being his wife, which is what I expected I'd be one day.

Boy, was I wrong. Once, when I brought up the subject, he made it clear I was his property, someone to have sex with but not good enough to marry."

Damn. Whit had a hard time not expressing out loud what he thought of someone who would do that to her.

"In the beginning he'd been so attentive," she said. "Then, suddenly, he started talking about this woman Gretchen that he worked with or knew at one of the offices. I got the impression she was an American, but she could've worked anywhere in the world."

"They were lovers?"

"I don't know. But something about her fascinated him. He used her to torment me, to destroy what little self-worth I had left. Gretchen was beautiful. Gretchen was clever. Gretchen was classy. The implication being, of course, that I *wasn't* beautiful, clever or classy. Then, in one of his rages, he delivered another shock—that if I was ever stupid enough to get myself 'knocked up,' he'd kill me and the baby. I believed him. The problem was, I was already pregnant."

"So you took Susan's identity and ran."

"As fast and as far as I could. Despite how I'd come to feel about the man, my unborn child was a real person to me. I loved him. I would have done anything to protect him."

"Did your lover ever find out?"

"I don't think so. For several years, I lived in fear that he'd find me and kill me for leaving him, not because he loved me but to prove that he could. He was that twisted. But as time passed and he didn't show up on the doorstep, I realized I had no reason to keep hiding, that my Susan Roberts Wright identity had worked."

"Why didn't you become Emma again? Your lover wouldn't have known."

"For Tom's sake. By the time I felt safe from my past, he was ready to go to kindergarten and he would've been too confused by a sudden name change. I'd been passing myself off as a widow and Tom's birth certificate listed *Wright* as his last name, so I had to keep up with the charade. I had respectability and that was important to me. I paid a guy to create the phony papers I needed to maintain our identities. I made up the story about Tom's father dying in a military accident and the body being lost, in case Tom ever asked to visit his grave."

"Who was William Wright?"

"Nobody. A name I pulled out of the air.

"Where is Tom's real father now?"

"Dead."

"Emma."

"No, I promise, he really is dead. The bastard got himself hit by a car a few years ago."

"Is there anything else about your past you need to tell me?"

"I can't think of anything."

"No big scams? No major thefts? No outstanding criminal charges anywhere in any fictitious name?"

"No."

"Swear to me."

"Whit, I swear. Like I told you, I was a small-time thief. Except when I was working with my father, I never scammed more than a few hundred dollars off anybody, and I've never been charged with a crime. I quit running cons when I had Tom and became Susan. I got a nice, boring job as a waitress."

"But that's not all you did, as I recall."

"Okay, you're right. Waitressing wasn't the only thing I did to make a paycheck. I had a job washing cars in a bikini, and selling crappy makeup door-to-door for ten times what it was probably worth. I've been a magician's assistant and let myself be sawed in half. I've mucked out barns and washed more dishes than any human should have to in a lifetime. Once, for two weeks, I danced topless. Tom had an ear infection and I needed money the pay the doctor. I'm not proud of those things, but I'm not ashamed of them either. I did what I had to do. And the only *crime* I'm guilty of in the past seventeen years is stealing Susan's identity. Believe me or not—it's your choice."

"I believe you."

"Thank you."

"I want you always to be totally honest with me."

"I will if you'll do the same."

"I will."

"Tell me about this break-in at your restaurant."

She gave Whit details, how the thief had easily bypassed her sophisticated security system and had even been in her safe nosing around.

"Abby didn't open the safe or move the papers?"

"Whit, give me some credit, please. I locked up at one o'clock and was the last person out. When I came down at nine-thirty the next morning, I was the first one there and things had been moved. Abby hadn't been back in. I checked with her to be sure. And no one else has a key to my office. Abby doesn't even have access to the safe or my office after hours. I lock both."

"The system's a Beizer-Denz, isn't it?" Whit asked. From habit, he'd noticed one of the boxes by the back door.

"Yes. They don't come any better. And it's customized. Four different zones can be set independently and controlled from my apartment."

"What's the zone pattern?"

"One zone for each floor—the restaurant, my apartment, the third-floor storage room—and then the front and back stairways and the halls connecting them are on a fourth zone."

"You have cameras above your front and back doors. Did you review the tapes?"

"Not completely yet, but I've fast-forwarded through one and I'm working on the other. So far, there's nothing unusual."

"How often do you rotate?"

"I keep fifteen tapes per camera so that when I tape over them, I always have the prior two weeks."

"I want to see the tapes from last night for both cameras. What about your safe? What's the brand?"

She gave him the name. A good model. Secure. Very difficult to crack.

"This guy was a real pro," Whit told her. "Definitely not an average burglar or one of your homeless friends. Only a handful of people could both disable that system and crack your safe in one night, and their services don't come cheap."

"I already know that."

"Then you also know that short of putting armed

guards inside at night, there's not a whole lot we can do to keep this guy out if he wants to come in. You could install cameras with laser detectors, but he's already bypassing your system somehow without setting it off or even alerting you or the police to the tampering."

"He makes me feel defenseless."

"You could upgrade to a museum-grade system, but the cost wouldn't be practical for a restaurant."

"How much?"

"We're talking hundreds of thousands of dollars. It likely wouldn't stop someone with his expertise, anyway."

"I don't have that kind of money."

"Few people do."

"Have you had much experience with master thieves?"

"Not as an investigator. My specialty is missing people, not thefts. But I had some familiarity with them in my last job."

"Which was?"

"I used to work for the FBI."

She groaned. "Please tell me you're kidding."

"No, I was a special agent for nearly eight years."

With another, louder groan she fell sideways on the bed. "Just go ahead and shoot me now. This gets worse by the minute."

He chuckled. "The news isn't that bad. Besides, I didn't bring a gun."

"I've been tracked down by the FBI."

"Former FBI."

She sat up. "A cop is a cop, former or not. It's in the blood."

"I'm not here to arrest you, Emma."

"First *you* show up, and now there's a thief. My luck keeps getting better and better."

"Do you have any idea what he's after?"

She shook her head. "No, not unless he thinks I have some high-priced original costumes. Could that be it?"

"Maybe." But that didn't explain why the burglar would go into the safe.

He considered pointing it out, but she was already distraught. No use upsetting her more. Cliff was en route to look into the situation, and in a couple of days, Whit hoped to know more.

"I'm really baffled," she said, yawning. Her eyelids were beginning to droop. "Although it does seem a strange coincidence that someone decided to burglarize me only a few days after you showed up. I've never had any trouble before. It's almost like you brought it with you."

Whit frowned, not liking her theory.

He mentally reviewed his steps in California. He'd talked to a lot of people, asked questions about her and her various identities and flashed the old photograph he'd had. But, as part of his normal routine, he'd covered his tracks when he'd left Hollywood and flown to Saint Augustine to check out a lead.

Damn! The answer hit him like a baseball bat to the head.

"Hinky" Allen Morrow and his nonexistent cop-killer case. Morrow hadn't contacted his office because he wanted Whit's help finding a witness; he'd wanted Whit's *location.*

And Whit had inadvertently supplied it. He'd returned Morrow's call using the motel phone instead of a secure one. All the man had to do was use Caller ID to get the number, then call back and ask the motel operator for the name of the city. Either Morrow or his people had probably flown to Florida, staked out the motel and tailed Whit to the restaurant.

"Shit!"

"What?"

"I think you may be right about me bringing the trouble," he said, knowing in his gut she was. He explained to her about the bogus call.

Someone had wanted to find her; he'd led them here. Now he had to figure out if it was Emma they were after or one of her false identities. And why.

CHAPTER EIGHT

EMMA DRIFTED IN AND OUT of sleep. She hadn't meant to doze, but the bed was warm and exhaustion had overtaken her. She thought she remembered Whit pulling up the covers and stroking her head, but maybe that was part of the delicious dream she'd fallen into.

She could hear him now on the phone in the living room, the clacking of computer keys accompanying his deep voice. He was working, probably checking out the validity of her story.

Yawning, she looked at her watch. After two o'clock. She was supposed to do employment interviews at four and discuss menus with Abby for upcoming parties.

Thinking about work was impossible, but she had to force herself. If she acted differently, Abby would suspect something was amiss. Tom would, too, and she couldn't afford that. Abby was probably already wondering what had happened to her. Emma had left her a note saying she'd be out for a couple of hours running errands, yet she'd been gone much longer.

She went to the bathroom and washed her face. Agh! Not a pretty sight. No makeup, puffy eyes, a blotched complexion. Her hair was wet when she'd fallen asleep, so it stuck out in every direction. Using

Whit's comb, she tried unsuccessfully to smooth it down.

She walked to the kitchen and examined her clothes. He'd draped them over two chairs in front of the open electric oven, but they still felt damp. Not relishing the idea of putting on the jeans, she decided to wait until she was ready to leave. She turned off the oven and slipped into the boxers. Wet clothes or not, she couldn't walk around bare-bottomed.

Whit was off the phone when she stepped into the living room.

"Hey," he said. He had his laptop on the coffee table. As soon as he saw her, he stopped typing and got to his feet. "Did you have a good nap?"

"I didn't mean to fall asleep. Sorry."

"You seemed to need the rest."

"I guess I did."

"You look great."

Self-consciously, she fingered her crazy hair. "Liar. I resemble something out of a horror movie, a cross between Leatherface and that kid in *The Exorcist* after the demon possessed her."

He smiled. "Not quite that bad. The porcupine thing you've got going with your hair is kind of cute."

"You're so full of it."

"I like the kinky wardrobe. You look better in my shirt than I do."

"Now I know you're nuts."

"Sit and we'll finish our conversation. You must have questions about your brother."

"I do. A million of them. And I want to hear step by step how you connected me with Susan. Right now, though, I have to get to work. Could we possibly meet later tonight? And would it be too much trouble for you to come by the restaurant? With what's been going on, I don't like the idea of leaving Tom upstairs at night when I'm not in the building. I worry about his safety."

"Sure, I can do that."

"The crowd is thinned by nine, if that's a convenient time for you. I'll even fix us a late dinner. Afterward, we can find a quiet place to talk."

"That sounds good. I want to take a look inside after you close, anyway, and see if I can figure out how your burglar got in."

"Okay. Maybe you can find something I didn't. When I feed Brownie and the others tonight, should I ask them if they've seen anything suspicious?"

"No, don't say anything to them yet. Give me their names and let me run checks."

"Whit, you said yourself the thief is a pro and not a homeless person."

"True, but he might disguise himself to case the building."

"But I know all these people."

"Okay, what about staff? Do you run background checks on them?"

"The employment agency does."

"I'm not sure I'd trust them to do a thorough job."

His computer beeped and a voice came on to tell him he had an e-mail message.

"What are you working on?" she asked.

"Some fact-checking."

"On my story?"

"Partly, yes." When she frowned, he quickly

added, "Hey, that doesn't mean I don't trust you, only that I'm doing my job. For the protection of your brother and his family, I can't simply take what you tell me at face value. I have to investigate every piece of information."

"But I told you the truth."

"I know you did. I believe you, although I'll admit I had my doubts in the beginning about whether contacting you was wise. I expressed those to your brother and his wife. That's why his location and current name weren't mentioned in the material I gave you."

"He's living under a different name?"

"Legally, though. He changed it years ago."

"I thought something strange was going on. The letter and the video didn't contain any details. Where is he? What does he do? What's his wife's name? I'm dying to know everything about him."

"Until I'm sure there's no danger to them, it's best I continue to withhold some information."

"You mean you still won't tell me where he is?"

"No, not yet. At least not until I can talk to him again and relay what you've said."

"That stinks."

"I know it does."

"And it's not fair, Whit. You're worrying about danger to them, but what about danger to me and Tom? What assurances do I have that J.T. didn't grow up to be like Ray? I don't want to bring a criminal element back into my life when I've worked so hard to get away from it."

"I give you my word your brother doesn't have

any hidden skeletons in his closet. I investigated his background before I agreed to take this case.''

''Then tell me about him.''

''Like I said, *I* feel comfortable with your story, and I'll tell him that, but the decision to release his information to you has to be his. I've had a chance to make a few calls, and everything you told me about Susan's death checks out. But some things still worry me, and I'll tell him that, too. Like this thief you've acquired, for one. I want to make sure I'm not involving your brother in anything that might hurt him or his wife and daughter.''

She nodded. ''All right. The thief worries me, too.''

''And it makes me nervous that somebody besides me has apparently been looking for you.''

''That downright terrifies me.''

''The thief and this mysterious somebody with a sudden interest in your whereabouts may be linked.''

''How?''

''I don't know yet.''

''It doesn't make—'' She thought of something and gasped. ''Oh, no, Whit. What if...? No, it couldn't be related.''

''If you know something, Emma, tell me, even if you think it's inconsequential. We can't disregard any possibility.''

''Do you remember the couple I mentioned earlier who owned the costume and prop company? They used to let me help out. Actually, I got very close to them. They were like parents to me, and since they had no living children, they gave me their inventory when they retired. That's what I'm using in the restaurant."

"Would that be the late Bert and Marie Marshall?"

"You know about them? Of course you do," she said immediately. "That's how you found me, isn't it? Marie was the only person who knew me as Rachel and Susan. You somehow connected both identities to her."

"Yes, using Marie's will. I came here on a hunch that the mysterious Rachel who had once helped Marie in the store and the Susan Wright named as her beneficiary were the same person. I was already pretty certain that Rachel had also once been Emma."

"I want the details of how you figured this out, but you can tell me later. What I have to say is more important and I don't have much time right now. Bert died several years ago of a stroke. Marie died eighteen month ago. She was murdered when she surprised a *burglar* in her home. But the police didn't find anything missing."

His expression changed, showing his deep concern. "I knew she'd died, but I didn't ask the circumstances. I assumed it was of natural causes."

"She was killed horribly. A knife. Police said the man was small but very strong. From the way he used the knife, he likely had military training. The profile in the newspaper listed him as male, thirty to forty, white, meticulous, very cold. He didn't have to kill Marie, but he chose to. And he knew how to use the knife to torture her, which is why they thought he might have once served in Special Forces."

"How did he enter?"

"He easily bypassed her security system. I read

that when authorities looked at the tape from the video camera she had over her front entrance, it had been... Oh, I can't remember the word."

"Looped?"

"That's it. Looped. What does that mean?"

"You create a loop by taking a few minutes of prerecorded, uneventful videotape and duplicating it a number of times to create hours of tape where nothing appears to have gone on. When the burglar entered, he took the original with his image on it and stuck in a cassette of looped videotape. And he created it using one of her own tapes."

"But how did he get it?"

"Easily. He stole it. He got invited in by posing as a telephone repairman or the gas man or some other worker who wouldn't arouse her suspicion. While he was in the house, he cased the place for his job and pocketed one of her older tapes. He then used that to make his loop. If Marie hadn't surprised him in the act of breaking in later, it would likely never have been detected. He didn't expect her to be there."

"Bingo."

"Yes."

"No, I mean *bingo.* Every Thursday night, rain or shine, hell or high water, she played bingo at the Elks Lodge until ten, but that Thursday night she didn't, because the friend who usually picked her up at seven had car trouble."

"Have *you* had any tapes go missing lately?"

"No."

"Think carefully. How about any that were temporarily misplaced but then showed up? Or that weren't where they should've been?"

"Now that you put it that way—yes. One day, a couple were gone from the shelf. I keep them in a closet in the office. The next night I found them under some papers on my desk. I shrugged it off, thinking I'd gotten them out for some reason and forgotten, or that Abby had been searching for a blank tape to record a private party. We do that for our customers."

"Were the tapes missing for each of the two exterior cameras?"

"Yes, they were."

"And when was this?"

"About a week or so ago. If I look at my office calendar, I can pinpoint the exact day, because I remember I was wearing these really long fake nails with a costume and when I picked up one of the cassettes, I broke a nail off."

"Look for that date, and give it to me with the tapes."

"Okay."

"Emma, listen to me carefully. I know you don't want to tell me about Tom's father, but the similarities between Marie's burglary and yours makes it more imperative that you do. Are you sure he's dead?"

"Positive. No doubt."

"If you'd give me his name, I could recheck."

She blew out a ragged breath, not sure what to do. Her instincts told her she could trust him, but a lifetime of lies had taught her that no one was ever completely trustworthy. Marie was the only person who had ever known that Patrick was Tom's father, and she could no longer tell.

Patrick was dead. Marie had sent her his obituary.

Emma was so certain of his death that not for an instant had she considered he might have been her burglar. Until now. Regardless of her uncertainty about that, she was absolutely positive he'd had nothing to do with Marie's murder. And he would have no reason to search for *her* after all these years unless...oh, God! Unless he'd found out about Tom.

Should she tell the truth about Patrick, the *whole* truth about his hidden career? Not yet. She'd give Whit his name. If Patrick was truly dead, Whit didn't need to know the rest.

Whit came and stood in front of her. He took her by the shoulders and leaned so she'd have to look him in the eye.

"Emma, tell me his name. If there's any chance he's responsible for the Marshall burglary and death..."

"No, he couldn't be. He was already dead by then."

"You said yourself he was capable of murder."

"He was, but... Even if it turns out he's alive, it *had* to be someone else."

"How can you be so sure?" He gave her a strange look. "Wait a minute. British accent. When I talked to the man who owned a business near the Marshalls', he referred to them as 'the Brits' down the street.'"

"Yes, they were originally from London. Marie had been married before, but the marriage fell apart and she was left with a small child to raise. Years later, she fell in love with Bertrand, and they moved to the States. Only the marriage and the move apparently caused a change in her son and led to an estrangement. They barely spoke. He returned to England to live.'' Emma made a decision she hoped wouldn't come back to haunt her. ''My lover's name was Patrick Logan. He couldn't have killed Marie Marshall. She was his mother.''

WHIT GOT TO ILLUSIONS shortly before nine. The rain had stopped, and the rising moon cast an eerie glow on the remaining clouds.

Thoughts of Emma made anticipation prowl in his stomach as he crossed the portico and went through the door. He pushed away the emotion. The woman aroused him to the point of madness with her ever-changing appearance and personality, but he had to stay alert tonight and not be sidetracked.

He spotted her and groaned. Staying focused on the job wouldn't be easy. As always, she was a knockout. She'd dressed simply in clothes reminiscent of the 1960s—an orange minidress and shoes with tall, square heels. A long, straight wig covered her short hair.

The dress had two loosely woven crochetlike inserts running horizontally. One exposed the soft skin of her middle from under her breasts to below her navel. The other went from about the crotch to the dress's hem, showing off nearly every inch of her shapely legs. She didn't have on stockings, but she was so tanned she didn't need them. The flesh spilling out over the low-cut bust line was definitely all her and not padding.

One thing that was different tonight: she hadn't bothered to put on any extra makeup.

''I didn't want to have to sit around in an uncomfortable appliance mask while we talked,'' she explained as they walked up the front staircase. "I'm supposed to be Heather Graham playing Felicity Shagwell. From the second Austin Powers movie, not the new one."

"I'm not usually a movie buff, but I'll definitely have to rent it."

"The costumes are great fun. Miniskirts, go-go boots. Vinyl. Wild colors."

"Do you have to get permission to use costumes from movies?"

"Sometimes. We don't represent characters that are licensed, or if we do use them, we get the appropriate permissions and pay a fee."

They reached her door. Loud music started up, vibrating the walls. "Tom's here, I take it," Whit commented.

"His friend Tony is spending the night." She leaned into him so he could hear. "I didn't know how to explain you to them, so I said I had a male friend coming over. You'll have to pretend to be my date. I'm sorry."

Sorry? He didn't think so.

"Is this a first date or are we lovers?" he asked. He put his hands on her waist, drawing her body flush with his.

Her eyes widened. She put her palms against his chest. "What are you doing?"

"Trying to understand the role I'm playing." He stuck his fingers through the holes in the dress insert and slid them over the soft skin covering her spine. The bare little number had his testosterone pumping like an oil well. "Which date is this supposed to be for us?"

"Second date, I guess, since Tom's already seen you once." Her voice remained unchanged, but her breathing had accelerated.

"Ah, so I liked you enough to ask you out again within twenty-four hours. We must have chemistry. We've likely already kissed at least once, maybe even sneaked away to some quiet spot to touch each other. We're close to making love."

"Are we?"

"You've been overwhelmed by my masculine charms."

She laughed. "You're really getting into this part, aren't you?"

"I'm willing to give it my all."

CHAPTER NINE

THE NEW Limp Bizkit CD was cool. Tom cranked up the volume and tried to follow along on his electric guitar. Tony, sitting on the floor in front of the couch, drummed on the coffee table with his hands.

His mom came in with the guy she'd introduced him to on the stairs yesterday, her big "date" she'd gotten all foxed up for.

She waved her arms around in the air and said something, but he couldn't hear. Putting her hands over her ears, she screwed up her face. He got the message and turned down the music.

"Are you guys trying to wake the dead?" she asked.

"Sorry, Mom."

"Whoa, Mrs. W.!" Tony said. He looked her up and down. "That outfit's bitchin'."

Tom rolled his eyes. Tony thought his mom was hot, and he acted like a goofball whenever he was around her.

"Thank you, Tony. I think." She motioned to the man. "This is Mr. Lewis. Tom, you remember meeting him."

"Sure. Hi." He raised his hand.

"And this is Tony."

"Hey," Tony said.

The man smiled and nodded.

"Whit, have a seat and I'll fix us a drink. Wine okay? I have a bottle of muscadine you might enjoy. It's bottled by a local winery."

"Sounds interesting. Sure."

Houdini started making a fuss in the bedroom, and Tom went and closed the drape over his cage so he'd go to sleep. "He's been loud all night," Tom said, coming back to the living room.

"Funny, he said the same about you," his mom joked.

"Good one, Mrs. W."

"Have you boys eaten?"

"Corn chips is all," Tom told her. "We were about to call down and get Santiago to send us up something."

She walked to the kitchen, opened the refrigerator and bent over, showing her butt. She had on some kind of orange short-shorts or something that matched the dress and covered more than her bathing suit did, but still, she was his mother, for God's sake, and neither Tony nor Mr. Lewis was turning away from the view.

"I can't decide whether to get plates sent up or cook," she said. "I could make some quick spaghetti, enough for four. I'm not that great a cook, but my meals will do in a pinch."

Tom and Tony looked at each other.

"That's okay," Tom called out. "Don't bother."

"It's no bother."

"Why don't you let me cook? Or I'll get plates for Tony and me. We already told Santiago we might do that. He's probably fixed something."

"Are you sure you don't want me to make spaghetti?"

"Positive."

"Well, okay. I'll just fix dinner for Whit and me."

She still had her head in the refrigerator. Tom hurriedly turned to Mr. Lewis. "Get a plate for yourself," he told him in a whisper.

"Why?"

"You don't want to eat anything she makes."

"How come?"

"She jokes about her cooking not being good, but she doesn't understand how awful it really is."

"It can't be that bad."

Tony jumped in. "Oh, yeah, it is. Barfsville." He stuck his finger in his mouth in a gagging gesture.

Mr. Lewis seemed to find that really funny. "Thanks for the warning." He said, "Hey, Susan?"

She straightened and turned. "Yes?"

"You must be tired from working all day. Let's get something from the restaurant like the boys. That way we'll have more time to spend together."

"Okay. Suits me." She closed the refrigerator and went to the intercom to order.

Tom held up his hand, and Mr. Lewis gave him a high five.

The guy seemed to be pretty cool, even if he did keep looking at his mom during dinner like he wanted to do the wild thing with her. Way too much smiling and touching was going on. They had to be hot for each other. Tom had never heard his mom giggle like that. He thought only the stupid girls his own age did it.

Tom mentioned that Tony's dad was a diving instructor and that he was willing to give Tom lessons. Mr. Lewis, or Whit as he'd asked them to call him, said he'd done some diving himself.

"How hard is it to learn?" Tom asked him.

"Not hard. Are you comfortable in the water? A good swimmer?" Tom said he was. "Then it's only a matter of learning the rules and remembering to follow them."

"See, Mom. There's nothing to it."

"Mmm." She didn't seem convinced.

Tom got Whit to tell him what equipment was best and about some of the dives he'd made. Whit had explored wrecks off the coast of North Carolina and Florida, and had even been to the Great Barrier Reef. He'd been up close to all kinds of sharks, and even a whale.

"Who taught you to dive?" Tom asked him.

"My grandmother."

"No way!" Tom and Tony said in unison.

"That's the truth. She's an adventuress of sorts, an only child, and was heir to her father's small airline. He treated her like a son. Growing up, she traveled all over the world with him. One of the first women to climb Everest, she's also a pilot, a crack shot and an exceptional skier, swimmer and sailor. My grandmother used to take me and my sisters on trips with her during summer vacation, and she taught us how to do everything her father had taught her."

"Where all did you go?" his mom asked Whit.

"One summer we crossed the Atlantic by sailboat. Another time, we traced the last flight of Amelia Earhart and flew it in an antique plane. When I was thirteen, we did a cross-country trip with my grandmother piloting a hot-air balloon. The next year, we hiked part of the Appalachian trail."

"Good Lord!" she said. "Where was your grandfather when all this was going on?"

"He died before my sisters and I were born. An influenza epidemic. Grandmother never remarried."

"Wasn't all that adventure a bit dangerous for four young people?"

"I'm sure it was, but my grandmother's a larger-than-life person and my parents trusted her with our lives. The experience of seeing other places and doing things we otherwise wouldn't have had the chance to do was always worth the risk."

"That's awesome," Tom told him. "My dad was in the navy. He probably traveled to a lot of different countries and did cool things, too. That's what I want to do."

Whit and his mom exchanged looks.

"Your mom mentioned your dad had been a diver," Whit said.

"I want to be just like him."

His mom smiled at him and patted his hand across the table, like she used to do when he was a little kid and he asked to do something she thought was too old for him or too scary.

He hated that pat; it meant she didn't take him seriously.

Well, she'd better. He wasn't a little kid anymore. In nine weeks, he'd be a man, at least according to the U.S. navy. She might not think he was up to following in his dad's footsteps, but he wanted the chance to try.

She stood. "That fish was delicious. Who wants dessert?"

A little pissed off by her attitude, Tom asked if he and Tony could just be excused.

She tried to tempt him with Spanish almond cookies. "We have Grenadines."

"I don't want any."

"But they're your favorite."

"Mom! I'm old enough to know if I want cookies. And I'm old enough to know what I want to do with my life, too. When are you going to stop treating me like I'm five years old?"

"I didn't realize I was," she answered stiffly.

"Can we be excused now?"

"As soon as you apologize for your rude behavior in front of our company."

He gritted his teeth. He was already in trouble for Rambo getting out of his cage this morning. He'd better not press his luck. "I'm sorry."

She let him get away with that. "All right. You can be excused. Don't stay up too late and don't leave the apartment. Whit and I will be in the garden if you need us."

Tony followed him to his room. "Hey man, what's up with you?" he asked. "She was only offering you cookies, and you bit her head off."

"Nothing. Drop it."

AFTER TOM'S OUTBURST, he and his friend closed themselves off in the boy's room.

"I'm sorry if I caused a problem by talking about diving," Whit told Emma, helping her clear off the table.

"It's not your fault. He's angry at me about these stupid diving lessons. We've been around and around about them for weeks."

"He seems pretty set on taking them."

"Because he thinks he's going to enlist in the navy when he's eighteen. I've got news for him—he's not going anywhere."

"Are you opposed to the military or to him joining so young?"

"Both."

"The navy's not a bad life for a young man who wants to travel."

"I want Tom to finish high school and college. And I don't believe he's really interested in diving, only in trying to emulate William Wright. Ironic, isn't it? A monster of my own creation."

"Must be tough not telling him the truth."

"The truth would be tougher."

She rinsed the dishes and stuck them in the dumbwaiter. Whit studied it more closely. The electric mini elevator was about two feet square. "Does this go up to the third floor?"

"Yes."

A very small person could get in there, but not a full-grown man or woman.

"Is there any access to the other floors aside from the front and back staircases?"

"A fire escape that comes off the roof. Come on and we'll look at it. I want to show you my garden, anyway."

She sent the dumbwaiter back down to the restaurant kitchen, then grabbed a towel and a flashlight. They locked the apartment and double-checked the outside doors before climbing to the roof by the back staircase.

The access door had a dead bolt lock. Using the flashlight, he examined the door inside and out and didn't find signs of tampering.

"You keep this locked when you're not using it?"

"Always. I leave the key in the lock, though, in case there's a fire and Tom and I have to get out this way."

"You haven't come up here at any time and found it unlocked or the key gone?"

"No. Other than Abby and Santiago, my chef, the staff never goes above the first floor. They have their own break room off the kitchen."

She flipped a switch. Thousands of tiny white lights came on.

"Welcome to fairyland."

"Wow!"

The sight bowled him over. Herbs, flowers and small trees in containers covered the entire roof and fringed a deck about twenty by twenty. She had a barbecue grill, a picnic table and a glider set up. The lights had been woven through the plants and across the tree limbs.

He'd been able to tell from street level that there was something up here. He'd seen the glow from the lights while doing surveillance. But he hadn't imagined a garden.

"My mother would go crazy over this," Whit said.

"I've always wanted to dig around in the earth but never owned property before. This isn't ideal. It can get very hot up here on midsummer days, and I have to be careful I don't add too much weight to the roof.

But I drape shading material when I need to, and my contractor says the garden actually helps protect this flat surface. Standing water was a problem before, but now the plants absorb a lot of the runoff. We channel the rest using those low pyramid lights."

"I thought those were art."

"They are, but they're also part of a drainage system. The rain runs down them and is siphoned off."

"Do you use the plants in the restaurant?"

"No, this is strictly for my pleasure. We harvest the courtyard herbs for the kitchen."

"Who has access from the business?"

"Only me. Tom uses it, of course. He loves grilling. Actually cooking of any kind. He's always been the cook in the family. He insists."

Whit tried not to smile. Figuring out why Tom insisted wasn't hard. But how Emma could have spent her entire adult life working in restaurants and never learned to cook was a mystery.

He looked at the fire escape, a fixed metal ladder that ended at the second floor but had an extension that could be lowered to the ground during an emergency. It didn't appear to have been used in years, but a clever thief could create that illusion.

"Everything seems secure," he told her.

Using the towel to wipe the glider of moisture, she invited him to sit down next to her.

"I love it here late at night." She pushed the glider into a gentle motion. "This is the tallest building for a block so I don't have to worry about anyone looking down at me. I come up to relax."

"It's nice," he said, stifling a yawn. His lack of sleep was catching up to him. "Excuse me."

"Tired?" she asked.

"A little."

"Me, too. I confess I took a second short nap this afternoon, but it didn't help much."

"Do you ever get to bed before one in the morning?"

"Never, but I rarely wake up before nine, except when Tom's in school. Then I get him going and go back to bed for an hour. Or I come up here to weed and water. Or just lie around. I've worked night shifts and split shifts for years. My body's adjusted to working after four in the afternoon."

"I'm more of a morning person. I live on a small private lake outside Pittsburgh, where I have the only house. I often get up at daylight and fish before going into the office. When I'm not working a case, I'm in bed by ten."

"We lead very different lives."

"Yeah, I guess we do."

"Did you rent the house on the beach so you could do some fishing?"

"That was my plan. Plus, the motel room was too small for an extended stay."

"Do you anticipate being here long?"

"Eager to get rid of me?"

"No, the opposite, actually. Despite who you are and the news you've brought, I've enjoyed being with you. I wish..."

"What do you wish, Emma?"

"That we were other people. That you really were a tourist. And that I really was Susan."

"I wish that, too."

A spurt of wind raced across the roof and rustled

the plant leaves. Emma rubbed her upper arms. The sleeves of her dress were made of the same open weave as the inserts and offered no protection against the night air. He took off his sport coat and draped it across her shoulders.

"Thank you. I didn't expect it to be cool."

"You can lean against me for extra warmth if you want." Surprisingly, she did, so he put his right arm around her shoulders and brought her closer. "Better?"

"Yes, thanks. I'm sorry we haven't had a chance to talk. The boys are best friends and spend a lot of time together, but I didn't know they'd both be here tonight."

"I'm glad they are."

"Why?"

"Otherwise, I might've been tempted to be bad at dinner."

"Worse than you already were?"

"Much worse."

"What would you have done?"

"Probably stuck my tongue through each of the little holes in this dress and licked you all over until you climaxed."

She made a choking sound and abruptly sat up.

"Too blunt?" he asked.

"No, it's just—Lord! I didn't expect anything so...intriguing."

He chuckled, delighted that she liked the idea.

"When this case is over, if you're still intrigued, I'll give you a demonstration. But I was teasing you about being bad tonight. As long as I'm working for your brother, I need to watch where I put my tongue."

"Oh." She bit her lip.

"Conflict of interest," he told her.

"Is that why you turned me down the other night? Or did I come on too strong?"

"Emma, the job is what stopped me from taking you up on the offer. I had to force myself to get in the car and leave."

"After you did, I worried that you might've gotten the wrong idea about me. Normally, I don't invite men up for sex. I particularly don't invite men I've only known twelve hours."

"We both acted differently than we would have under normal circumstances. Let's accept that and not beat ourselves up over it."

"I was lonely. And it's been a long time since I've been physically attracted to a man."

"I'm flattered."

"Only twice since Tom was born have I had relationships involving sex, and they were so brief they're hardly worth mentioning. But you probably already know that."

"I guessed as much from talking to your ex-neighbors and landlords. Nice lady, they all said. Never any trouble. Paid her rent on time. Didn't seem to have men friends."

"Ugh! How pathetic that sounds."

"Come here." He pulled her down into the crook of his arm but turned her toward him so he could better see her face. "That's not pathetic. What would you rather they'd said?"

"I don't know. Something more exciting than 'pays her rent on time.' Good Lord, how boring."

"Emma, no one could ever accuse you of having a boring life."

"Well, maybe not boring, but it isn't a life I'm proud of. Emma Webster. Thief. Con artist. Runaway. Tenth-grade education."

"Hey, look at me. Don't you understand how incredible you are? You got yourself out of a situation most kids would never have survived. You've built a unique and thriving business. And you've raised a child all by yourself. On top of that, you're the most attractive, desirable woman I've ever met."

"You really think so?"

"Does this answer your question?"

Those sweet lips of hers were only inches away, and he couldn't help himself. He touched them with his own, lightly at first to see if she minded being kissed, then more strongly when she made it known that she didn't. She became pliable in his arms.

"So desirable, you've been driving me crazy all night," he murmured. "The way you look, the way you smell, could make any man do the wrong thing." He ran his free hand up her thigh to finger the edge of the little orange thingies she was wearing under the dress. "You don't have boxers on beneath these, do you?"

She stifled a laugh. "No."

"You picked this outfit to torment me."

"I did not."

"Maybe we should get you out of it so I can retain my sanity."

"Oh, now there's a man's logic for you."

"My logic went out the window the moment I met you."

He kissed her again and slipped his fingers beneath the hem of the shorts. He expected to find fabric. Instead, he encountered the lovely bare skin of a hip. Maybe she wore a thong or high-cut panties.

"Damn! Are you wearing anything under here?"

"No, I'm naked."

Now it was his turn to choke.

"I never got around to washing clothes," she explained innocently. "Remember?"

Whit let out a deep groan. She was killing him. He'd gone as hard as an iron spike. A picture rolled through his head: Emma riding him in her little dress, pants discarded.

"I thought we weren't going to do this," she pointed out.

"We're not doing anything bad, only kissing."

"Tongues are involved."

"That doesn't count. My tongue in your mouth is legal. My tongue anywhere else isn't."

"Who wrote these stupid rules?"

"I did," he grumbled, but he could already see he was going to have a hell of a time living with them.

CHAPTER TEN

"THEY DID IT," Tony speculated the next morning. "He probably banged her on the picnic table."

"Shut up. He did not." The thought of his mother having sex made Tom want to hurl. If she'd done it on the roof last night with Whitaker Lewis, Tom didn't want to know about it. Or picture it. Nasty.

The object of the argument suddenly came into the kitchen humming, two hours before her normal time to get up. She was already dressed and alert, which was strange. Most of the time she dragged herself to the table in her gown or robe, looking and acting like a zombie.

"Good morning, boys," she chirped.

Tom slouched against the counter with a mug, waiting for the coffee to quit dripping out of the machine. She came over and kissed him, then kissed Tony, who was drinking milk at the table. Majorly weird.

"You look really happy this morning, Mrs. W.," Tony told her. He gave Tom a knowing wink.

"I feel wonderful. How are you boys? Okay?"

"Sure," Tom told her.

"When do you have to be at the bike shop?"

"Nine for both of us."

She opened the doors to the porch and took a loud,

deep breath. "Ah, isn't it a gorgeous morning? I love this time of day."

Tony smirked, and Tom threw a pot holder at his head.

"What's with you?" Tom asked her. "Why are you conscious?"

"Aren't I usually conscious?"

"Not before nine, Mrs. W." Tony said. "Sometimes not fully until noon."

She laughed. "I'm not quite *that* bad."

Walking to the dryer, she emptied it of jeans and then dumped in a load of towels she must've washed last night before going to bed.

"Would you boys like some breakfast? I think there's enough bacon and eggs in the refrigerator."

"We've already eaten cereal," Tony told her.

"Want me to cook you some?" Tom asked.

"No, thanks, I'll get a bite later. Tom, I've been thinking about the diving lessons, and I've decided to let you take them."

"Honest?" He straightened in surprise.

"This doesn't mean I've changed my mind about the navy, but if you're dead set on learning to dive I want you to do it safely with someone I trust. Have Mr. Parker get you the necessary equipment, then let me know how much I owe him for the rental and the lessons."

"Great! Thanks."

Diving! She was finally going to let him take lessons. All right!

He couldn't wait to call Tony's dad and tell him the news. Mr. Parker had taught Tony and his little brother years ago, and the three of them were always going out on weekends, having fun. Maybe now they'd invite him along.

"Mom?"

"Yes, sweetie?"

"I'm really sorry about last night."

"I'm sorry, too. I forget you're not a child anymore. I'll try to do better. But please don't be in too much of a hurry to become an adult, okay?"

"Okay."

She walked over and gave him a hug. Tony, the idiot, raised his arms and wanted to know where his hug was, so she gave him one, too.

After filling her thermos with coffee, she headed out.

"Yeah, they did it," Tony said. "No doubt about it."

EMMA JOGGED down the stairs smiling, glad to be on a better footing with Tom this morning. Her good mood was also a hold-over from last night and her time spent with Whit. He'd helped her close up and check the security of the building, even looked at her phone lines to make sure the burglar hadn't tapped them, but they'd never gotten around to having their talk. They'd spent too much time kissing.

Short kisses. Long kisses. Sweet kisses. Long, wet kisses. Mouth, eyelids, throat, forehead, ears, nose… He'd kissed each one.

Below the neck had been off-limits, to her disappointment. Those bizarre rules of his. She had yet to decipher them. He *had* kissed her hand, though.

She'd discovered that the hand could be a very erotic place, particularly the palm and the underside of the wrist. A little shiver went through her at the memory of his lips pressed to the pulse there.

Today, sadly, kissing was out. Getting information had to be foremost in her thoughts. She wanted to know if he'd talked to J.T. yet and what her brother had said. Another priority was learning what Whit had found out about Patrick.

She turned off the burglar alarm and did a quick inspection of the restaurant, kitchen and all the auxiliary rooms. Everything looked okay, the same as they'd left them last night.

Whit had taped a small piece of clear fishing line to the bottom of her door after she'd locked up. She carefully examined it. Still intact. No one had opened the door during the night, thank God.

Taking advantage of the isolation, Emma spent the next hour studying. Math was still giving her fits, and she was determined to master it.

She wasn't stupid. Daily she fed close to six-hundred people, more if she and Abby were doing a party. She helped create menus, calculate portions, order stock and keep up with staffing, breakage, linen, equipment and a hundred other things. And although she let an accounting firm handle the books, she always knew how the business was doing, which services were profitable and which weren't. Surely she couldn't be stupid and do all that.

But common sense was different from book-learning sense. She wanted both.

"Let's see." The next question asked her to figure the areas of a square, rectangle, circle and parallelogram and state which was largest. She worked on it for nearly fifteen minutes, but still came up with the wrong answer. "Ah, hell."

The phone rang and she welcomed the distraction.

"Illusions. May I help you?"

"Are you still intrigued?" Whit asked.

The sound of his voice slid across her body like a caress, making heat rush to her face and between her legs. "Very intrigued."

"Hold that thought. This case can't last forever."

"I hope not."

"You got going early today. I called upstairs expecting to find you still in bed, and Tom said you'd been up since before seven."

"I woke up and felt rested. It seemed silly to lie there."

"How did you find things this morning? Any problems?"

"Seems fine. The thread was still in place."

"Good. I had someone doing surveillance and he didn't report anything unusual, either."

"You have someone watching my building?"

"One of my investigators. He flew in late yesterday."

"Whit, this must be costing my brother a fortune. When he hired you, I'm sure he didn't figure that resolving my problems would be part of the deal."

"The bill's already paid. Don't worry about it."

"I am worried. Can't *I* hire you? That would relieve J.T. of the expense."

"No, you can't hire me."

"Why not?"

"Conflict of interest."

"I thought that only had to do with where you put your tongue."

"No, it also keeps me from working for you and your brother at the same time."

"Oh. But Whit—"

"I have news about Tom's father. We can sit here and argue about money, or I can fill you in on what I found out. Your choice."

"Please don't tell me Patrick's alive."

"I don't see any chance of that. The newspaper clipping you gave me was genuine. Authorities had no suspicion or doubt about his death, and there wasn't even an inquiry. He was supposedly in Egypt on business for the shipping company when he was struck by a car and killed. Several people witnessed it and the driver stopped."

"Yes, I know. Marie told me all this in a letter she sent with the clipping. She and Bert were coincidentally working on a TV movie in Egypt at the time, some Agatha Christie novel adaptation, and Patrick showed up out of the blue to see her on the set. She said she'd gotten her hopes up that they might reconcile, only to have them dashed. The next day he was killed. However, Marie didn't learn about it for several months."

"The authorities didn't contact her?"

"No. Patrick always said his parents were dead and that he didn't have any other family. When he died, they notified his company. The people there arranged for his body to be sent back to England and buried. Months later, Marie got a sympathy card with the newspaper clipping from an old friend in London who wrote to say she was sorry to hear about Patrick's death."

"That's a tough way to find out about your kid dying."

"I know. I felt so sorry for her."

"If the two of them were estranged and she didn't introduce you to Patrick, how did you end up knowing both of them?"

"Well, they weren't completely estranged. They'd talk occasionally, and a few times he came by her shop, although never, thank God, when I was there. He would've killed me if he'd known I was friends with her."

"Why didn't he know?"

"Because I met Marie first, you see. The Marshalls' business was across the street from the diner where I'd sometimes sweep or wipe down tables in exchange for food. Studios have their own wardrobe and prop departments, but they often go outside to private contractors when they need things they don't have in stock. That's what Bert and Marie did. They rented to movie companies, then collected, packed and shipped the costumes and props back to California when shooting was over. Afterward, they'd rent them again or, if the movie was very successful, sell them as memorabilia. I was naturally fascinated by all that. I started hanging around her shop to look at all the pretty things, and once she discovered I had a knack for putting together costumes, she let me help sometimes."

"This diner is the same one where you met Patrick?"

"Yes. I guess he'd been to see Marie at the shop

and walked across the street to eat lunch. I didn't find out he was Marie's son until a few weeks after we got together. He came home furious one day, raving about his 'bitch of a mother' and how much he hated her. Until then, I'd thought his mother was dead. Certain things he said made me realize it was Marie he was talking about."

"When did you tell her about the relationship with her son?"

"I went to her immediately. She'd treated me like a daughter, and it didn't feel right to lie to her. She warned me not to tell Patrick, though, that he'd see it as a sign of my disloyalty. I agreed in the beginning because I thought he'd make me stop being friends with her. Later, after Patrick's true nature began to surface, I realized he wouldn't simply stop me from seeing Marie—he'd kill me for having lied to him. Marie kept my secret. When I discovered I was pregnant and needed to get away from Patrick, she's the one who helped me."

"And you kept in touch because Tom was her grandchild."

"Yes, and because I loved her. We used postal drop boxes so the letters couldn't be traced if Patrick ever came across them. Over the years I sent photographs and updates about Tom. Twice, when he was little and she was still getting around okay, I took the chance of meeting her for the weekend a hundred miles up the coast. But she was already in her late seventies by then. Later, it was impossible to set up anything in person because physically she couldn't travel, and I couldn't take the chance of going there and running into Patrick if he happened to be in L.A."

"Marie's husband never knew all this?"

"I think he must have known. When they retired, they gave me their entire inventory instead of selling it. I doubt Bert would've done that unless he'd had an idea that Tom was Marie's grandson."

"Patrick was already dead by then, right?"

"Yes, this was in late 1990 and Patrick died in July of 1989. Bert died of natural causes a couple of years later. When Marie was killed eighteen months ago, any remaining money she had went to charity—the local humane society. That's what was so confusing about her murder. She didn't have anything valuable for the burglar to be interested in. I received a small bequest of jewelry, collectively not worth more than $5,000, and she gave Tom her pets. It was all written in her will."

"I know. That's how I ended up finding you. One of Marie and Bert's business neighbors thought a composite I showed him looked like a girl named Rachel Stanton who used to do some work for the Marshalls. When I discovered Marie had died not too long ago, I checked probate records and got the name of her attorney. He didn't know of a Rachel, but he said a Susan Wright and her son had received a small inheritance and that Mrs. Wright might have information about Rachel. He gave me your address."

"You're pretty smart."

"I got lucky."

"And now someone else has found me."

"Because I was careless."

"I don't blame you for that, Whit, despite my initial anger. As long as it's not Patrick looking for me, I can cope. I was worried that if it *was* Patrick, he might've learned about Tom's birth. But I've had time to think about it rationally, and I can't imagine him caring after all these years. He never wanted children, and he'd be fifty-eight now. That's a bit old to suddenly want to play daddy."

"You don't have to worry about Patrick. He's definitely dead."

"Thank God."

"I have more good news for you. I talked briefly to your brother, Jack, this morning."

"Jack? Is that the name he's using now?"

"Yes. Jack Cahill."

"I thought you weren't supposed to tell me that."

"I wasn't until I checked out your story about Susan Roberts. Now that we both know how Susan died and that you didn't have anything to do with it, Jack's instructed me to answer any questions you have about him."

"Really? That's wonderful!"

"He also wants to see you."

Her heart lunged. For a moment, she couldn't say anything. She wanted to see him, too, but the idea was frightening. Would he agree to keep her identity secret?

"Emma?"

"I'm here."

"I told him it's a bad idea until we know who's looking for you and who broke into your building, but he's waited so long to have his sister back that he no longer cares. He's insistent, being bullheaded about it."

"That sounds exactly like the J.T. I remember."

"He wants to help, if he can."

"He can't help."

"Well, he might be able to. He has experience in these things."

"I know he does. J.T. was always a better thief than Ray. He had what Ray always called *perfect touch.* He could remove any item from a pocket and the mark would never feel a thing. And he was so quick, he could lift merchandise from a store right in front of a cashier and they'd never catch him. Nobody could pick a lock faster than J.T."

"No, I mean, he has experience with burglary and theft now."

"But you swore to me he'd gone straight!"

"He has, about as straight as you can get. He's a cop, Emma."

Emma made a sound of disgust. "That's not funny."

"I'm not joking."

She had to digest that for few seconds. Uh-uh. No way.

"Whit, I'll kill you if you're playing with me."

"Sweetheart, I want nothing more than to play with you, but I'm telling the truth about this. Your brother's a captain with a police force in a town in Alabama."

"He's in the next state?"

"About twelve hours away by car. Less than three by small plane."

This was all too overwhelming to handle at once. J.T. was a cop. And he lived so close.

She felt faint and had to put her head down on the desk. A small groan escaped her lips.

"Are you okay?" he asked.

"I feel sick. This is too much, too fast. I only found out a few days ago that he was searching for me, and now he wants to meet."

"As I said, Jack's not the most patient person in the world. He wanted to book a flight this morning and come see you."

"Oh, no, he can't do that!"

"Don't worry. He won't. Lucky helped me convince him to take a breath and let you decide the next step. She threatened to leave him if he barged into your life without an invitation, and that's not an idle threat. She's a pistol."

"Lucky's his wife?"

"Yes. Erin is her given name."

"I hear admiration in your voice."

"Yeah, I like her. You'd like her, too."

"I don't know what to do, Whit. I *do* want to see them, but Tom can't know. And I'm worried what J.T. will think of me. I never dreamed he'd grow up to be in law enforcement. Won't he... Would he turn me in?"

"No, that's not an issue. If you want him to keep your secret, he will. If you want help getting back your true identity, he'll help. So will I."

"I'm so confused."

"Why not start with a call?" He gave her several sets of numbers where she could reach her brother. "Talk to Jack. Get to know him. Let yourself adjust to this new reality. Then, if you feel you want to see him, I'll set it up. I can take you there, or Jack says he, Lucky and the baby will gladly come down here."

"I'm not sure I can even talk to him by phone. If I do that, there's no going back. I won't be able to stand not seeing him."

"You don't have to make a decision right this minute. We can discuss this later."

"Will I see you today?"

"No. That's one reason I'm calling. I have another case needing my attention, and I'm about to fly out."

"You're leaving town?"

"Only for a few days. You have my cell number, and you can call it day or night. An associate of mine, Cliff Hodges, is here to take care of you."

He gave her the man's cell number and told her to program it into speed dial on all her phones.

"But how will I know this Cliff?" she asked.

"You won't."

"Oh."

"He'll keep a watch on your building at night and on you and Tom, but he won't identify himself unless he has to."

"Okay."

"If anything happens, he can be there within a minute or so."

"That's reassuring."

"I want you to take extra precautions while I'm gone. Stay inside and off the roof after dark. Encourage Tom and Tony to do the same. Have someone with you when you feed your mice."

She let out a long sigh.

"I know my leaving comes at a bad time," he added, "but it can't be helped."

"Am I allowed to say I'll miss you?"

"Yeah, you're allowed. I'll miss you, too."

AFTER HANGING UP, Emma checked in a delivery of produce at the back door. The kitchen staff began to come in along with Abby, who quizzed her about her "date" the night before.

"Did you have a good time?" she asked.

"A very good time."

They walked to Abby's office. Abby unlocked her door and they went inside. "He's so cute. He must like you a whole lot to extend his vacation."

"Mmm, I suppose."

"It's about time you met a nice man and had a relationship."

"I'm not sure how much of a relationship there's going to be with him living in another state, but I plan to enjoy it while it lasts."

"Good girl." She put her purse in the bottom drawer of the desk. "What have you got going today? Are you doing more employment interviews?"

"This afternoon I am. I hired four of the people I interviewed yesterday. Two will start today and two on Monday."

"Great. Which ones? The bartender, I hope."

"Yes, Cade Wesson."

"I hear he's pretty good. His body ain't too bad to look at, either. He does triathlons, or so one of the waitresses told me."

"I didn't hire him for his body."

"I know. But it doesn't hurt to have attractive people as servers. We could use another bartender, you know. Even a couple more who could also wait tables."

"I'll look into that."

"Who else did you hire?"

"The two college students whose applications you liked and the older woman."

"The grandmother?"

"Yes. Eve Vincent."

"Oh, Susan, you didn't. She hasn't got any experience, she's half-crippled and she has to be at least sixty."

"She's fifty-seven."

"Ancient."

Abby was thirty-two. To her, anyone over forty was old.

"The fifties are the prime of life," Emma told her. At least she hoped they were. She wanted something to look forward to. Her teens, twenties and thirties had all been pretty bad. "And she's not half-crippled. She's probably in better shape than the two of us put together."

"I'm sure," Abby said, "that fifty-seven won't feel *prime* to her after she's stood on her feet for hours and had to keep up with multiple orders."

"I'm not going to discriminate against her because she's older, Abby. It's against the law. And anyway, it's not right. She really needs this job. Her daughter dumped two grandchildren on her and disappeared. Poor Eve is raising them."

"And you're a sucker for every sob story."

"No, I'm not. I thought about it logically. She's mature and needs the money, so is therefore stable. And while she hasn't been employed outside the home, she's been a wife and raised a family. She's used to taking care of people."

Abby rolled her eyes.

"Don't give me that look," Emma told her. "I'll bet she turns out to be the hardest worker we have."

"If you say so, but if she has a coronary one night and keels over into the salad bar, don't come to me for sympathy."

"I'll remember that. Now, she'll be here shortly and I'll be busy, so you need to put her to work."

"Oh, wonderful. Geriatric baby-sitting. Did you even bother to ask her why she was limping?"

"The law says I can't."

"Wonderful."

"But she volunteered. She sprained a muscle. She says it's a minor injury and will heal in a few weeks."

Abby snorted. "I bet it's really something like arthritis, and if it is, it's going to be a constant aggravation."

"Abby, when you get to be her age, I'll remind you of this conversation and how stupid you're talking. We'll see if you still consider fifty-seven ancient."

On that note, Emma left, telling Abby she was headed upstairs to work on costumes and to call her on the intercom if there was anything she couldn't handle.

She made a list of outfits she wanted to wear over the next several days. In her apartment, she poured five latex masks and set the molds on the kitchen table to dry, then took the stairs to the third floor.

An Elizabethan theme was what she had in mind for the upcoming weekend, and because nothing in her private dressing room would do, she decided to look in storage. Her collection index listed several dresses, wigs and shoes. She also thought that for one or two nights, something cartoonish might be fun, like Betty Rubble from *The Flintstones.* Or she had a futuristic Jane Jetson outfit she was dying to try.

She punched in her code and turned off the alarm. Two steps into the room, she stopped and sniffed several times, having gotten a whiff of an odor she couldn't identify. Stale air? She didn't think so. Nor did it seem to be drifting up from the kitchen or caused by anything electrical.

The odor was very faint, and familiar somehow, but she couldn't say why. This wasn't her perfume lingering, nor was it the woodsy aftershave Whit had been wearing when he was up here. That had smelled nice, masculine. This wasn't exactly unpleasant, but it didn't strike her as a body scent.

She made her way through the aisles of costumes and looked around. The smell made her uncomfortable.

Not finding anything out of place after an exhaustive search, she went about her business. She picked up the swords and ninja costumes she and Whit had dragged out, and returned them to their places, then found the new costumes and accessories she wanted.

Back in the apartment, she did the preliminary painting of her "faces" and pressed her clothes for tonight. The final coats of paint would wait until she had the appliances glued on.

Walking back downstairs, she made a quick trip through the kitchen to see if everything was okay. In her absence, the place had come alive. Fresh bread was about to go into the oven. The staff was hard at work preparing lunch, including the delicious tapas that Santiago had introduced them to.

In Spain, he had explained, where dinner wasn't served until nine or later, these small dishes were eaten late in the afternoon. Illusions offered ten different kinds for both lunch and dinner.

Santiago wasn't scheduled to come in today, so Emma was surprised when she walked toward the cooler and heard him speaking in a low tone.

"Your hair reminds me of a sunset. And your skin is the color of a pale, delicate flower." He spoke a few words in Spanish and a feminine giggle followed.

"Santiago?" Emma called out.

"Susan, I am here," he said. He stepped out, followed by—she should have guessed—Abby.

Her friend grinned. Santiago, at least, had the good sense to act embarrassed.

"Was there something you needed, Susan?" Santiago asked.

"No, I was, uh, coming to check if the meat delivery got here, and heard voices."

"Yes, it has arrived. Abigail and I have made certain."

"Great. Isn't this one of your days off?"

"*Sé.*" He didn't offer further explanation.

"Well, I'll—" she pointed behind her "—be going now."

"I'll come with you," Abby said. She turned to Santiago. "Don't leave. I'll be back in minute."

Emma waited until they were in Abby's office before she questioned her. "What was that all about? Did I interrupt something?"

Abby grinned again, wider. ''Like he said—'' she wiggled her eyebrows ''—I was helping him check his meat.''

''I'll just bet you were.''

They burst out laughing. Emma got herself under control and wiped her eyes. They should both be ashamed of themselves for acting like adolescents.

''Seriously,'' Abby said, ''we were only talking.''

''What was he saying to you? I didn't think you understood Spanish.''

''I don't, but the way he speaks it melts my bones. Have you ever heard anything so sensual?''

''You're incorrigible. I thought you didn't like him. Only a few days ago, you said he was crazy.''

''I was wrong. He's not crazy, he's *passionate.* I figure any man who puts that much of himself into his cooking probably does the same with relationships. You don't mind, do you? I promise we'll be discreet.''

''Abby, I don't want him thinking he has to go to another restaurant if things don't work out between you two. That's my only concern. I paid through the nose to lure him away from that place in Miami. I don't want to lose him. I *can't* lose him.''

''We already talked about this, and we both agreed that we won't let our personal lives get in the way of our jobs. I swear to you it won't. Okay?''

''All right.'' She turned to leave. ''Oh, did Eve Vincent get here?''

''Yes, I put her to work doing the setups for lunch. Harold's supervising her and teaching her the ropes.''

''Thanks. And I wanted to ask you...have you been

in my storage room for any reason the last couple of days?''

''Uh-uh. Why?''

''I thought you might've gone in looking for something.''

''Wasn't me.''

A crash from the dining room had them both hurrying in to investigate. Pieces of glass were strewn across the tile floor. Eve Vincent stood in the middle of it holding an empty tray and looking as if she wanted to cry. ''I dropped the water glasses,'' she said forlornly. ''I'm so sorry, Mrs. Wright.''

''That's okay. Everyone breaks a few glasses at first. Harold will show you where the brooms and dustpans are.'' The woman followed him toward the cleaning closet.

Emma glanced at Abby, who was shaking her head.

''Don't you dare say it,'' Emma warned.

''She'll have a coronary and do a nosedive into the salad bar. You wait and see.''

EARLY THAT EVENING, after Tom had gone to a movie with friends, Emma took out the sticky note on which she'd written J.T.'s numbers and carried it upstairs. Her whole body was a roiling mass of emotions, and she wasn't sure, even as she sat down with the phone in her hand, what she was going to say.

All day she'd argued with herself. But she knew she had to do this. Twenty-three years ago she had abandoned her little brother. She couldn't do it a second time.

Shaking, she said a prayer for strength and punched

in J.T.'s private cell phone number. It rang twice before he answered.

"Jack Cahill."

The sound of the rich, bold voice made her go mute. Although her mind accepted that he was now thirty-five and a man, in her memory he was still a twelve-year-old boy.

"Hello?"

"J.T.," Emma said softly. "I *do* still love you best."

CHAPTER ELEVEN

WHIT'S TRIP TOOK much longer than he'd expected. Two weeks passed before he could get back to Florida, but he returned having wrapped up the Goldblum case. The two hundred and fifty thousand dollars he deposited to the company bank account went a long way toward making him feel better about the money and manpower he'd used to find and take care of Emma.

He unpacked his bags, then immediately contacted Cliff and asked him to come over to the bungalow. He and Cliff had stayed in touch by phone, but Whit had taken an unexpected side trip to Nova Scotia to pick up the missing Goldblum heir and hand-deliver him to the estate attorneys. That had monopolized his time.

Now, before Cliff flew home, Whit wanted a face-to-face update on what Cliff said were a couple of new developments in the search for Emma's cat burglar.

"Like I told you, no after-hours activity at the restaurant while you were gone," Cliff told him, throwing himself down on the couch. He lifted his feet to rest them on the coffee table. "I started to think your lady friend might have cooked up her break-in, or the burglar already got what he was looking for."

"But?"

"But she's right. Something strange is going on. Three nights ago a rented sedan showed up around closing. Your ilk inside."

"FBI?"

"Yep. Two guys. They watched the building. I watched them. Nothing happened. At daybreak, they were relieved by a duplicate set, another two guys in a second car, this one with government plates."

"Round-the-clock surveillance."

"I thought so at first, but last night, I went a little early. I took the six p.m. to six a.m. shift to see if I could confirm they were really double-teaming her. This is where things get screwy. Car number two is still there, and I expect it to be until midnight. But at seven-fifteen, the first car comes back. Only the suits aren't there to relieve their buddies. They're *tailing* a guy."

"Ah, hell." Whit rubbed his face, exhausted from his trip, and not wanting to hear there were new players in the game.

"It hits me that I've seen this guy more than once. He's been eating there every night. And it's *him* the suits are keeping tabs on."

"Tell me about him."

"He goes inside the restaurant and eats. The suits follow him. So I follow the suits."

"Did he have any contact with Emma?"

"No words were exchanged, but he didn't take his eyes off her."

"Damn!"

Cliff laughed. "Hey, I didn't either. She's hot! I think I'm in love."

Stand in line. "Who was she dressed as?"

"Julia Roberts. *Pretty Woman.* The big smile, the red dress. Man! she was perfect. If she hadn't been so much shorter, I swear I wouldn't have known it wasn't really Julia."

"I warned you she's as good as they come." Whit tried not to dwell on the image, or he'd lose his concentration. "So the guy never spoke to her or approached her in any way?"

"No."

"Did he talk to anyone else?"

"Not that I saw. He ordered. He ate. He left. The suits followed. They tailed him to the Ocean Blue Motel." He handed Whit three photographs of a large man exiting a car. "These aren't very good. I still had infrared film in the big camera, so I had to take these with the little spy cam and it was nearly dark. Here are photos of the suits." He handed him a second set.

"Do you have an ID on this guy?"

"Al Juneau. Better known as 'Big Al' Juneau. He works for Martin Charles Taylor as a bodyguard and gofer."

"*The* Martin Charles Taylor?"

"Same one."

"I didn't realize he was still alive."

"Oh, yeah, the old guy's living it up with wife number six. He's eighty-three. She's thirty-one. I'm making him my new hero."

Taylor was a colorful character, a native Californian who'd built a billion-dollar-a-year food company based on his father's steak sauce recipe. He'd twice run unsuccessfully for governor and had frequently been listed as one of the richest men in America.

"Is there a chance this Juneau guy is Emma's burglar?" Whit asked.

"Doesn't have the brains. He's strictly muscle and a messenger boy. Taylor tells him what to do, and he does it."

"Any idea why the FBI has an interest in him? Or how this ties to Emma?"

"No clear idea about the FBI. Your contacts at the bureau might help us there."

Whit nodded. He'd have to make some calls, remind a former colleague or two of favors owed.

"There's another twist to this story," Cliff added, "but first let me finish with Juneau. I checked on Juneau's arrival. He got here from L.A. the morning after you were contacted by the nonexistent Allen Morrow. I'm guessing Taylor sent him after he found out you were looking for Emma."

"Or more likely her Rachel identity."

"Yeah, or Rachel. He followed you, hoping you'd lead him to her."

"Which I did."

Cliff shrugged.

"This has the makings of a Laurel and Hardy movie," Whit muttered. "I was watching Emma, Juneau was watching me, and the feds were watching Juneau."

Cliff laughed. "Yeah, and now I've been watching the feds. Pretty funny."

"Did any of them make you?"

"No, they were too busy keeping an eye on Juneau to notice that someone was keeping an eye on them. I've been careful."

"I'm wondering if the feds have been here from

day one. If so, they might have witnessed the burglary."

"I have a theory on that. Hear me out. Let's start at the beginning. You asked questions about Emma—Rachel—in California. We have to assume that tipped off whoever was looking for her besides you."

"For argument's sake, let's say it *is* Martin Charles Taylor."

"Agreed. Maybe Taylor doesn't find out about your inquiries quickly enough to have you followed. You've already left town. But he has your name, maybe a business card you've left behind."

"I left my card with several people."

"Martin calls our office pretending to be Allen Morrow needing your help on the cop-killer case. When he talks to you by phone, he discovers your location. The next morning he puts Juneau on a plane to Florida to tail you."

"Our burglar is probably on the same plane."

"Good point. I hadn't thought of that."

"I'll pull the whole passenger list and see if I can tie any other names to Taylor. Go on with your theory."

"Juneau follows you to the restaurant. He maybe even follows you when you're with Emma on the boat, and he IDs her for his boss. The burglar now has a confirmed target. He waits in the wings for his opportunity."

"Which came when I left town. I flew over to see Jack and Lucky, and the burglar hit that night."

"But he obviously didn't get what he was looking for, because Juneau is still here."

"Which one—Juneau or Taylor—do you think is my hinky Allen Morrow?"

"When you talked to Morrow, did he seem to have an accent?"

"No."

"Juneau does. I heard it when he ordered."

"Then he's not Morrow. But I'm not sure Taylor is Morrow, either. Morrow didn't sound like an older person when I talked to him on the phone."

"An assistant maybe?"

"More likely. Check that out. When and how do you think the feds came into play?"

"Well, they could have followed Juneau from California, but since you didn't notice them while you were doing surveillance, and I didn't see them the first few nights I was on stakeout, I think they probably followed Martin—who led them to Juneau."

"Martin? He's here?"

"*Was* here. That's the second twist. Out of curiosity, I decided to track Martin's whereabouts. He flew in on his private jet three days ago."

"The same day the feds showed up."

"Exactly. He stayed several hours, then flew back out, according to the flight plan his pilot filed. The guy who pumped his fuel confirmed he was definitely on the plane when it arrived and left. He never got off. I suspect Juneau came to the airport and met with Martin aboard the jet. When Martin flew off again, that's when the feds picked up on Juneau and began following him. After Juneau started skulking about, showing an unusual interest in Emma's place, the suits must've brought in backup to watch it, too."

Whit nodded. The FBI in California could easily

have called the local guys, told them Martin was headed this way and asked them to watch the airport.

"It fits," he said. "The trick is confirming it."

"Now that you have Taylor as a possible instigator, you can get Deborah to work backward and see if she can tie the office used by the bogus Morrow to Taylor. Or I can do that for you."

"No, Cliff, you've done enough, and I'm grateful, but I can take it from here. It's time for you to go home."

"What about you?"

"I'm going to stay and see if I can figure out what all these people are after. Emma swears she doesn't know."

"Do you believe her?"

"Yes."

Cliff's lips thinned. "We've been friends a long time, Whit, and I've never known you to let your dick rule your head, but are you sure you're not doing it here? You're putting a lot of faith in a woman you've just met."

"*Because* we've been friends a long time and I know you're only looking out for my welfare, I won't beat the shit out of you for that 'dick' remark."

Cliff held up his hands. "I had to say it."

"Noted."

WHIT TRIED TO LET the comment slide, but he had a hard time shaking it off after Cliff left. What bugged him most was that his friend was right. The simple favor of finding Emma had turned into a challenge. The challenge had become curiosity. The curiosity had grown into admiration. And the admiration had shifted into something he wasn't yet ready to label.

Calling it simple lust wasn't honest. Calling it love was premature. He floated in a gray area where he'd never been before, where he could *imagine* caring enough for a woman to want to be with her every day. The realization surprised him.

Three weeks ago, he'd seen Emma for the first time. Yet two months of looking into every aspect of her life had given him a clearer picture of this woman than any he'd ever known, especially any he'd dated. He *knew* her. And he trusted her.

But yeah, he was fighting a losing battle with his emotions. He was smart enough to accept it. The problem was what to do about it.

Walking away from this case was out of the question. He'd given his word to Jack that he'd find his sister and facilitate his reunion with her. And he wouldn't rest until he knew Emma was safe. But staying meant that, sooner or later, he'd give in to temptation. The best he could do was try to minimize the damage to his professional ethics.

He punched in Jack's number and left a message on his voice mail. Fifteen minutes later, Jack returned the call.

"Hey, buddy, what's up?"

"I wanted to let you know I'm back in Florida and on my way to see Emma. You two still getting to know each other?"

"Yeah, we've talked every night since she first contacted me. She and Lucky are fast becoming good friends."

"I'm not surprised. Have you told her about your father?"

"No, she still assumes he's in prison. She's agreed to get together in person as soon as we can both swing it, but if she knew Ray was out on parole and part of my life again, she might back out. Then, again, she has a right to know he's free and wants to see her."

"Lucky still of the opinion that you should tell her?"

"Yeah, and I don't like going against her instincts, but she loves Ray and has only ever seen his good side. She can't comprehend what Emma's been through because of him. Ray's been working on her, too, trying to get her to convince me that he should come with us when we meet Emma. I'm between a rock and a hard place. I don't know what to do."

"Don't wait too long to decide. Ray doesn't strike me as being any more patient than you are."

"I won't."

Jack filled him in on what Cliff had uncovered and about the government stakeout.

"Damn! How much do you think they know?" Jack asked.

"Right now, I have no idea."

"If they find out about her background, we've got trouble. I hope to God they haven't already figured it out."

"I'll stay on top of the situation and call you if I learn anything more. I haven't mentioned any of this to Emma yet, and I wonder if it wouldn't be best to keep it between us until I can get some information. What do you think?"

"Will she freak if she finds out she's being watched by the FBI?"

"Definitely."

"Then let's hold off. She has enough on her plate, like worrying about Tom and what to tell him about me. We also don't want her doing anything crazy and giving herself away to the feds."

"Can you keep this from Lucky? I don't want her inadvertently letting something slip."

"It'll be hard, but yeah. Do you think this connects to the burglary?"

"Probably. They seem to be waiting for something to happen, so I don't think it's her they're after."

"Emma must have something Taylor wants."

"I doubt it's her salad dressing recipe. My job is to find out what."

"*Our* job. I want to help."

Good. He needed Jack and told him so. With Cliff flying home, Whit was working solo again. Except for Deborah. He wanted her to continue following up on the hinky Allen Morrow, to try to confirm that he indeed worked for Taylor. That case could be considered separate from Jack's and involved someone providing fraudulent credentials to gain information from the firm. He had zero tolerance for that.

"What can I do?" Jack asked.

"See what you can pull up on Taylor. Be very discreet. I want to know how clean he is, but we can't afford to alert the feds that you're asking. Let's try and keep your name disassociated from Taylor's."

"Got it. Anything else?"

Whit cleared his throat. "One last thing…hell, this isn't easy. I need a favor, and I'm not sure how you're going to take my request. I don't want it to injure our friendship."

"It would take a lot to do that. Name your favor."

"Fire me from the case."

A low chuckle sounded in his ear. "Okay, you're fired."

"I'm serious. You don't need my services anymore. I'll still go on with this case and I'll help Emma any way I can, but I want all work I do from now on to be unofficial."

"Okay. Consider it done. You're fired."

Whit wasn't sure how to take his casualness. "Why aren't you surprised? Or asking me for a reason?"

"Because Lucky warned me to expect it. She sensed something when you were here."

Hell! "I don't know what to say."

"Are you falling for my sister, Whit?"

He let out the breath he'd been holding. "Boy, Lucky doesn't miss much, does she?"

"Not often."

"If I *am* falling for Emma, how would you feel about it?"

"I'd be happy...as long as you didn't hurt her. Is this an itch you need to scratch, or is it more likely you'll become my brother-in-law?"

"I honestly don't know."

"I'll give you some of your own advice. Don't wait too long to decide."

TRAFFIC WAS HEAVY and the spaces along the bay front road were nearly full, but Whit had no trouble spotting the dark sedan parked half a block up from Illusions.

He didn't try to conceal himself from the two men inside. After a lot of consideration, he'd decided he *wanted* them to see him, get used to him going in and out. They would prove useful, even if they didn't know it yet.

Emma had made herself up to look like a young Bette Davis in a black strapless dress and long gloves minus the fingers. The dress was split all the way up one leg so that when she walked, a silk-encased leg peeped through. A black garter belt held the stockings in place.

He didn't recognize the character, but it made no difference to his body. The instant he saw her, he experienced a low clench of muscles, an escalation in temperature and the kind of raw sexual yearning that had caused men to make fools of themselves for thousands of years.

She spotted him, and her face lit up, adding to his internal battle for self-control. Every sense he had was aware of her as she walked over to him. Even his skin seemed to seek her out and want to connect with hers.

"Can you get away?" he asked.

"Yes."

They only made it to the landing on the second floor before his willpower failed him. He pulled her into his arms and ran his hands roughly down her body, bending to cup her sweet little ass. With those outrageously high heels she had on, she was tall enough to nearly match his height for a change. He was able to nestle himself right between her thighs.

It took every ounce of strength he had not to back her against the wall, hike up the slinky scrap of fabric and make love to her right there in the hallway.

"You've missed me," she said, laughing.

"Yeah, dammit, I've missed you. Did you miss me?"

"Very much."

"Good, because I got your brother to fire me this afternoon."

She drew back. "What?"

"Don't worry. I'm not dropping your case. Officially, though, my firm is no longer working for him."

"But, I don't—" Her forehead wrinkled in thought, but when her brain finally put it all together she grinned. "Oh! You're no longer worried about a conflict of interest!"

"That's right. I'm only a private investigator helping out a couple of friends. Is Tom home?"

"He won't be back until midnight. He's out on a date."

"Can we finish this in your apartment?"

"Absolutely."

PATRICK HAD TAKEN her virginity in a painful, loveless act devoid of romance. Sex after that hadn't been much better. With Whit, Emma had higher expectations.

At his request, she took off her "Jezebel" makeup and slipped into the little orange minidress with its matching shorts—minus her panties underneath. Whit had expressed a fantasy about that dress, and she didn't mind acting it out. She'd been dreaming of his tongue pressing through each of the little holes and touching her flesh ever since he'd suggested it.

He was in the bed when she emerged from the

dressing room, sitting against the headboard breathtakingly male and naked, without a trace of embarrassment visible on his face. She tried not to stare, but curiosity *was* a part of her nature.

"Oh, my, will that fit?" she said, which was stupid but made him laugh, breaking the ice.

"It'll definitely fit, but to try it out, you have to come a whole lot closer." She'd stopped ten feet away.

With nervousness tumbling in her stomach, she walked to the bed and lay down. Immediately he moved beside her, bringing them together, nearly covering her body with his. He kissed her, not once, but several times, then began to lick her stomach through the holes in the dress.

Scalding waves of desire washed across her skin. She'd never experienced anything so erotic in her life. When he began to lick and kiss her legs, she nearly leapt off the bed.

"Let's get rid of these," he said, pulling the shorts down, using his fingers to stroke her thighs as he did. No man had ever put his face there before, and she was apprehensive when he moved between her knees and parted them.

"Whit, wait. No one's ever...you know. Done this."

"Never?"

She shook her head. "I don't know what to do."

"Relax and enjoy. Believe me, you'll catch on."

Oh, she did. She couldn't believe she'd waited this long to experience such pleasure. When she climaxed twice in rapid succession, she was embarrassed, but he told her that was the whole point of his kissing her there.

"Can I do that to you?" she asked.

He grinned. "Oh, yeah."

"Will you show me how?"

She was awkward when she took him into her mouth, but his arousal seemed heightened by being able to give her directions—touch here, lick there, this feels better than that. She quickly realized that just about anything you did to a man's penis he was going to enjoy, as long as you watched where you put your teeth.

Pretty soon, she had him puffing in measured breaths like a freight engine climbing an incline.

"You're killing me," he moaned.

She smiled, pleased with herself. "How about this? Does it feel good?"

"Damn!" Hurriedly he sat up on the side of the bed and slipped on a condom.

Still clad in only her dress, she found herself suddenly in his lap, impaled, being made love to better than she'd known was possible. The sound of moist flesh sliding against moist flesh was wonderful, the best music in the world.

She vocalized her enjoyment. Houdini mimicked her from the other room. "Harder, harder."

Whit laughed. "Tom's going to love hearing that."

"Oh, no! He'll know we've been having sex."

"You're thirty-eight years old, Emma. You're entitled."

His hands were under the dress, on her hips, and he rocked her faster, pushed himself deeper. Her fears about Tom melted as the pressure built inside her.

"Oh, Whit!"

"Let it come, sweetheart."

They climaxed together, and it was so strong it made her whole body arch as if shot through with electricity. She screamed her release.

"I never even got undressed," she pointed out, collapsing on his shoulder.

"Next time," he said.

TRUE TO HIS WORD, the next time he made love to her, he undressed her completely and spent a leisurely hour exploring every inch of her body with his hands and tongue, particularly her breasts, since he hadn't had access to them earlier. He took his time, bringing her slowly and deliberately to orgasm.

Afterward, lying in his arms, she knew she'd never been happier.

"I should get back downstairs."

"So soon?" he asked, stroking her hair.

"I've been gone two hours."

"They know where you are."

"They also probably know what I'm doing up here with you. I'll never hear the end of it from Abby."

"So what? Like I said, you're a grown woman. I'm sure she's had sex before."

"I think she's having sex with my chef."

"The Spanish guy?"

"Yes, Santiago Chaves."

"What do you know about his background?"

"Why?"

"I'm checking up on all your employees from that list you gave me."

"I need to update that. I've hired more since you left. Six of them."

"Do that for me tomorrow. Now, tell me about Chaves."

"I lured Santiago away from a restaurant in Miami. He'd been working there since he came over from Spain two years ago."

"You approached him, and not the other way around?"

"Uh-huh. I'd heard fabulous things about him, so when I decided to open the restaurant I took a trip down there to see if he lived up to his reputation. I was so impressed I called him the next day and made an outrageous offer."

With her fingers, she traced the pattern of hair across his chest. He was nicely built. Muscular. Strong shoulders. She loved his narrow waist and nice butt. His abs were like taut little hills.

"Tomorrow I also want to go through your inventory list and see if I can match it to everything in your storage room."

"All right. That's no problem."

"Cliff's gone back to Pittsburgh, but I don't think you have to worry about anyone breaking in. He didn't detect any attempts in the past ten days. You still have my cell phone on speed dial, right?"

"Yes."

"If you get scared or hear anything, I'm only a mile or so away. You can call me and I'll come over. Unless, of course, you want me to spend my nights here."

"Much as I'd like that, I doubt I could explain it to Tom."

"I could sleep downstairs on the couch in your office."

"Heavens, no. I don't want you doing that. We'll be fine. Like you said, I can call you if anything happens, or nine-one-one for that matter. I've got your number programmed in right next to the main one for J.T.—Jack—on all my phones. Lord, I'm never going to get used to calling him Jack."

"I understand you've been talking to him regularly."

"Ooh, I'm glad you said that. I want to call him before it gets too late. It's an hour earlier there, but Lucky goes to bed at nine because she's up by five-thirty. I don't want to risk waking her."

"Jack said you've decided to get together. When are you planning it?"

"Week after next. Tom's going to be with the Parkers on his first weekend scuba trip, so it works out perfectly. They're planning to stay several days. Both of them took the whole week off."

"So you decided to let Tom take the lessons?"

"I thought I'd told you. Mr. Parker's been working with him every day in their pool. This will be Tom's first time to actually practice what he's learned in the ocean, and he's thrilled about it."

"Too bad he can't meet his uncle and aunt."

Emma didn't know what to say to that, so she kept her mouth shut.

"Are you nervous about seeing Jack?" he asked.

"Terrified. But also excited. I can't wait to talk to him and Lucky in person and to hold that baby." Her voice broke and she swallowed a sob. "I'm sorry."

He rubbed her back. "You've earned the right to cry."

They lay quietly, not talking, Whit giving her comfort with his gentle strokes. Emma stroked, too, first across his chest, then under the sheet where he began to spring to life again.

She'd never had this, an intimate sharing of time and space with a man. A sharing of thoughts and dreams. Joys.

"I'm shameless," she said, "jumping into bed with a man I hardly know."

"Ask me anything, and I'll tell you."

"Um, okay. How old were you when you first had sex?"

"Sixteen. She was my seventeen-year-old neighbor, and we did it on her couch one night when her parents weren't home."

"Where's the craziest place you ever had sex?"

"My mother's kitchen table. Same girl."

"Boy, she must have been something."

"Biggest breasts I'd ever seen. I lusted after her nearly a whole year before she let me get in her pants."

She playfully slapped him for that crude remark. "Is that all you saw in her, big breasts?"

"At sixteen, that's all I saw in any girl."

"Did your mother ever find out about the kitchen table?"

"God, I hope not, but I still can't eat at it without laughing."

"Besides brainless sex at sixteen, what's your deepest, darkest secret?"

He was silent for a moment, and then he said the

last thing she'd expected. "I killed a man once in the line of duty, and I never got over it. That's why I left the bureau. I tell myself I resigned because I felt confined by their rules, but that was only part of the problem. After the shooting, I realized there were some parts of the job I wasn't going to be very good at."

"Is that why you don't carry a gun?"

"I carry one when it's absolutely necessary. I have my pistol in a locked box in the closet of the bungalow, and I'm licensed to carry it in Florida. If it came down to killing or being killed, I'd use it. But at least now I have a choice about carrying, and I try to keep myself out of dangerous situations."

"I'm glad about that. What happened? I mean, why did you have to kill him?"

"He'd kidnapped and sodomized a little boy. I worked around the clock for days to figure out who might be hiding him. We surrounded the house. He came out holding a knife to the child's throat, and I had no doubt he'd use it. When I got a chance to shoot him, I took it."

"He deserved to die."

"Knowing that didn't make it any easier to watch. He bled to death before the paramedics arrived." His fingers found their way to her breast and began to tease her nipple. "Your turn. What's your deepest, darkest secret?"

"Whit, how can you ask that? You know more about me than I do myself."

"How'd you get that scar on your elbow?"

"Tripped, fell down some steps and cut it."

"Was that your book I took off the bed?"

"What book?"

"The school workbook."

"Oh, that."

"Come on. Confess. You've gone back to school, haven't you?"

"Sort of. I'm studying to take the GED. But I don't want anyone to know in case I fail the tests."

"You won't."

"I especially don't want Tom to know. He thinks I graduated from high school."

She told him what she was studying, and how she hoped to pass before Tom graduated.

"Sweetheart?" he interrupted. His voice sounded tense. "Be very still."

"What's wrong?"

"I don't want to panic you, but there's something big moving between my legs under this sheet."

She giggled. "Mmm, I know. I'm holding it."

"No, I mean there's *something else* moving under here. Oh, shit!"

He jumped straight up and off the bed, and was on the other side of the room with one of her shoes raised above his head like a club before Emma could even react.

She dissolved into laughter. The big, tough FBI agent turned P.I. was scared of a lizard. Well, a *big* lizard, but still a lizard.

"What the hell is that?" he asked. "The damn thing licked my knee."

She picked up the iguana and gave him a kiss. "Meet Rambo."

CHAPTER TWELVE

THREE NIGHTS LATER, when Whit stepped out of his car on his way to see Emma, two men came up on either side and guided him into the alcove of a nearby building. He recognized them as one of the stakeout teams.

The white guy had the body and expression of a bulldog, like he'd tear your throat out if you looked at him wrong. He was missing his jacket and had sweaty circles under his arms. The other guy was black, slender and impeccably dressed in what seemed to be a hand-tailored suit. Both seemed out of place on a hot Florida street where almost everyone else wore shorts and T-shirts.

"Could we have a word with you, Mr. Lewis?" the black guy asked politely. His accent was cultured, British.

"I was wondering when you boys would get around to asking."

"Our vehicle is over here. If you please."

"Identification first."

They both pulled their shields. The white guy was Special Agent Lawrence Ebeckie of the FBI. The other, Inspector Wallace Singleton of Interpol. Oh, boy.

"Lead the way."

In the car, they were silent. They drove him to a room at the Red Carpet Inn. Ebeckie offered him a seat at a small table by the window and took the chair across from him. Singleton chose to stand.

"Something to drink, Mr. Lewis?" Singleton asked. "Coffee? Tea, perhaps?"

"No, thanks."

A brown file folder with Whit's name on it lay on the table next to a tape recorder. Ebeckie didn't open it, but the implication was clear: we know everything about you. Whit had pulled the same stunt himself while he was an agent.

Whit's FBI contacts had already confirmed that Martin Charles Taylor was the target of an investigation, but beyond that, they didn't know much. A special task force was handling the case. Whit was curious as to what these two guys would reveal.

He'd already uncovered that Taylor collected rare and expensive works of art—paintings, furniture, statues, jewelry, clothing and funerary objects. He assumed that Taylor's "hobby," rather than his business, was under scrutiny, since he'd retired years ago.

Thanks to Deborah's superior talents, Whit now knew for certain that Taylor's personal assistant, Craig Hardesty, had rented the office "Allen Morrow" had used to call him. Hardesty was Morrow.

Ebeckie turned on the tape recorder. "No use beatin' around the bush here, Lewis," he said, his accent pure Jersey. "You know we've got the restaurant and its owner, Susan Wright, under surveillance. What's your connection to her?"

Whit was careful how he answered. "The lady and I are friends. We're involved."

"Lovers?"

"Yeah, if it's any of your business." He looked casually at his watch. "In fact, you're spoiling my date with her. Is this going to take long?"

"How'd you meet?"

"I ate dinner at Illusions one night. Saw her. Liked what I saw very much, and asked her out. The relationship grew from there."

"Your interest is personal rather than professional?"

"Mrs. Wright hasn't retained my services, if that's what you mean."

"You've been asking your former FBI buddies questions about us."

"Well, of course I have. Wouldn't you if *your* girlfriend was being watched by suits?" Ebeckie didn't answer, but Singleton nodded. "By the way, you guys need to brush up on your surveillance techniques."

"We'll keep that in mind. You met Mrs. Wright when?"

"A few weeks back while I was in the city on business."

"What kind of business?"

"A missing person's case."

"And you're here now for what?"

"I thought I made that clear. To continue my relationship with Mrs. Wright."

"And she's the only reason?"

"Buddy, if you've seen her, you know that's reason enough."

Singleton liked his answer. His smile widened.

"We want you to look at something," Ebeckie said. He motioned to Singleton, who took a photograph out of a white cardboard storage box on one of the beds and put it in front of Whit. He recognized the man as Juneau. "Have you ever seen this man inside the restaurant?"

"No," Whit answered honestly.

"His name is Al Juneau."

"Never met him."

"Do you know if Mrs. Wright has ever had occasion to talk to Juneau? Or if she knows him?"

"Susan sees and talks with hundreds of people every day as part of her business. If he's a customer, she's probably talked to him."

"What about this man?" Ebeckie put a second photograph in front of him. "Do you recognize him?"

"Sure. That's Martin Charles Taylor, the industrialist."

"Ever seen him in the restaurant or heard Mrs. Wright mention him?"

"No. I seriously doubt Mrs. Wright would have any reason to know a billionaire. They don't travel in the same circles. Are you guys going to tell me what this is all about?"

The agents exchanged quick glances. Singleton nodded, proof to Whit that he, and not Ebeckie, was in charge. Ebeckie leaned forward in the chair. "Whitaker. Can I call you that?"

"Sure, Lawrence, but I prefer Whit."

"You're one of us. Your record with the bureau was damn good. I'd like to think we can talk man-to-man without worrying that you'll leave here and say or do anything that might screw up an ongoing investigation."

"I'd like to think so, too."

"Juneau works for Taylor. We've been keeping tabs on both of them for over a year. A joint task force of the FBI and Interpol is looking into allegations that, since at least 1970, Taylor has commissioned the theft of works of art worth hundreds of millions of dollars from galleries in the U.S. and a number of foreign countries."

He showed Whit a long list from the Art Loss Register. At the top was an oil on canvas by J.M.W. Turner, stolen in 1994 from an exhibition in Frankfurt, Germany, and worth twenty-four million pounds. That was followed by a Gutenberg Bible taken from a Paris museum in 1987 and worth eight million dollars and a Yuan vase from Boston valued at five hundred thousand dollars.

The list went on and on, and included every imaginable item—English pocket watches, Tiffany pitchers, a Ming gilt-bronze Buddha, a Tibetan silver butter lamp, antique pistols, jewels. All were wildly expensive, some priceless. The list covered countless countries, museums, bank vaults and private residences.

Whit's experience told him that thefts like these occur for three main reasons: so the objects can be ransomed back to the owners; so they can be sold to finance illegal activities like drugs, weapons and terrorism; and so some rich, greedy bastard can hide them away in his private vault and gaze at them at his leisure. Taylor probably fell into the third category.

"This is all very fascinating," Whit said, "but what's it got to do with Susan?"

"Maybe nothing. But Juneau has eaten at her place six times in the past five days. We find that a little strange."

"Hey, maybe he just likes the food."

Singleton chuckled.

"And maybe he's helping to set up the next victim for the thief," Ebeckie said.

"You think Susan's place is next?" A bead of sweat rolled down his face. Damn! He'd nearly slipped up and called her Emma.

"We're hoping you can tell us that, and what Taylor might be after." Ebeckie asked Singleton to get a folder from the box and put it on the table. The name on it was *Susan R. Wright.* Whit's heart fell to his knees, but he kept his face passive.

He flipped through the pages. Vital info, employment records, credit history. Routine stuff he'd already gathered himself. All the information was about *Susan,* not Emma or her other identities.

He almost wanted to laugh out loud. They had no idea who Susan Wright really was.

"Nothing in here suggests any link to Taylor, other than that they once lived in the same state," Ebeckie said.

"That was nearly twenty years ago," Whit pointed out.

"She's been making a lot of calls to the home of a police detective in Alabama. What do you know about that?"

Whit shrugged. "She has a woman friend in Alabama whose husband's a cop. That's probably who she's calling."

He made a couple of mental notes, one to tell Jack

to stick to that story if contacted, and two, to get Emma a secure phone. Because they'd asked about Jack, it meant they hadn't yet tapped Emma's lines or monitored her conversations, only pulled her record of calls. But that situation could change.

"She has no criminal record," Ebeckie continued. "We don't, at the current time, have any evidence to suggest she's involved in the thefts. That leaves her as a possible target. I ask again, do you know why Juneau might be interested in her and her business?"

"I have no idea. I'm positive she doesn't own anything even remotely close to the value of objects I see on this list. She's accumulated a few movie costumes and props for her business, but the top item is worth only a few thousand dollars."

"You've seen them?"

"Yes. And so have you, if you've been inside. All the valuable ones are on public display in cases in the dining room."

"And the rest?"

"In storage on the third floor. She has an itemized list I can get for you, if you'd like. I'm sure she'd be happy to help."

Whit thought lightning might strike him for that last comment.

"We'd appreciate it."

"You could come over and look at her collection and talk to Susan."

Whit held his breath, praying he'd played his cards correctly. If he appeared cooperative, they might leave Emma alone. He didn't want them bringing her in for questioning.

"No, we don't want to tip off Juneau that we're on to him," Ebeckie said.

"Are you sure he doesn't know?"

"Yes."

Whit nodded. They were probably right. If Juneau had smelled a tail, he'd have split by now.

"We'd rather you didn't mention this little chat to your lady friend," Ebeckie asked. "We want her to go about her normal routine, and she might not do that if she knew about us."

"No problem. Anyway, I wouldn't want to frighten her unnecessarily."

"But that list would be helpful, if you can secure it without tipping her off."

"Sure. I'll get it to you tomorrow. I have a couple of requests in return, though."

"Which are?"

"That you not put Mrs. Wright or her son in danger. I'll help you any way I can, but I expect you to watch out for their safety. And I want to be alerted to any possible problems concerning them. Agreed?"

Ebeckie rose, so Whit did, too. Ebeckie and Singleton conferred.

"Agreed," Ebeckie said, turning back to him.

"This Juneau..." Whit tapped the photo still in front of him. "Is he a thief? He looks a bit beefy to be squeezing through air-conditioning ducts and scampering over rooftops."

Singleton chuckled appreciatively. "Beefy. Very apt description, Mr. Lewis. You Yanks have an interesting way of phrasing things. No, Juneau is not a thief. We suspect that at least two persons have been involved in the actual thefts over the years, but not necessarily at the same time. These are rare individuals. Highly skilled. The elite of the elite. And because they command a great deal of money for their services, only a select few can afford to hire them."

"You're clueless about their identities?"

He smiled. "Not clueless, Mr. Lewis, but not positive, either. We plan to catch him or them in the act."

"I wish you luck."

"We'll need it, Mr. Lewis. This thief won't give up until he has what he's after. He can't afford to. And we can't afford to keep letting him get away. Now, if you'd be so kind as to come with me, we'll take you back to the restaurant and your engagement with the fetching Mrs. Wright."

ON THE DAY Jack and Lucky were due to arrive, Emma could hardly contain her excitement. At four they called her at the office pretending to be a Mr. and Mrs. Johnson wanting directions to the restaurant, alerting her that they'd checked into their room. The code had been prearranged.

They planned to meet at Whit's. He offered to come by and get Emma. For some odd reason, he parked quite far from the building and made her walk through several stores on the way to the car. He also wouldn't let her talk.

Finally, unable to stand it any longer, she asked, "Care to tell me why all this cloak-and-dagger is necessary?"

He put his finger to her lips to warn her to be silent, then pulled her into a pub crowded with chatting tourists.

"I'm being cautious," he said.

"Why are we talking so low?"

"Are we talking low?"

Lately, he'd fallen into a pattern of either answering questions with a question or not really answering them at all. She appreciated that he was watching out for her but sometimes felt as if she was living in a James Bond movie. He'd even insisted that Jack and Lucky make reservations at a motel of his choosing.

"If I'd known you were going to make me carry all this junk," he said, "I'd have reconsidered and picked you up at the door." He shifted the shopping bag he was holding to the other arm; it was one of two she'd packed. "What is all this?"

"Food from the restaurant in my bag. A few gifts for the baby in yours."

"A few? The damn thing must weigh fifty pounds."

"Oh, don't exaggerate. Now tell me who's following us."

"Nobody that I'm aware of, but if they are, I'd rather they think we're out shopping, returning merchandise."

"You've never made me do this before when I've gone to your bungalow. What's different now?"

"Before, we were always alone, or it was only you, me and Tom."

"But I haven't had any more trouble. And why would anyone follow me?"

"Maybe no reason."

"Are you purposely trying to be difficult?"

"Am I being difficult?"

"You know you are."

He just shrugged.

"Whit, I don't see the need for all this intrigue. I haven't had any problems other than that one time. I'm beginning to think I imagined the burglary."

"You didn't. Your security tapes were looped. I got the report this morning."

"So a master thief *was* in the building that night. But why hasn't he been back? Do you think he got what he wanted and left?"

"That's a possibility, but I doubt it. What's more likely is that he searched, couldn't find what he was after and is waiting, hoping for some new bit of information that will lead him to it."

"You know something? I'm glad. If there's a chance he's still here, maybe you'll stick around."

"Have I said anything about leaving?"

"No, but we both know that sooner or later you'll have to. You can't stay here indefinitely."

"As long as I have my laptop, a phone line and a fax machine, I can work anywhere."

"But beach rentals aren't cheap. And your family must miss you terribly."

"Have you been using the secure phone I gave you to call Jack at home?"

There he went, changing the subject, being aggravating.

"Yes, but I still don't understand why I have it, or why you keeping checking my wiring box. Has someone tapped my lines?"

"No, but that would be an easy way for your thief to get information about when you'll be in the building. I want to keep you safe."

Warmth infused her. "You always wait to say

something sweet until we're in public and I can't kiss you.''

''I'll remind you when we're alone.''

HER LIFE HAD BEEN MARKED by happy and tragic events, memories strung like beads upon a string. She knew that when she grew old and looked back at her time on earth, the moment she saw her brother again would rank among the best.

As soon as she and Whit pulled up to the bungalow, Jack was off the porch and striding to the car. She got out and he scooped her up in his arms, lifting her off the ground.

She'd vowed not to cry, but the tears wouldn't obey. They poured out in great heaving sobs until she'd completely soaked his shirt. Ever since she'd left him behind, she'd felt as if she'd lost part of her soul. Finally she had it back.

He put her down and pulled out his handkerchief. ''Hey, now, there's no reason to cry. This is a happy day, a time to celebrate.''

''I *am* happy.'' She wiped her face.

''Lord, you're beautiful. The pictures Whit gave us didn't do you justice.''

''Oh, I'm not—I'm a mess.'' She took a step back. ''You're the beautiful one. Look at you! So tall and handsome.'' Behind him, Lucky stood with the baby on her hip, smiling. She had tears on her face, too. ''Lucky.'' Emma held out her arms. They embraced, newfound sisters with a bond as strong as blood.

''And this is Grace,'' Lucky said. She rubbed her hand lovingly across her daughter's curly head.

"Gracie, this is your Aunt Emma. Can you give her a kiss?"

The baby was adorable. She stuck out her precious little lips for a kiss.

"Hello, Grace. Will you let Aunt Emma hold you?"

Grace shook her head and clutched her mother tightly.

"Maybe when she gets used to you," Lucky said.

Whit and Jack brought in the shopping bags, and soon wrapping paper was flying around the living room as Grace opened her presents.

"You shouldn't have gotten all these things," Jack told Emma. "She'll be spoiled rotten."

Lucky, sitting on the arm of his chair, laughed. "As if you haven't already done that." She turned to Emma. "He takes her to the store and all she has to do is point, and he buys it." She poked him, and he captured her hands, forcing her down for a kiss.

Emma watched the two of them, the easy way they had with each other, the touches and smiles they shared. A fierce longing seared her. She wanted what they had, not simply to love and be loved by a man, but to be one half of a perfect whole.

Her gaze met Whit's, and he winked. She smiled back. What they had was wonderful—friendship, affection, attraction, mutual respect—but she wanted love, the deep, forever-after love of a husband and wife. How could she ever have that when she was living a lie? And when the man she was falling in love with would soon leave?

She didn't know how to go on without him. Even Tom was starting to care for Whit. She could tell by the way he acted when the three of them were together. They'd cooked out on the beach a few times recently, and since Tom was a movie freak like her, Whit had bought a VCR and hooked it up at the bungalow.

They'd sit on the couch sharing a bowl of popcorn and watch a horror flick, Tom's favorite. Those evenings made her feel as if they were becoming a family. Only, like everything else in her life, it was an illusion.

Her sadness must have shown on her face because Whit frowned and gave her a questioning look. She shook her head, as if to say *it's nothing.* She pushed her unhappy thoughts aside. Like Jack had said, this was a day of celebration, and she refused to let anything bring her down.

Not until after supper did Emma have a chance to talk to her brother alone. They took a stroll along the beach and spoke of things pleasant and unpleasant.

"What was it like for you after I left?" Emma asked. "Tell me the truth."

"Hard. With you gone, I got caught up in the idea of pleasing Ray, and I found myself helping him burglarize stores."

"I'm sorry. I never meant to hurt you."

"Hey, it wasn't your fault. Even if you hadn't left I probably would've done it anyway."

"Damn Ray! I hope they keep him in prison the rest of his pathetic life."

"Don't hate him, Emma. He's not bad, just misguided. And he's sorry for what he did to both of us."

"You've been in touch with him?"

"Yes."

She stopped walking, stunned. "My God, how can you, after what he did to you?"

"At first, I thought it was guilt driving me because I'm the reason he got arrested, but I came to realize I still cared for him."

"I don't understand? What happened that makes you responsible for his incarceration?"

"I decided in my infinite wisdom at fourteen that Mama and I would be better off without Ray. He and I were supposed to do a job together, only I feigned being sick after we got there, and I wouldn't go inside the building. As soon as I knew Ray was in, I tipped off the police." His tortured face told her that telling the story was painful.

"I don't know what to say. That took guts."

"It turned out to be a really stupid move."

"Ray must've been furious."

"Emma...Ray confessed so I wouldn't have to testify or be dragged into court. He willingly went to prison to protect me. He was afraid Mama would find out I'd been helping him."

She shook her head in confusion. "That doesn't sound like Ray. He never owned up to anything in his life."

"Well, he did. He even pretended to believe the silent alarm caught him. Until a couple of years ago, I wasn't aware that he knew I'd snitched on him."

"I'm glad you did. He's right where he needs to be."

"Honey, have some empathy. He's still your father. And he loves you."

"He was never any father to me. He never caused

me anything but grief and pain. And as far as love goes—he doesn't understand the meaning of the word."

"Are you telling me you never loved him? Remember, we're both being honest here."

The question made her heart ache.

"Yes," she said sadly. "I loved him. I adored him at one point in my life. But he disappointed me so many times that I stopped letting myself care. All I ever wanted was for us to be a normal family. But Ray valued other things over being a father."

"Do you think you could ever forgive him?"

"I don't know."

"MMM, HAVE YOU EVER SEEN better-lookin' male specimens in your whole life?" Lucky asked.

Emma chuckled. "Not at the same time, no."

"If those two were bulls, cows would be leaning over the fence sighing."

"Kind of like we're doing right now?"

"Uh-huh."

They stood at the bar that divided the living room from the kitchen, heads propped on their palms, watching the men talk. Whit and Jack were on the sofa, their dark heads bent over some papers, oblivious to their female admirers. Whatever the discussion, it had to be intense.

Lucky was right. Both men were incredibly easy on the eyes.

"I fell in love with Jack almost instantly," Lucky said, "like the love was so strong and so tired of waiting to be shared, it couldn't hold itself back anymore. We didn't have an easy time of it, though. I guess he told you we got married fast and then separated almost as fast."

"He said you'd lived apart for several months."

"Until I got pregnant with Grace. Even after he moved back in, things weren't perfect. My Mema—my grandmother—says that great passion demands great commitment."

"She sounds like a smart lady."

"She is. I hope you'll come sometime and stay with us so you can meet her and the rest of my family. They're your family now, Emma. I already feel you're one of my sisters."

"I'd like that, but I can't promise. I have to be careful about Tom. He can't know."

"What do you think he'd do if he learned the truth about you?"

"Probably run off and join the navy. He's been threatening that all summer. At the very least he'd hate me."

"Or maybe he'd understand."

"I doubt it."

"Isn't it worth the chance for you and him to have a family? Please don't take offense at this, but it saddens me to think of him never knowing he has an aunt and uncle, or getting to meet Grace. He should know he has a grandfather, too."

"Lucky, you don't understand. You're part of a big, loving family. You can't imagine what it's like to have your father constantly disappoint you."

"Emma, you don't have the monopoly on disappointment. The people you love the most are also the ones who hurt you the most." The baby tugged at her pant leg and she set her on the counter. "I found out that my father had an affair a few years ago. Here was a man I'd worshiped since the day I was born, and I suddenly realized he wasn't perfect.''

''What did you do?''

''I forgave him, like I did Jack for keeping his past a secret from me when we were first married. When you truly love someone and they make a horrible mistake, you have to find a way to let go of the pain. Otherwise, life will be very long, and very lonely.''

''It's too late for me.''

''No, it's not. Start by offering forgiveness to the one person who needs it most.''

''And who is that?''

''Yourself.''

''RAY'S HERE,'' Jack said quietly to Whit when the women went outside to sit on the porch. ''He refused to stay home. I was afraid if we left him behind he'd show up on his own, so I got permission from his parole officer to bring him.''

''Damn, I had a feeling this might happen.''

''I should've seen it coming. The old coot pulled the same stunt on me when he got out of prison.'' Affection was obvious in his voice.

''You never told me the details of that.''

''Lucky complained about a guy following her, so I set a trap to catch him. It turned out to be Ray. Until then, I thought he was still serving time. I'd told Lucky my parents were both dead. Of course, it didn't take her two seconds to figure out that he was my father.''

''I don't suppose so, given the resemblance. He

won't do that here, will he? Follow Emma? Or try to contact her?''

''So far he hasn't had the chance, and I've told him he absolutely can't until I've told her about him. But Ray isn't great about taking orders.''

''I've noticed.''

''And, shit...I chickened out today when I talked to Emma. I couldn't tell her.''

''We have a ticking bomb on our hands.''

''Yeah, well, welcome to the Webster family, my friend. Trouble is our motto.''

CHAPTER THIRTEEN

EMMA WAS SILENT on the ride home and Whit didn't know what to make of it. She sat as rigid as a tree, holding a box in her lap that Lucky had given her for Tom. Whit knew it contained fossils and arrowheads Lucky had found along the Black Warrior River, but he wasn't sure how Emma intended to explain the items' origins.

"Who will you tell Tom his present came from?" he asked.

"I have no idea. A customer, I guess." Her voice sounded flat. "What's one more lie when I've told so many."

"Is something wrong? You seemed so happy all day, but now you're miserable. What happened to depress you?"

"I got a good look at myself today through the eyes of other people, and I didn't like what I saw. Am I wrong, Whit, in continuing to withhold the truth from Tom? I didn't think so, but I'm no longer sure."

"That's a tough one. I understand why you've done it, and I can't honestly say I wouldn't have made the same choice in your position, but you admit you live in fear of him finding out. Maybe it would be best to tell him before he does."

"Lucky thinks he deserves to know about them, and about Ray."

"I'd want to know."

"Would you? Truly? You'd want to be part of a family of thieves, to know that your only living grandparent is in prison?"

"*Ex*-thieves. And no, I wouldn't *want* it, but I'd accept it."

"If I lost him..."

"He might be angry and hurt, but he loves you. I doubt you'd lose him."

"I don't know what to do."

"The decision is yours to make. Right or wrong."

"Are you aware that Jack's been in touch with Ray in prison?"

"He mentioned it." Whit swallowed hard. They were getting into territory that could get him in trouble. "How do you feel about the two of them reconciling?"

"Confused. Alarmed. I'm furious at Ray for how he treated Jack after I left, yet sad about what's happened to him. Thirty-five years is a long time to be locked up."

"Yes, it is."

"I also feel a bit ashamed."

"Why?"

"Because I don't seem to have the capacity to forgive him like Jack does."

"Maybe that will come with time."

"I'm afraid it makes me a bad person."

"No, it makes you a person who's been badly hurt."

She reached over and squeezed his arm. "Thank

you for understanding. And for everything you've done for me, not only today, but in these past few weeks. Thank you for giving me back my family.''

''You're welcome.'' He hoped she felt the same way when she found out Ray was out of prison...and in Saint Augustine.

THEY PULLED IN by the back door at nine o'clock. Emma said she planned to work until closing, and that she'd see Whit in the morning.

''You don't want me to stay?'' he asked, surprised when she said no, she wanted to do some thinking.

Finding time to be alone together had been hard lately. She had to oversee things in the restaurant at night. During the day, Tom was often home. He'd given up his part-time job last week when football practice started.

With Tom away this weekend, Whit had been looking forward to making love to Emma for most of the night, waking up next to her in the morning.

He parked the car and shut off the engine, but didn't immediately get out. ''I don't like the idea of you being here alone. The building's too large. You could scream and no one would hear you, not even if the restaurant was full.''

''I'll be fine. I installed that second set of locks on the front door of my apartment like you suggested, and I also lock my bedroom door at night.''

''Call me before you go to sleep. And keep your cell phone on the nightstand. Leave a light on so you don't have to fumble around.''

''Yes, sir. Phone. Speed dial. Light. Locks. Got it.''

"Can I at least have a kiss before you send me on my way to a cold shower?"

"Of course you can."

She scooted over and into his arms. He liked the feel of her skin, and the light, airy smell of the perfume she wore behind her ears and at her wrists. Her lips softened under his, and as the kiss intensified, she moaned. A few minutes of this and he might talk her into letting him stay.

A couple of hard raps on the driver's window had them jumping apart like two guilty teenagers. Brownie stood there with his face against the glass.

"Damn," Whit said, his voice nearly a growl. "I'm going to shoot that guy one day."

He opened the door. Emma leaned over. "What is it, Brownie? We won't have the plates ready for a couple of hours."

"I need to talk to you, Miss Susan. It's important." He looked right and left, as if he was afraid of something.

"Okay." Emma and Whit both got out of the car. Emma came around to Whit's side. "What's wrong?"

"I'm worried about you. I've seen men in a black car watching your place at night. Sometimes it's a light car. They're out front right now."

Whit hastily pulled him up under the dark of the stairs. Emma followed.

"Mr. Brown, don't worry," Whit told him. "We know about the men."

"We do?" Emma asked.

"Yes, we do," Whit said, then to Brownie, "Go on about your business and forget about them.

They're watching Miss Susan, but only to make sure nothing happens to her. The businesses around here have reported some break-ins."

"Wasn't me. I swear."

"We know that, Mr. Brown. We're trying to catch the people responsible. You can help Susan by not telling anyone about the men out front. Understand? Can it be our secret?" He took a twenty from his wallet and gave it to the man.

"Our secret. Yes, sir."

"You haven't noticed anyone else watching Miss Susan besides them, have you? Or seen anything unusual?"

"No, sir."

"If you do, I want you to let me know. Can you do that?"

"I sure can. I'd be glad to help out Miss Susan."

"Thank you, Brownie," Emma told him. "You're a good friend."

Brownie left, but Whit still had to deal with Emma. And from the expression on her face, he wasn't going to get by with a half-assed explanation this time.

"Upstairs," she ordered.

He followed her up to the second-floor landing. She punched in her security code, opened the outer door and stepped into the hallway, but she stopped a few feet inside.

"Do you smell that?" she asked.

He lifted his head and took a sniff. "I don't smell anything."

"A very faint odor." She turned off the alarm to her apartment and opened the door. "In here it's stronger."

He walked inside as she flipped on the lights. She was right. There was something, some scent, but it was too faint for him to identify.

"One day I went up to the storage room, and I thought I detected an odd smell. Later, I decided I was only spooking myself. But this is the same. Whit, I think the burglar's been in here."

"Wait in the hall." He cursed himself for not having his weapon.

"Hell, no! I'm not staying out there by myself. I'm coming with you."

"Then get behind me."

He searched every room, every closet and cabinet where someone might hide, but it wasn't easy with Emma plastered to his back and gripping his shirt.

They looked around Tom's room. "Stick 'em up," Houdini squawked.

Nothing seemed to be out of place or missing, so Whit relaxed.

"If anyone was here, they're gone," he said.

"If? You don't believe me?"

"Wait, now. I didn't say that. But you're not sure the smell is associated with the thief. You live above a restaurant."

"No, this isn't from the kitchen. The odor is…I don't know, familiar somehow. I've smelled it before, upstairs in the storeroom, but I can't identify it."

"You should have mentioned that first incident to me."

"I think it happened while you were in Pittsburgh, or maybe it was the day you left. I don't remember."

"I'll stay here tonight. If my being in your bed will bother you, I'll sleep in Tom's or on the couch."

She wrapped her arms around his waist and put her head on his chest. "I want you in my bed. But tonight, could you simply hold me? I don't feel too amorous."

He rubbed her back. "Yeah, I could do that."

"Your guys outside weren't much help, were they?"

Whit stiffened. "No, not much."

"You said you sent Cliff home to Pittsburgh. Did you bring him back, or are these new people from your office?"

"Emma, honey...about the men outside... You'd better sit down."

THE FBI! INTERPOL! Oh, Lord!

Emma bent over and took several rapid breaths, drawing air out of the paper sack Whit had placed over her nose and mouth. She'd never hyperventilated before, and the experience wasn't pleasant. Her hands and feet had gone numb, and now a prickly sensation was moving up her arms. She felt dizzy.

"Take slower breaths," Whit warned. "That's it. Try to relax and breathe normally. You're taking in too much oxygen."

Once she felt better, he outlined the whole story, how the FBI suspected Martin Charles Taylor of hiring a thief to steal something from Emma's building.

Now, *that* was a name she hadn't heard in a long time.

"Oh, God!" She jumped to her feet. "I can't believe this is happening. Taylor is behind this?"

"You know him?"

"Not personally, but Whit, I do have a connection

to him, and if the FBI finds out about it—oh, sweet Lord! They'll think I'm an accomplice and put me in prison."

In her agitation, she bounced around the room, unable to sit still. Whit finally grabbed her by the forearms and made her sit down.

"Hold on a minute. What's the link between you and Taylor?"

"I'm afraid to tell you."

"Dammit, Emma, this isn't the time to be holding anything back. What's your link to Taylor?"

"Patrick."

Whit groaned loudly. "Hell."

"He worked for Taylor. At least I think he did. I'm not absolutely sure."

"That would mean Taylor owned the shipping company where Patrick was employed, and nothing suggesting that turned up in my background check."

"No, he worked *privately* for him. One night I was watching the news and it showed a clip of Taylor attending a benefit dinner. He had this really young woman with him, and I made some catty comment about old men always seeming to like very young girls. Patrick said something like 'yeah, but the old lecher pays good money.'"

"If you tell me Patrick had a second job as a master thief, I'm going to strangle you."

She winced. "Okay, I won't tell you."

"Ah, shit!"

WHIT PACED, trying to work out his anger and frustration. She'd promised to be honest with him, yet she'd withheld information crucial to the case.

"Dammit, Emma, you swore to me that you weren't hiding anything else. If you'd told me about Patrick weeks ago, we might know what Taylor's after. You could have saved us both a lot of grief."

"I'm sorry."

"Being sorry doesn't mean shit right now. You *lied* to me."

"No, I didn't."

"A lie of omission."

"Okay, you're right. I should've told you everything. But I didn't see any need after you found out definitely that Patrick was dead. Obviously, he can't be the thief."

"But these thefts go back more than thirty years, which means Patrick could have given you something when you and he were together. Taylor probably only found out recently that Rachel and Susan are the same person."

"No, I don't think so, at least the part about him giving me something. Patrick bought me nice things, sure, but always clothes, or furniture for the apartment. He never gave me any expensive art."

"What about jewelry?"

"No."

"Knickknacks?"

"Yes, but I didn't take anything when I left. I walked out in disguise. I only had the clothes on my back, my makeup kit and an extra costume. Marie lent me five thousand dollars, and I used that to get away and start fresh out of state."

"It could be something else you're not aware of. Maybe it even got into the things Marie gave you later, a prop or an article he put inside a prop."

He wasn't sure he was on the right track. Maybe Patrick *hadn't* hidden anything with her. But it seemed the most logical reason for Taylor's interest.

He ran his hand over his hair. Damn! She should have told him the truth. He was so pissed off at her right now he could...well, he didn't know what, but he was thankful he wasn't a violent person.

He suddenly had an idea, but he needed his computer and files to check it out.

"I'm driving over to the bungalow to get my laptop," he told her. "You close up downstairs. When I get back, I'll help you feed your mice. Then we'll try to figure out how to get you out of this mess."

"I wouldn't blame you if you walked away and never came back. I've been nothing but trouble from the beginning."

"That's an understatement."

Tears welled up in her eyes, making him regret his words. She looked so vulnerable standing there, pain marring her pretty face, that he had to go to her, despite his anger. He held her tightly. "I didn't mean that. I'm angry because I'm afraid for you."

"No, you were being honest. I *am* too much trouble. You should go home to Pittsburgh before I involve you any deeper."

"I'd never leave you."

"Whit, you *should* leave. If the FBI finds out who I am, that Patrick was my lover and Tom's father, they'll think I helped him steal. They'll assume you're covering up for me. I don't want you to get in trouble."

"I'm not going anywhere. We're in this together."

"But you can't risk your good name, your business's reputation, by being dragged through the mud because of me."

"Hush. I'm not abandoning you."

He kissed her and whispered reassuring words. He'd fix this, he promised. But at the moment he didn't have any idea how.

WHIT RETRIEVED his computer, portable printer and briefcase of files from the bungalow, then returned to the restaurant to help Emma distribute her nightly dinners to the homeless. Upstairs, he hooked up his laptop to his satellite phone and went on-line.

"Will it bother you if I watch?" she asked. He told her no, and she sat next to him at the kitchen table. "What are you looking for?"

"Patrick has to be the key to all this. I'm going to start with his death and work back from there. His supposed business trip to Egypt may have been a cover for a job for Taylor. You said he visited his mother on the movie set while he was there. Maybe his purpose in showing up so unexpectedly was to give her what he'd stolen."

"Marie would never have accepted stolen goods."

"Who said she knew about it? If he needed to smuggle Egyptian artifacts or works of art back to the States, I can't think of a better way than to hide them in crates of Egyptian movie props controlled by his mother and stepfather."

"Whit, that's brilliant."

"All he had to do when he got back to the U.S. was go by Marie's business and retrieve his loot from the heist. Except that he was accidentally killed before he had a chance to do it."

"And Taylor wouldn't have known where he'd hidden it because Patrick didn't tell anyone that Marie Marshall was his mother."

"Exactly."

"Then that means I really *could* have what Patrick stole."

"Unless it was given away or sold before Marie retired and passed along her inventory to you."

"But why, after all these years, would Taylor suddenly be after me?"

"Maybe he's been looking for the stolen property since Patrick died, but he's only now learned that Patrick had family he might have given it to."

"Then Taylor's responsible for burglarizing Marie's place. He didn't know she no longer had the props."

"That's likely. And, since the FBI didn't mention her to me, I'm guessing they don't know her death could be connected."

"Taylor *is* guilty of murdering Marie."

"If we're correct in our assumptions, he could be an accomplice. He wouldn't have committed the burglary himself. He'd have ordered whatever master thief he had working for him to do the dirty work."

"Who is?"

"I don't know. It may or may not be the same person who broke in here, but it probably is. Taylor may have known about Patrick's mistress, Rachel Stanton, before now, but not where to find her. Then I came along and started asking questions about you—Rachel. Taylor followed that lead here."

"We're dealing with some very nasty people. Killers."

"Possibly. That's why we should consider going to the FBI."

"But I can't produce the stolen object, and I don't even know what it is to get rid of it. If they come in here, search and find it, they could arrest me for receiving and concealing stolen property, couldn't they?"

"Two statutes cover this kind of theft. The first is the Transportation of Stolen Goods Act, which has to do with objects valued at over five thousand dollars that cross state lines. The second, the Theft of Major Artwork Act, makes it a felony to steal museum objects more than a century old or worth at least a hundred thousand dollars. Of course, we don't know that this object, whatever it is, came from a museum. More than half of stolen art is from private estates."

"What's the penalty if it did come from a museum?"

"For both—imprisonment up to ten years and a possible fine."

She paled. "Twenty years?"

"Unless the terms are served concurrently. But the statute of limitations for the interstate law is five years, so even if they wanted to prosecute you on that, they couldn't."

"What about the other? Marie gave me her things twelve years ago."

"The limit there is twenty years."

"Oh, Lord!"

"Hey, this isn't anything to worry about. I doubt they could make a case against you. You had no knowledge of the theft. And this last statute was only added in 1994. I'm not sure it even applies to cases prior to that. That's something I need to brush up on.''

''But I can't prove I *didn't* steal anything. And do you really think they'll believe I wasn't involved? I'm a former thief with a father already serving a thirty-five year sentence for theft. I stole a dead woman's identity. When they figure all that out, I might as well pack my bags for the state pen.''

''I won't let you go to prison.''

''If we can find this stolen object, would it give me some bargaining power?''

''Maybe.''

''If we had the object, we could even set a trap for Taylor's thief, couldn't we?'' Her eyes lit up. ''Oh, Whit, that's what we have to do! We have to catch the thief.''

''Whoa! This is no game, Emma. If these people killed Marie Marshall, they wouldn't think twice about killing us *and* Tom.''

''You're right. I wouldn't want to risk his safety, or yours. I love you both too much. But couldn't we at least wait until we find what was stolen and then decide what to do? I don't want to approach the FBI empty-handed.''

He smiled. Did she even realize she'd admitted to loving him?

''If we...'' Her mouth sank into a frown. ''What was so funny about that? If I bargain from a position of power rather than weakness, I might stay out of jail.''

''Nothing was funny about it. I'll go along with waiting. Temporarily.''

He decided to let her other comment slide. The

immediate problems were more important. There'd be time later to discuss the future.

"What do we do next?" she asked.

"We look at when Patrick was in Cairo and see what objects were stolen during that period and never recovered."

"Well, let's do it."

He leaned over and gave her a quick kiss.

She smiled softly. "What was that for?"

"A down payment on better things to come."

THEY WORKED until the wee hours of the morning. Emma fell asleep about three o'clock, leaving Whit still at his computer. Now it was five hours later, and she awoke to find him sprawled naked in the bed next to her, lying on his stomach, his long legs hanging partly off the end.

She ran her hand lightly down his broad back, then across his butt. His cheeks were stark white next to the tan he'd gotten from fishing on the beach in nothing but shorts.

"The other side is much more fun to play with," he drawled without raising his head.

"I thought you were asleep."

"I only lay down two minutes ago."

"You worked all night?"

He grunted something that sounded like a yes.

"We're meeting Jack and Lucky at your place at eleven, so I'm going to set an alarm for ten in case I'm downstairs. Did you get their room number at the White Oaks? I forgot to ask, and I want to call them this morning." Another grunt. This one faded into a snore.

She kissed his shoulder, and tiptoed quietly from the room. She had a lot to do today and couldn't afford to sleep in.

Whit had been insistent last night that she pack clothing for her and Tom this morning. He wanted them to move into the bungalow until the thief was caught, and Emma had decided that was a good idea.

She could do it without arousing anyone's suspicion since her employees were used to seeing Whit around and knew they were dating. She'd mentioned to Abby that she and Tom spent quite a lot of time at Whit's place. Tom would be safe out on the island. He wouldn't think the move odd if she presented it as a mini-vacation and invited Tony. And without that worry about Tom's well-being, she and Whit could set a trap for the burglar.

While the coffee was brewing, she looked through the pages of information Whit had printed from several stolen-art databases he'd accessed. He'd made a list of possible items, but circled one that fit the time frame and had never been recovered. Attached were notes and newspaper articles about something called The Burning Eye of Ra. Emma began reading and quickly became absorbed.

According to the material, in 1473 B.C., Hatshepsut, the eldest daughter of Pharaoh Thutmose I and Queen Ahmose, became one of the few female pharaohs of Egypt. She wrested power away from her half brother's young son, Thutmose III, by declaring that she was a divine child, the daughter of Amon-Ra, god of the sun. Hatshepsut claimed the god took the form of her father, Thutmose I, and impregnated her mother. The story was inscribed on the walls of her temple at Deir el-Bahri.

Not written, but passed down through legend, was an accompanying story that Amon-Ra's descent from the sky came in a flaming ball of fire. Hatshepsut was said to possess evidence of his trip to earth, a stone with mystical powers, which she displayed as proof of her right to rule Egypt.

Scholars concluded that if this stone ever existed, it had likely been a meteorite whose fall was witnessed. Hatshepsut may have believed the story of Amon-Ra, or she may have cunningly used the incident and the meteorite to her advantage.

Hatshepsut mysteriously disappeared around 1458 B.C., when Thutmose III grew up and regained his title as Pharaoh. She was never buried in either of her constructed tombs.

In 1903, Howard Carter discovered a tomb in the Valley of the Kings. He declared it minor because it had already been robbed of its antiquities. He had it resealed.

In 1906, Edward Ayrton reentered it and removed one of the mummies, believed to be Hatshepsut's wet nurse, to the Cairo Museum, along with broken bits of burial equipment and stony debris. A second mummy was deemed unimportant for study and was left in the tomb. The tomb wasn't entered again until the 1980s, when the second mummy was more closely examined. Its position—right arm crossed over the breast—suggested royalty.

Another expedition, undertaken in July of 1989 by Pacific Lutheran University, fueled a debate as to whether the mummy could be that of the missing Hatshepsut. Interest in the burial equipment stored at the Cairo Museum was immediately renewed.

Among the items was a stone, about the size of a man's open hand and odd in color. Rather than the light, sandy composition of the cliff tombs, the stone was crusty and dark, typical of a meteorite.

Emma looked at the photograph. A rock. And not even a pretty one. Her hopes fell. Nothing in her collection looked like this Burning Eye of Ra.

She got her coffee and went back to the article to read more. The stone had disappeared from the museum before it could be examined. Whit had underlined the date of the theft: July 26, 1989, three days before Patrick was killed. She read:

> "As with the Hope Diamond, legend has increased the value of the Eye many times beyond its actual worth. Debate continues regarding its authenticity, but many consider it priceless. A five-million dollar reward is offered for its return."

Emma nearly choked. Holy cow! "Well, old girl, money like that won't do you any good in prison."

She restacked the papers, drank the rest of her coffee and took a shower. Once dressed, she went into Tom's room to check on Rambo's water and to feed Houdini, but she found the bird gone.

"Oh, no, not again." She searched every room and whistled for him but didn't get a peep in response. "Come on, Houdini. Don't do this to me today." He couldn't have gotten out of the apartment. The glass door to the dumbwaiter was closed, as were all the windows.

She made another thorough search of Tom's room, peering under the furniture, opening the drawers of the dresser in case he'd somehow gotten shut up in one. Once before, they'd found him in the closet, where he'd pulled all the shoelaces out of Tom's sneakers and torn them into shreds. He'd been missing for two days.

She dragged the desk chair over and began to look through the big wall unit of shelves. "Here birdy, birdy, birdy." Tom's books were a mess, shoved in every which way. When she pulled one out to straighten the row, two others that had been tossed on top fell to the carpet, along with a shower of papers.

Hopping down, she picked up the books. The first one was *Tracing Your Family History.* The second, *Finding Lost Relatives.* With growing horror, she looked at each of the papers. Among them was a form for requesting military records.

"No!"

Tom had already filled in the name of William Wright.

WHIT HAD TO STAND under the shower for a full fifteen minutes before he was awake enough to even soap his body. He was pleased with the information he'd dug up last night, but the hours he'd been keeping lately were killing him.

Normally he worked out every morning, doing a few minutes of tai chi, boxing or taking a short run, but he hadn't had time this week, and he was feeling the effects.

He dried off and slipped into his undershorts. Emma wasn't in the living room or in the kitchen. He called her name, but she'd apparently gone downstairs. He vaguely remembered her saying something about work.

She'd made coffee before she left, bless her, and he poured himself a cup. He sat down and packed his files. He was unplugging his laptop, getting ready to zip up the case, when he heard a key in the lock and the front door open and close.

"Hey, baby," he called out. "I'm in here."

"Hey, baby yourself," a male voice said as its owner came around the counter island.

"Tom!" Whit shot up, banging the table leg, sloshing coffee everywhere. "What are you doing home?" He grabbed the dish towel and began mopping up the liquid.

"Mr. Parker's mother had a stroke so our trip got canceled."

"I'm sorry. For Mr. Parker and for you. I know how much you were looking forward to this."

Beyond that, Whit didn't know what to say. He was standing there in nothing but his briefs, and obviously he couldn't pretend he'd just happened to drop by. The irony was that he and Emma hadn't even had sex last night.

He liked Tom. The young man, it turned out, wasn't just bright, he had a perfect grade-point average, pretty astounding given that he'd been in something like nine or ten different schools. Most kids would've fallen behind, even been put back a grade or two, but Tom was first in his class, excelled at sports, and seemed ten times more mature than other kids his age. He had a lot going for him.

They'd gotten along well the past couple of weeks. He and Tony had come over to the bungalow with Emma a number of times to swim and cook out. Twice Tom had showed up alone, which had surprised Whit.

They'd fished, talked about diving and his options for getting into the navy. He'd asked about exercises he could do to start putting some muscle on his lean body, and Whit had done his best to help him.

He and Tom were buddies. But Whit wasn't sure how Tom felt about him dating his mother—or doing anything else with her. How should he handle a confrontation? Leave? Try to talk with the boy?

"Your mom's already gone to work," he said.

"I'll call down later and tell her what happened." He tossed his duffel onto the floor and walked to the refrigerator, where he began rooting around for something to eat. "Hey, while you've got your laptop, can we go online and look at that Naval Academy stuff you were telling me about? My modem's fried. I want to download an application."

Whit let out his breath. "Sure."

"I'm seriously starved. Want breakfast? Bacon and eggs?"

"Yeah, that sounds great. I'll go put on some pants."

"Good move."

Whit returned to the kitchen a couple of minutes later, feeling not quite so vulnerable—until Tom asked him if he was going to marry his mother.

This was the second time someone had asked him

that question. He hadn't known the answer before. Now he did.

"Yeah, I am. If I can talk her into it."

"That would make you my dad in a way."

"I suppose it would. Are you cool with that?"

Tom shrugged. "I'm cool. Scrambled eggs or fried?"

CHAPTER FOURTEEN

THE CLERK AT THE FRONT DESK of the motel told Emma that the Cahills had adjoining rooms on the first floor, right side. Odd, she thought, that they'd gotten two. Maybe they'd done it so when they put Grace down for bed or a nap, they could talk in the other room without waking her.

Although she was supposed to see Jack and Lucky in only a few hours, Emma felt desperate to talk to Lucky now and in person. The books and papers she'd found in Tom's room had sent her into a panic. She needed to be with someone, a woman who knew what it was like to have a child.

She was closer to Abby than Lucky, but her secrets prevented her from seeking comfort from her good friend. Abby also didn't understand the responsibilities of motherhood.

Emma rapped heavily on the door to Room 119. Lucky stuck her head out of Room 120.

"Emma!" She stepped outside and pulled the door closed until only a crack showed. "What are you doing here?"

"I found papers. I didn't know he was even looking. Tell me what to do."

Lucky's face told her she wasn't making much sense.

"I'm sorry," Emma said, sagging. "This must be a terrible imposition, coming here so early."

"Oh, no, it's okay. I can see you're in a tizzy. What is it? Has Whit done something?"

"Tom. He's been searching for information about his father. I found forms in his room for requesting military records from the navy."

"Oh, dear." Lucky glanced back at the door. "How 'bout I dress Gracie and we go somewhere for coffee? You can tell me everything."

"That would be wonderful. Thank you."

They went inside. Emma hastily shut the connecting door to the other room. "Jack's sleeping," she explained. "Have a seat."

Emma sat on the bed while Lucky put clothes on Grace. She seemed nervous and mistakenly pulled the baby's shorts on inside out.

"Are you okay?" Emma asked. "You seem almost as rattled as I am this morning."

"Mmm, I'm okay."

"It's late for Jack to still be in bed, isn't it? Is he feeling all right?"

"He stayed up past midnight."

"Same here. And poor Whit didn't lie down until a couple of hours ago."

A bump against the wall from next door made Lucky jump. "Put these on right for me, would you?" she asked, handing the baby to Emma. "Be back in a minute."

She went into the other room and closed the door behind her. Emma heard the low drone of voices. While Lucky was gone, she tried to wrestle Grace back into her pants, but the child wasn't cooperating. She didn't like being handled by a stranger.

"Da," she cried. She wiggled until Emma was forced to set her down.

When Lucky came back, she asked, "All set?"

"No, Grace won't let me dress her. Is Jack up? I thought I heard him."

"He's moving around."

Lucky tried to pick up Grace, but she squealed in protest. "Da!"

"Grace, no," her mother scolded. "You can't have Da."

"Da!" She reached her hand toward the other room. "Want Da now!"

The twang of a key card tripping the lock drew Emma's and Lucky's attention to the outside door. Jack walked in carrying a McDonald's sack and a tray with three cups of coffee.

"Emma!" His face reflected panic.

"How did you...?" Emma tried to sort through her confusion. "Weren't you just in there? In bed?"

"I went to get coffee."

"That must've been one fast drive-through window."

He laughed nervously. "Yeah, they're pretty fast."

"Who's the third cup for?"

"Uh..."

Lucky came forward, took the sack and coffee from his hands and shut the door. "Oh, good grief, Jack, tell her the truth. I refuse to lie to her one more second."

"Da!" Grace cried. Jack picked up the child and tried to quiet her. She still wasn't happy and demanded to be put down. She toddled over to the connecting door and tried to push it open. She banged her tiny palm against the metal.

Jack expelled a breath. "Emma, I should have told you this right off. I wanted to yesterday when we talked, but I was afraid you'd leave and—"

"Mentioned *what?* What's going on with you two? You're both acting very strange."

"I told you I'd been talking to Ray." Emma froze at the name. "The truth is…he got out of prison two years ago, and he's been living in Potock. He's straightened himself out. He's got a job, consulting on security systems, of all things."

Emma's knees threatened to buckle.

"I swear he's changed," Jack continued.

"He's living in your hometown?" Emma asked.

"About ten miles from us. He's part of our family."

Another bump against the wall sent a cold chill down Emma's spine and Grace into a full-blown fit. The "Da" she was calling for obviously wasn't Jack but someone on the other side of the door. And Emma didn't have any trouble figuring out who it was.

A force she couldn't control compelled her feet across the carpet. She turned the handle, knowing who she'd find but needing to see him with her own eyes.

Grace immediately ran to her "Da" and was scooped up into Ray's arms. He smiled at Emma. "Hello, Princess."

WHIT GOT THE CALL from Jack as he was about to go downstairs. He'd blown it, Jack said. Emma had shown up unexpectedly at the motel and seen Ray.

Whit swore under his breath. "How'd she take it?"

"She tore out of here without a word and drove off before I could catch her. I'm worried about her, Whit. Lucky says she was already upset, something about finding out that Tom is looking for info about his father."

"Damn!"

"Should I stay here and hope she comes back, or come over?"

Whit glanced around the corner to see where Tom was. His pet bird was loose somewhere, and he was searching the apartment trying to find him.

"Don't come here. Tom's trip was canceled. He's home."

"Should we get out and look for her? Where would she go?"

"I can't leave Tom here alone. Too dangerous. You go on over to my place like we planned and take Ray with you. You know where the key is. I'll call you when I hear something."

Whit hung up. He still hadn't dressed completely, only slipped on his jeans. He put on his shirt and running shoes, then cleaned up the mess he and Tom had made in the kitchen. Emma apparently had her cell phone with her, because it wasn't on the counter where he remembered she'd left it last night. He called her number, but she didn't answer.

He found Tom in his bedroom, checking under the bed. "Tom, I'll be outside for a minute."

"Okay."

Whit walked across the hall, leaned out the rear door and had a look around. Thankfully, Emma's car was in her parking space. She'd come home.

Abby was on her way in, unlocking the service doors to the restaurant with her key. "Morning, Abby," he called out.

"Well, hello, handsome."

"Is Em—" He stopped himself before he said *Emma.* A couple of times lately he'd almost used the name in front of Tom. He cleared his throat to cover his mistake. "Is Susan down there?"

"Don't think so. Just let me shut off the alarm." She went inside for a minute and popped back out. "No, I don't see her. But her car's here. Try the storage room or better yet, the roof."

He came upon Emma working in her herb garden. She seemed calm, but she had a pair of hand clippers and was doing serious damage to a small tree. Bay, it looked like. By the time she got finished, it wouldn't have a leaf left.

"Jack told me what happened," he said. "You okay?"

"I'll survive." She hacked off several more of the delicate shoots.

"You have reason to be mad. We shouldn't have kept you in the dark about Ray. Jack was afraid you wouldn't want to see either of them if you knew."

"He's probably right. The last thing I need in my life is my convict father. I've got a thief trying to steal from me, the FBI about to put me in prison, a son going behind my back to find out about his dead father and a lover who demands honesty but doesn't give it."

Whit scratched his jaw. This wasn't going well.

He hunkered down next to her. "I couldn't tell you,

Em. I was still working for Jack when I made that promise."

"I see. Then, I apologize."

"No need."

She sighed heavily. "You've been overwhelmingly good to me, Whit, even when I didn't deserve it. I don't have the right to blame you for this. I'm not really angry at you, anyway."

"Who, then? Jack?"

"Ray. But mostly myself. The incident this morning put everything into perspective for me. My life is one big masquerade. I've played so many characters that I no longer know where the false people stop and the real me begins. I'm lost somewhere under a million different faces and disguises. Even Susan isn't completely me."

"I know."

"I want *Emma* back. I simply have to figure out who she is."

"You will."

She nodded. "I'm going to start by taking your advice. I don't want Tom finding out about me some other way, or learning about his father by having a paper come back from the military saying 'no such person.' He has a right to know about J.T. And about Ray, too, I suppose, difficult as that will be for him."

"You should know that the Parkers dropped Tom off this morning. He's downstairs. And I told Jack they should all go hang out at my place. They're hoping you'll come over."

She stopped attacking the tree. "What happened to Tom's trip?"

"Mr. Parker's mother had a stroke, so they postponed it."

"Oh, no!"

She said she'd call the Parkers and see if she could do anything to help.

"I still want you and Tom to pack some things and stay with me. If you need help explaining it to him, I can do that."

She stood and took off her gloves. "I'd rather do it myself. Send him up here, please. He might as well hear everything at once."

"Everything?"

"God help me, I don't want to do this, but it's time he knew the truth."

HIS MOM WAS all teary eyed and strange-acting when Tom went up to the roof. She was shaking. She hugged him and told him how much she loved him. When she didn't let go, he practically had to wrestle her to get away.

"I love you, too," he said.

"More than anything on this earth."

"Gee, Mom, I know that. What's with you? You're all weirded out."

"Sit down." She motioned to the glider. "I have something I need to tell you. Something unpleasant."

"Did Tony's grandmother die?"

"Oh, no, sweetheart. She's fine. I called Mr. Parker just now and the stroke was minor. She should recover fully."

"That's good. Tony was really freaked out about it. He's close to his granny."

"There's no need to worry. Everything's fine."

Tom relaxed, glad to hear it. He liked the Parkers. He especially liked being around Tony's dad because he treated him as if he were his son. The way Whit treated him.

"Are you scared I won't like Whit being my stepdad?" Tom asked. "Is that what this is about? Because it's okay. He's pretty sharp."

"Whit and I aren't getting married."

"He says you are."

She stared at him in surprise, then shook her head. "I'll deal with that later. This isn't about Whit. There's something... I don't know where to begin. I should have told you certain things a long time ago, but didn't. I thought you were too young to know the truth about your father. I was trying to protect you."

"You were never married to him, were you? I tried to look him up in the genealogy records they keep at the Mormon church, and he's not there. I couldn't find a death certificate for him, either."

"He *is* dead, Tom. But it didn't happen in a diving accident like I led you to believe. He was hit by a car. And you're right, I was never his wife, only his...girlfriend." She moistened her lips. "His name wasn't William Wright. It was Patrick Logan."

"Who was he?"

"If you're going to understand that, I need to go back a few years and tell you another story. This is about a fifteen-year-old girl. Her name was Emma Webster."

"HE CRIED when I revealed he has a grandfather," Emma told Whit, sobbing herself. She moved closer to him on the couch and curled against his shoulder, letting all her pain flow freely. "I haven't seen him bawl like that since he was a little boy. And he wouldn't let me comfort him, or even touch him. He said he'll never forgive me for lying."

"Hey, he doesn't mean it. Finding out the truth was a shock, but he'll deal with it. The kid's more resilient than you know."

"He wants to see Ray and Jack."

"That's good, isn't it? He's trying to accept what you've told him."

"I hope so. Will you go with him? I don't think I'm ready to face Ray again, but Tom needs someone there to support him, even if he doesn't think so. He made it clear he doesn't want me near him. He went straight to his room and locked the door."

"I'll take him if he wants me to, or he can follow me in his car. Did you explain to him about *staying* at the bungalow?"

"Yes, but I didn't go into the whole story. I told him simply that Patrick may have stolen something we think got hidden in my costumes and this thief must be looking for it. I didn't go into the whole FBI thing yet or tell him about his grandmother Marie being murdered. He has enough to digest for one day."

"When things calm down, I'll show him photos of the items I pulled up in my search. I'll ask if he remembers seeing any of them."

"I doubt it's that 'Eye' thing. I don't have any rocks in my house." She wiped her face and tried to get herself back under control.

"Let's not worry about that today. Deal with one crisis at a time. Do you plan to see Jack at all this afternoon? He'll be disappointed if you don't show up for the cookout. He and Lucky don't have much more time to spend here."

"Maybe I'll come over later. I think I'll go in and work for a few hours. I've been gone so much lately, I've put an unfair burden on Abby. Working always calms me, too, and I need that right now."

"Don't be up here alone, okay?"

"I won't. I'll stay downstairs."

"I'll see if I can get Tom to pack his clothes. You can take my bedroom, and he and I can bunk down in the living room in sleeping bags. Maybe we'll even get us a tent and sleep out on the beach."

"He'd probably enjoy camping. He likes you a great deal, you know. He told me."

"I like him, too. He's a damn fine kid."

"He seems to be under the impression that the two of us are getting married, though. How did that happen?"

"When he walked in this morning, I was sitting in the kitchen in my underwear. He asked me if I was going to marry you. I told him I plan on it."

"I appreciate your trying to protect my reputation, but he's aware that sex between two people doesn't always lead to marriage. You should have told him the truth."

"I did."

RAY SAT ON THE PORCH of the Lewis fella's house and, for once, tried to behave himself. J.T. was mad at him, and Sweet Pea hadn't had a whole lot to say either, which was bad. He reckoned he was in pretty big trouble for her to give him the silent treatment.

"You can't blame a fella for wantin' to see his kid," he told them.

"We don't," J.T. said. "But you could've done as I asked, old man, and stayed home. I wanted to prepare her for the shock of you being a free man."

"She didn't need no preparin'. That girl always was stronger than the rest of us put together. Besides, it worked out okay, didn't it?"

"No thanks to you."

Yeah, no thanks to him. But Emma *maybe* was coming over in a little while, and that was all that mattered to Ray. J.T. and Lucky could be mad at him all they wanted, but as long as he got to see his girl again, and talk to her, he could stand his son and daughter-in-law being a mite put out with him.

Ten minutes later, two cars pulled up out front. "They're here," Lucky said.

The Lewis fella got out of the first one. Ray didn't see Emma, but tears came to his eyes at the sight of a tall, lanky boy getting out of the second one. He mopped them up with his handkerchief.

Standing, he brushed the wrinkles from his shirt and pants. For once, he cared what he looked like. He wanted to make a good impression. He was about to meet his grandson.

EMMA MINDLESSLY CHOPPED vegetables. Santiago wasn't thrilled about her being in his kitchen, but she pulled rank, telling him she wanted to help with lunch preparations.

Her emotions were raw. She needed to keep busy. Tom. Ray. She didn't know what to do about either of them. Even Whit had her confused. He claimed he wanted to marry her, and the idea was terrifying. The last thing he needed was to tie himself to a woman with a notorious past and an uncertain future.

"Too big, too big," Santiago scolded from the other side of the stainless-steel counter. "The celery must be finely chopped. Like this." He demonstrated for the second time. "You are hopeless."

"Thank you very much. Exactly what I needed to hear today."

"You have had an upset? A trouble of the heart?"

"Something like that."

"Ah, Santiago suspected as much. You wear your misery like a costume. I hope your Mr. Lewis has not been unfaithful."

"Whit? No. Whit is wonderful."

"That is good. I like your friend because he makes you laugh. You did not laugh before he comes along."

"I didn't?"

"No, not so very much. Now you laugh and smile. You have very pretty smile, Susan. You must use it."

"I understand why Abby's so crazy about you, Santiago. You're very sweet."

"Sweet? I am handsome, charming and world's greatest chef. But I am never sweet."

Emma laughed out loud, and it felt good. "You *are* sweet, but I'll keep that our secret."

"I am grateful." He looked at his helpers at the other counter and lowered his voice. "I could not terrorize my staff if they thought I was sweet."

She came around the counter and kissed him on the cheek, but then her smile faded. A distinctive odor assaulted her. "What's that smell on you?"

"Ah, I am caught. I will tell you, but you must not give secret away to Abigail. I say to her it is lingering smell from chopping pungent herb for tapas, but not so. Last night, I want to be like big hero in old movie, Errol Flynn, and carry her up the stairs of my building. She is beautiful, and I am very much in love, but, alas, she is not light." Emma suppressed a giggle. "I wake up this morning and my back feels like I have carried a bull. Must rub medicine on it. It does not smell so good, but it helps."

Muscle ointment! That was the odor Emma had been trying to identify upstairs!

"Excuse me, Santiago. I need to check my costume for tonight. You don't need my help anymore, do you?"

He chuckled. "You are nice woman, Susan, and you are wonderful at the disguises, but you are a disaster in kitchen. That is why I feed Tom and help him cook better. So you will not make him sick."

"I'm that bad a cook?"

"Very bad. Go on. Check your costume. Leave cooking to those who can."

Emma didn't believe for a moment that Santiago was the thief, but he'd given her an idea. She went to her office and got her master key, then walked over to the dressing room for the male staff.

"Anyone in here?" she called out. When no one answered, she slipped into the room and locked the door behind her.

One of the new employees, the bartender Cade Wesson, was an athlete, and they used muscle ointments. He also matched the profile of Marie Marshall's killer—a white male, military type, thirty to forty years old.

Wesson had passed Whit's preliminary background search and that of the employment agency, but Whit had warned her not to put too much stock in either. He was in the process of doing more thorough searches on each worker.

Wesson's locker was in the fourth row. She was probably violating his constitutional rights or something, but she and Tom had constitutional rights, too—foremost to live upstairs without worrying about being murdered in their sleep.

Emma looked through the contents and didn't find anything suspicious. No ointments. No sports creams. No burglary tools.

She'd tell Whit her theory regardless, so he could investigate the man further. And the first chance she got, Emma was going to sniff Cade Wesson.

Carefully, she sneaked back out and returned her key, then helped with lunch, keeping a watchful eye on the staff. She hated being so suspicious, but her freedom could be at stake.

At four, she decided she'd worked and snooped enough. She'd finally garnered the courage to see Ray.

Abby was folding napkins in the kitchen with Eve Vincent, which Emma found comical given the way Abby had initially talked about the older woman. Eve had turned out to be one of their best employees, just as Emma had predicted.

"Abby, I'm taking off now to meet those friends of Whit's from out of town. Harold knows what to do, so you go on and leave at five like we planned."

"Are you sure?"

"No use you sticking around when he can handle it. I'll come back at eleven, close up and take care of distributing the extra dinners."

"I don't mind working until closing if you need me to."

"Absolutely not. You've been here all day, and you deserve a night off."

"Thanks, Susan. Especially for juggling the schedule."

"I didn't mind." Emma had rearranged Santiago's hours this week so that he and Abby were off at the same time. They probably had plans tonight—if Santiago's back held up. Emma suppressed a laugh at the image of him trying to carry Abby up a flight of stairs.

Eve interrupted her thoughts. "Mrs. Wright? I can stay if you need extra help. I'm supposed to get off at seven, but I could work later."

"That's nice of you, Eve, but I think we have enough people to cover tonight. Besides, those grandchildren of yours will be expecting you home, won't they?"

"Yes, ma'am, that's for sure. They don't like me being late to fix supper." She smiled widely. Dressed as Granny from *The Beverly Hillbillies,* she looked very cute with her apron, wire-rimmed glasses and clunky boots.

"Well, I'd better run," Emma told them both. "Tom and I will be at Whit's if anybody needs us. I have my cell phone."

"Have fun," Abby said.

A few minutes later, she arrived at Whit's and parked behind Tom's car. They were all around on the beach side of the house. Whit and Tom were putting up a tent and making what looked like a nice campsite, while Lucky and Jack played at the edge of the surf with the baby. Ray sat in a chair sipping a cold drink. The scene was right off a wall calendar.

For a moment, she watched them covertly and felt a strange tugging at her heart. All her life she'd dreamed of a warm, safe place to live and the perfect family surrounding her. This wasn't even close. But maybe it was as close as she'd ever get.

Taking off her sandals, she walked through the sand to the rear of Ray's chair and stopped.

He sensed her and glanced back. "Didn't much think you'd show up."

"I didn't much think I would either."

"You gonna hold a grudge your whole life, girl?"

"I don't know, Ray. I'm here. For now, that's all I can promise."

CHAPTER FIFTEEN

NEVER HAD THE HOURS PASSED so slowly for Emma. Tom was downright animated around the others, but he wouldn't look at her or get within ten feet of where she sat. If she asked him a question, he either pretended he hadn't heard, or he answered with a one-syllable word and without feeling.

And Ray—damn him. He wasn't *trying* to drive her nuts, but each time he called Lucky that stupid nickname—Sweet Pea—and showed her affection, Emma sank further and further into depression.

She would never have imagined herself jealous of someone else getting attention from Ray, but she was. He and Lucky laughed and shared private jokes and exhibited the kind of close, loving relationship that Emma had always longed for with him and never had. Watching them hurt.

Lucky giggled about something Ray said, and the sound grated on Emma's nerves like fingernails being dragged across a chalkboard.

"I forgot to get a few things when I packed my overnight bag," she said, plastering a false smile on her face. She had to get out of there before she lost her mind. "I'm going to the apartment. Be right back."

"Wait and get them when you close up," Whit suggested. "No use making two trips."

"I'd rather do it now." She stood and grabbed her purse.

"I'll go with you."

"No, stay and enjoy yourself. I'm only going to run in—two minutes." But in that two minutes she planned to pour herself a whiskey in the largest glass she could find.

Whit walked her to the car. "Don't go sniffing the bartender," he warned. She'd told Whit about the muscle ointment.

"Can't anyway. I don't think Cade's working tonight."

"Come right back. Promise me. No more than fifteen minutes."

"I promise."

WHIT LOOKED at his watch for the third time. Twenty minutes. Emma should have been able to drive over the bridge and back in ten.

He called her cell phone. It rang and rang. Finally her voice mail picked up. That worried him more.

The others were talking in the living room. Whit walked to the bedroom and slipped into his shoulder holster and gun, putting a sports jacket on as cover. That didn't fool Jack, who saw through the ruse right away.

"Why are you carrying?" he asked when Whit returned.

"Emma's taking too long. And I can't reach her on her cell. I'm headed to her place."

"I'm going with you."

Ray piped up, "Me, too. And don't tell me no, 'cause I ain't stayin' here if my girl's in trouble."

THE LAST THING Emma remembered thinking was that she'd made a deadly mistake. Like some ditzy female in a B horror movie, she hadn't backed out of the apartment and run when she'd unlocked the door and found the burglar alarm off. Confusion had made her freeze. Those few seconds had given the thief time to slam the heavy door into her side and throw her off balance.

The blow to the shoulder had knocked her into the door frame, where she'd struck her temple. She'd fallen backward into the hallway. The thief had dragged her inside, and for several minutes she'd drifted in and out of consciousness, aware of movement beyond her but unable to move.

Now clarity began to return. The scattered contents of her purse lay before her on the carpet. Hairbrush, wallet, keys, phone. She remembered the phone ringing, but she wasn't sure how long ago that had been. Whit was trying to reach her; of that she was sure. He would come when she didn't answer, when she didn't return. But would she live long enough for him to arrive?

The last light of sunset gave everything an orange glow. A dark figure frantically searched cabinets and drawers, not caring if he left behind evidence of his appearance. He growled in frustration under his breath each time he came up empty-handed.

Watching, Emma noticed two important details about the thief. First, that he was desperate, which didn't bode well for her survival. And second, that *he* was a *she.* Eve Vincent. The granny costume was gone, replaced with dark pants and a shirt.

Eve turned and caught her with her eyes open. Emma scrambled for the door, but Eve was across the room in a flash, tackling her, sending her reeling against the wall. The crash must have hurt her, as well, because she came up limping.

Emma broke free, but Eve blocked the exit, and she ran toward the kitchen. If she could get out the double doors to the porch, she could scream and be heard. People were on the street. The FBI was out there, too, or so she hoped.

Eve was too fast for her, even with her hurt leg. She slid across the counter separating the kitchen from the living room, and was in front of Emma before she could react. She drew a knife from her ankle boot. And smiled.

Emma ran back the other way. In a split second, she had to decide what to do. She could head for Tom's room and go through his double doors to the porch. Or she could try the front and take her chances on outrunning Eve in the hallway.

Neither option was promising. Although the woman outweighed her by twenty-five pounds, she moved as quickly as a cat.

Emma chose the front door but didn't make it. Eve got to her before she could even touch the knob.

"Cooperate, and I'll let you live," she said, catching Emma by the hair. She whirled her around and pushed her back against the door. With the blade pressed to her throat, Emma halted her struggles. "Be stupid, and you'll never see your son again. In fact, after you're dead, I might kill him for fun."

"What do you want?"

"You know what I want. Where is the Eye?"

Whit had been right. A lot of good it would do her now. "Kill me and you'll never get it."

"I don't have time for any more games. Where have you hidden it?"

"Eve, please."

"The name is Gretchen."

Emma sucked in a breath. "Patrick's Gretchen?"

"That's right."

"You were his lover?"

Her expression hardened. "His partner. We were a team."

"You stole together for Martin Charles Taylor, didn't you?"

"You're not as stupid as Patrick said you were, although for the life of me I can't understand why he found you attractive."

"If you stole the Eye with him, why don't you have it? And how did you trace it to me?"

"That's none of your business. Now, stop stalling and give it to me."

Emma needed time. She calculated how long she'd been gone from Whit's bungalow and weighed it against his impatience. She figured he had to be on his way by now. If she could last a few minutes longer…

"You'll never find the Eye unless I tell you where it is," she said. "You've already searched and haven't found it."

"I wondered if you'd guessed I'd broken in."

"It wasn't too difficult. You're not that good."

She nipped Emma's throat with the blade, drawing blood. "I should kill you for that remark alone."

"I knew immediately that someone had been in the office. And you left your smell behind when you searched in here and the storage room."

Gretchen didn't immediately understand, but when she did, she laughed. "Well, well, the dumb little mouse isn't so dumb."

"How did you hurt your leg?"

"I pulled a muscle climbing across your roof one night."

"Too bad you didn't fall off and break your neck."

Gretchen placed a second nick next to the first one. "Keep it up and I'll practice my carving."

"I'll make a deal with you, Gretchen. Tell me what I want to know, and I'll give you the Eye. There's no need to hurt me. I'll cooperate. I won't even tell the authorities. I have reason to hide from them myself."

Gretchen acquiesced, or at least pretended to. "All right. You've intrigued me. I have a few questions myself—like why Rachel Stanton is calling herself Susan Wright. But first, a warning. If you try anything I'll gut you. Are we clear?"

"Yes, we're very clear."

"Good. Remember that I hold your life in my hands."

"I do. Now, please, take the knife off my throat. I can't talk like this."

She stepped back, but held the blade close enough that Emma was still in danger.

"How did you lose the artifact?" Emma asked.

"The pressure from the authorities in Egypt was too great to get the Eye out of the country cleanly.

They don't like people making off with their national treasures. Patrick said he knew how we could ship it to the States, and in a way that no one would ever suspect."

"But he didn't tell you how, did he? And he died with the secret."

"I thought I'd lost the stone. It's priceless, you know. Taylor offered me six million if I could find it. I searched for years. Then finally, two years ago, an old business card for a movie properties shop in California fell out of a book I'd borrowed from Patrick and never had the chance to return. The shop, I discovered, had closed, but the old woman who'd run it was still alive. Only she wasn't very cooperative. She admitted she'd been in Egypt working in the summer of 1989, but she didn't want to tell me where the props from the movie had gone. I had to torture her to get the name Rachel Stanton. She protected you until the very end."

"My God." In most ways, the FBI had been correct in their profile of Marie's killer, but they'd missed the most important detail—the sex. This woman was more deadly than any male.

"The name struck a cord with me," Gretchen continued. "A number of years earlier, Patrick had taken a lover with that name, a sniveling, needy little thing he used for his amusement. He used to tell me stories about her to make me laugh. 'How stupid she is,' he'd say. 'She has no grace. No education.'"

"But he still preferred me over you, didn't he, Gretchen?" The woman's eyes narrowed. "That must've really stuck in your craw, to be in love with him and know he'd rather be with some sniveling, needy little thing twenty years younger."

"I didn't say I loved him!"

"But you did. I see it in your eyes. You loved him, and he didn't have any feelings for you at all. He used you like he used everyone."

"He cared, in his own way. Patrick liked my 'lack of conscience,' as he called it."

Yes, Emma thought to herself, *he would.* That coldness would attract him.

"Patrick was my mentor," Gretchen went on. "Everything I know I learned from him, even how to kill. He'd be proud of how I took down the old lady, for all the good it did me. Rachel Stanton was nowhere to be found. You'd disappeared. Who was the woman to you? A friend? Your mother, I hope."

Emma tried to stay calm. The pain of knowing that Marie had died so violently while trying to protect her and Tom was too much. She wouldn't die the same way.

"You're unbelievably vile and stupid," Emma told her.

"I'd watch my tongue, if I were you. I might cut it out."

"You really don't know who Marie Marshall was, do you?"

"What do you mean?"

"Patrick wouldn't be proud of you for killing her. She was his mother, you dumb bitch."

Gretchen's eyes widened in shock. Her hand dropped a couple of inches. "You're lying!"

While she was off guard, Emma lunged. Gretchen

would probably kill her, but she was going down fighting.

WHIT RACED through the service doors of the restaurant with Jack and Ray on his heels. The outer door to the second floor would be locked, but Whit knew he could go up an inside staircase.

No one in the kitchen tried to stop him. But when he got to the apartment, he faced the barrier of not having a key. He thought of the extra locks he'd made her install on this door, and cursed. He prayed they weren't all engaged.

"Emma!" He pounded with his fists on the door. From inside he heard her scream his name, nearly stopping his heart. Sounds of a violent scuffle came from the apartment.

Whit drew his gun. He and Jack tried to shoulder their way through the door, then kick it down, but it was reinforced steel. Ray, the cowardly bastard, took off running back the way they'd come.

"Paper clip," Jack yelled, frantically searching his pockets. "Knife with a corkscrew. Something." Whit quickly realized what he was talking about. He wanted a tool to pick the lock.

When he pulled his coat back, Jack lunged for the pen in the breast pocket of his shirt. Quickly he unscrewed it, pulled out a tiny spiral wire and stuck it in the lock. Two seconds the later, door sprung open.

"Stay behind me," Whit ordered, rolling through the opening in front of him with his gun ready. Inside, Emma wrestled a woman for a knife, but she was outpowered. The woman grabbed her around the neck and put the knife to her throat.

"Come closer and she's dead!"

"Let her go," Whit warned. One swipe of that knife to an artery and Emma would bleed to death before help could arrive.

Jack had followed him into the apartment, and he fanned out to the right. He didn't have a gun, but Whit wasn't worried about him. He was an expert at tae kwon do, and could easily take the woman down, knife or no knife, if she came at him.

Whit went to the left, gun pointed at the woman's head. His blood thundered through his veins. He couldn't possible get a clean shot before Eve Vincent—he recognized the face now—used the knife.

"I mean it, boys. I'll slit her throat if either of you tries anything."

"Put down the knife, Eve," Whit told her. "There's no way out."

"We'll see about that."

She backed toward the bedrooms, roughly dragging Emma down the dark hall. He guessed her intention. Tom's room. The doors to the veranda. Whit and Jack kept pace as they moved, following them footstep for footstep.

The light was only slightly better in the bedroom. Whit could see their silhouettes against the glass-paneled doors. But he was still in shadow, which might give him an advantage. He dropped to the floor. Beside him, he felt Jack do the same.

What happened next had to be sorted out later. An object soared across the room, both women screamed and the doors seemed to explode from the outside, spraying glass everywhere.

A voice from above yelled, "Hold it, scumbag!"

Almost simultaneously, the FBI burst into the room.

TWO HOURS LATER, the apartment remained in chaos. FBI, police and emergency rescue personnel milled about, studying measurements and taking statements from Jack and Ray. Whit and Emma had already given theirs but had been told not to leave.

Whit held her in his arms in the kitchen and tried to quiet her shaking. "Are you sure you don't want to go to the hospital?" he asked. "They should look at those cuts on your throat and do X-rays. Bruises are coming up all over you."

"I'm all right. The paramedics said I don't have a concussion. My head was all I was worried about. Did they check Ray's cuts?"

"Yes, and they're only superficial. Both he and Jack are fine."

"Poor Tom. He must be terrified by all this."

Lucky had shown up with Tom and the baby more than an hour ago but had not been let in. Nor had anyone else. The police had closed the restaurant and sent the staff and customers home, pretending a gas leak had been detected under the street.

Jack had managed to get a call out to Lucky to let her know they were all safe.

No one had been hurt except for Eve Vincent. Her real name was Gretchen LeSeur, according to Inspector Singleton from Interpol.

She'd sustained injuries from being hit twice, the first time by the wrought-iron chair Ray had thrown through the glass door leading to the veranda, the second by the rock he'd picked up and used to clobber her once he'd stepped inside.

Ray had found the rock next to the door of Houdini's bird cage. The Burning Eye of Ra, a priceless meteorite, had been used by Tom to weight down a board to try and keep his pet contained. Still affixed to it were two classification tags with inventory numbers, placed there years ago by the museum in Cairo. They attested to its authenticity.

Singleton came in and sat down at the table. They were pleased to have Gretchen LeSeur in custody, he said. She was the suspect in a number of thefts in Germany, France and England, but they'd had no idea she was in the U.S. or involved with Martin Charles Taylor. Their surveillance hadn't detected her.

"Mrs. Wright—Ms. Webster," he corrected himself, for he now knew the whole story of her background, "you're a very lucky woman. When our people saw a man climbing the side of your building, they naturally assumed it was the thief and moved in."

"I think my father did all right without your help, Inspector, as much as I appreciate it."

"Yes, quite so. He not only recovered stolen property and caught a killer, but he saved your life, as well."

"Yes, he did. With help from my brother and Mr. Lewis here." She thought of someone else who had contributed. "*And* Houdini," she added. "If he hadn't flown across the room and talked when he did, scaring Gretchen into dropping the knife, I think she would've killed me."

"Your father's background suggests he shouldn't

be climbing buildings, breaking into houses and flinging rocks at people. And I'm left with the puzzling problem of what to do about you."

"Emma wasn't involved in the theft," Whit said quickly. "Nor did she know she had the Eye. We've already explained that."

"Yet she did have it in her possession, and she concealed her identity and her relationship with Patrick Logan from you and therefore us. Had she not done that, we might have recovered the object sooner."

"That's an interesting position," Whit said, trying to remain cordial. He sensed an ally in Singleton, and he wanted to be careful how he handled this. "As I recall, you didn't even know what Taylor was after until we handed it to you. You might say we saved your bacon."

Singleton smiled. "Another one of your colorful expressions, Mr. Lewis, and unfortunately one with which I cannot argue. You did, indeed 'save my bacon.'"

"Is Emma a suspect? Because if she is, this discussion ends here and we request a lawyer."

"We have no plans at the moment to file charges against her—or you. Ms. Webster is not a suspect. Nor is her father in trouble."

"Good, because it seems to me that you ought to be going after Al Juneau and Martin Charles Taylor rather than sitting here wondering what to do about one small female and one old ex-con."

"Yes, you're right, of course. We've taken Mr. Juneau into custody, and he'll be questioned about his involvement. He's already attempting to make a deal in return for information on Mr. Taylor."

"Will he get a deal?" Emma asked.

"Perhaps. Taylor is the one we want, although I'm not convinced we have sufficient evidence to move on him, even with Juneau's cooperation."

That sent Emma flying into a rage. "Not enough evidence? My God! He commissioned the theft of the Eye *twice,* he got Marie Marshall killed and he's behind my attempted murder. What the hell else do you people need?"

Whit put his hand on her arm, a signal to calm down and not inflame the situation.

"Ms. Webster, you must understand that Mr. Taylor is a respected businessman of an advanced age. He also has a vast fortune, and that provides him with a certain amount of...sympathy...among elected officials in your government. We must deal with authorities in Egypt, as well. We cannot accuse Mr. Taylor of any crime based on circumstantial evidence. Juneau has agreed to testify against him, but it is still Juneau's word against Mr. Taylor's. And Juneau isn't the insider LeSeur is. He is a helper, a facilitator. Not a thief. His tenure with Taylor has also been shorter than LeSeur's."

"What about my testimony? Gretchen admitted to me that Taylor is her employer, that he offered her six million dollars to steal the Eye."

"Alas, given your theft of the identity of Susan Roberts, a court would say your credibility leaves a great deal to be desired. Your testimony would be of value only if backed with hard evidence."

"Oh, this is just great! Taylor's behind everything,

and you're telling me you're going to sit on your ass and let him get away with it. This is too much. What do you need to tie him to the theft, to any of the thefts? I want him to pay for what happened to Marie.''

''A taped confession would be nice,'' Singleton said. Whit snorted. They were daydreaming if they thought *that* would ever happen. ''We need irrefutable evidence of his involvement in the crime, and we need to know where he's hiding the objects he's previously stolen. Those two things would give us leverage for securing the search warrants we need.''

''What about Gretchen LeSeur?'' Whit asked. ''Will she turn on Taylor?''

''It's possible but unlikely, since she's facing charges of murder and attempted murder. Unfortunately, we don't have her cooperation. She could provide information about crimes going back far more years than Juneau could.''

''At least back to 1983,'' Emma said. ''She admitted to me she was working with Patrick then, and Patrick was working for Taylor at that time, because he told me so himself.''

''Our window of opportunity is quickly closing,'' Singleton continued. ''We've put out a cover story for what happened here tonight, but that will hold only so long. We have perhaps forty-eight hours before Mr. Taylor learns that Juneau and Ms. LeSeur are in custody. With Ms. LeSeur in the hospital, that eliminates any chance of her cooperation within our time frame.''

''She'd never cooperate, anyway,'' Emma said.

"And I wouldn't advise you to trust her if she offered."

"You're very likely right in that assumption, Ms. Webster. Using her in a sting against Taylor was a remote possibility from the outset."

"A sting?" Emma asked.

"Yes. It means—"

"Inspector Singleton, I already know what *sting* means. It was probably the first word I learned as a child."

"Yes, forgive me. I'd forgotten your...former occupation. What we need is Gretchen LeSeur, a *cooperative* Gretchen LeSeur, to help us set up Taylor. But we don't have that."

Emma seemed thoughtful for a moment, and then a strange expression came over her face. She looked at Whit, then at the inspector. Her mouth curved into a truly evil grin.

"Ah, but you do."

"NO!" WHIT SAID, raising his voice. "You're not doing this."

Emma ignored him. "If you think I'm letting that bastard get away with allowing Marie to be killed because of his greed, you don't know me very well."

"And you're crazy if you think you can waltz in there pretending to be Gretchen and pull it off."

"I can do it. I know what she looks like, how she talks and acts. With photos I can easily duplicate her face and body. Singleton said he can supply those."

Gently he grabbed her shoulders and gazed into her eyes. "Emma, honey, it's too dangerous. If anything happened to you, I swear I'd die."

"Whit, he's an old man in his eighties with bad eyesight. What's he going to do, jump out of his wheelchair and chase me down?"

He threw up his hands in frustration. "You're not getting my point. He has people around him all the time, trained people who could break your neck with one hand if anything goes wrong. And Singleton says Taylor's personal assistant rarely leaves his side. He's probably seen Gretchen more than once. And *his* eyesight's fine."

Okay, that was a problem. "Then we'll have to get rid of him somehow."

"How are you going to get Taylor to cooperate?"

"One of the first things Ray taught me was that if you dangle the right carrot, the rabbit will always bite."

"What kind of carrot are you talking about?"

"I don't know yet. Planning isn't my strength, but luckily I know somebody who's really good at it."

"Oh, God, don't tell me. You and Ray working together again, pulling a scam. That's all we need."

It *was* pretty ironic—but she had the opportunity to use her skills for the right reason, and she wasn't going to lose it. "Whit, please back me up. I've been running away from who I am all my life, but I'm no longer ashamed to be Emma Webster, because I'm the only one who can do this. I can bring Taylor down."

He wasn't easily persuaded. They argued for more than twenty minutes. But he was a reasonable man. He accepted that Taylor wouldn't be brought to justice unless she pulled this scam.

"Okay, you've convinced me," he said finally. "If

you're determined, I'll help, but I want you to let me negotiate with Singleton for what you'll get out of the deal. I'm not letting you put your life on the line for nothing.''

''Thank you. I knew you'd come through for me. Now, tell that cop at the door that if I don't get to see my son in the next five minutes, I'm going to flip out and do bodily harm to someone.''

''I'll see what I can do.''

AUNT LUCKY SAID no one had been hurt, but Tom still worried. He paced the restaurant kitchen, unable to sit still any longer. The cops hadn't let him go upstairs or even use the intercom. The later the night grew, the more upset he became.

He was ashamed of how he'd acted before, not talking to his mom, telling her he hated her and would never forgive her. He just wanted her to be okay.

He looked up and saw her standing in the doorway.

He rushed to her, not caring that he was supposed to be a man, and that men didn't cry in public. ''I'm sorry,'' he said, clinging to her. ''I didn't mean it before. I don't hate you.''

She held him and cried, too. ''I know you don't.'' She rubbed his back and patted it, like she had done when he was little and had fallen off his bicycle or scraped an elbow. ''It's okay, baby. Everything's going to be all right.''

Tom closed his eyes and held on tight, afraid to let her go. For once, he didn't mind being treated like her little boy.

CHAPTER SIXTEEN

THE STRATEGY WAS SIMPLE. Put a wire on Emma. Fool Taylor into thinking she was Gretchen. Get him to confess on tape.

Whit knew, though, that implementing it would be much harder. First, in order to control the game and eliminate the variables, they had to convince Taylor to come to them. Next, they had to keep Taylor's assistant from getting on Taylor's private jet in Los Angeles, making sure his absence didn't arouse his boss's suspicions. When Taylor arrived in Saint Augustine, Emma's job would begin. She'd have to bluff her way past Taylor's bodyguards.

They spent Sunday and Monday getting ready. The California team included Ray, Jack and members of the joint FBI-Interpol task force, one of them being Special Agent Lawrence Ebeckie. The three flew out Monday night and would be assisted by the authorities in L.A.

Since Ray was on parole, Inspector Singleton had secured permission for him to travel. If this scam worked, though, Ray would be sitting pretty. Whit had extracted a promise from Singleton and Ebeckie that they'd both do what they could to have the remaining year of Ray's probation canceled. The Florida team included Singleton, more FBI agents to be used as backup at the hotel, Emma and Whit.

Lucky was miffed at not being allowed by Singleton or Jack to help—until Emma said she needed her to play Marilyn on Monday night. Illusions was offering free dinners to the patrons evacuated on Saturday by the fake gas leak. Emma needed her to pretend to be Susan Wright and schmooze with the crowd while she worked on her disguise. Tom would baby-sit Grace.

Getting Taylor to agree to come to Florida proved to be easier than expected. Juneau dangled the carrot. Gretchen had recovered the Eye, Juneau told him in a coded telephone call, but she had another buyer offering more money. If Taylor wanted the artifact, he needed to fly in on Tuesday and personally handle the negotiations. The trap was set. Emma only had to spring it.

RAY HAD GOTTEN his start in crime early, stealing from the corner store and shilling. He'd run carny cons, bar games, tried gambling stings and worked every hustle invented, even invented a few himself, all the while trying to avoid the cops. This was the first time he'd ever worked *for* them.

The Lewis fella had explained what he had to do. He needed to take this assistant of Taylor's—Hardesty was his name—out of commission for a couple of hours so he'd miss the plane and Emma wouldn't have to worry about her cover being blown. The FBI could put him on ice, but that was risky. If Taylor didn't hear from the guy, or didn't think his excuse was legit, he might not make the trip to Florida.

Ray had to find a way to keep Hardesty busy, at least until Taylor was in the air, and not make him or Taylor suspicious while Emma did her job. No problem. When you wanted to tie somebody up, Ray had learned that the best approach was to use red tape.

Hardesty came to work at Taylor's mansion every morning at nine, using the same route, or so Ray'd been told by the FBI guy. Ray waited for the signal from the lookout, watched the white Mercedes turn the corner and timed his walk into the street perfectly. He banged the side of the car hard with his fist and fell to the ground screaming.

The car squealed to a stop. Hardesty jumped out. A crowd had already started to form and Ray did the best acting job of his life, groaning and carrying on like he was about to kick the bucket right then and there.

When the cops came, J.T. stepped forward right on cue. "I saw the whole thing," he told the officer in charge. He pointed at Hardesty. "That man there hit this poor old guy trying to cross the street."

"I didn't even see him," Hardesty said. He kept saying that over and over. Even as they tested him for alcohol consumption and took him to the squad car, he said to anybody who'd listen, "I didn't even see him."

"Can I call my employer?" he asked the cop.

"From the station. Then we need your statement."

"But I'm supposed to leave town on a business trip in an hour."

"You're not going anywhere today, buddy."

Paramedics put Ray on a stretcher. Before the doors closed, he lifted his head, looked at J.T. and winked.

EMMA HAD CONCERNS about her disguise. Excessive sweat could make the latex appliance slip and look false. With no means for a touch-up, she'd have to get in and out quickly. *And* remain calm. Another, bigger problem was adding twenty-five pounds to her figure. Normally she used a padded bodysuit when she needed to appear larger, or she stuffed her clothing. Neither was an option this time. Whit warned she had to *feel* as well as look, talk and act like Gretchen. Taylor's bodyguards might search her.

She chose a modified suit, padding covered with a poured latex outer shell. She'd gotten the idea for partial molding from watching a horror film five or six years ago where the creature creators had used it to make vampires. The same technique would work here. The molded latex would feel like skin under the dark pants and shirt she'd wear to mimic Gretchen's.

When she put on her new body, she was like a big rubber doll. From her knees to her shoulders was latex, except for a space cut out to allow her to go to the bathroom. The appliance was cumbersome and heavy, but the effect was perfect. It even had a place to conceal the transmitter for the wire she'd wear, and keep it insulated so it wouldn't set off any metal detectors. The microphone would be hidden in a brooch pinned to her shirt. She asked Whit for his opinion.

"Good job," he said, "but let's put it to the test." He did a thorough search, as a guard might, running his hands all over her. She thought he was enjoying his task a bit too much. When he touched her breasts, she protested.

"They won't do that!"

"Don't bet on it. You're a woman. They'll probably be men. Which means they'll cop a feel if they can get away with it. You need to be prepared."

"The joke's on them. My breasts aren't real."

"They look it. They even have nipples. I could get off on this."

"Well, don't. Not right now."

"It's like feeling up a life-sized Barbie. I always did have a thing for her as a kid. My sisters had twenty or more of them and I'd sneak in and take off their clothes."

"Why, you little pervert." He moved to the crotch of her pants. She sucked in her breath. "Now, I *know* they won't try that."

"No, that's the Lewis touch."

"Oh, is that how you searched female prisoners when you were in the FBI?"

"Only the special ones," he joked, leaning over to rake her earlobe gently with his teeth, knowing that drove her nuts. His fingers continued to stroke and tease. "I'm very good at certain types of interrogation. I'll bet I can have you squealing in no time."

She had to bite her tongue to keep from begging him to do it. "I don't doubt you can. But later, please. I'll put on something naughty and you can strip-search me. I'll play the thief and you can be the big, bad policeman who catches me."

"Mmm," he said, grinning.

"Right now, though, you need to stop arousing me. I have to finish my face. And I want you to go to the storeroom and find me a knife, something that looks realistic but that I won't accidentally cut myself with."

His hand fell away. "You can't go in armed."

"Have to. Juneau says Gretchen never goes anywhere without that knife concealed in her boot, and the FBI won't let me have the real one because it's evidence. If Taylor's bodyguards have searched her before, they'll know about it and be expecting it. Right?"

"Right," he said with reluctance.

"Then let's get on with it. Taylor's plane will be here in two hours."

MENTAL PREPARATION WAS as important as the disguise. By the time Emma took the elevator to Taylor's third-floor suite at the Ritz-Carlton, she had become Gretchen, right down to the bitchy attitude. Juneau commented on it as they rode up. So did the FBI agent assigned to keep Juneau from escaping.

She told Juneau she didn't want his damn compliments. All she wanted him to do was get her inside and shut the hell up. The man gave her the creeps. True, he'd supplied her with information on how Gretchen would talk to Taylor and how she'd act, but he was as bad as both of them, as far as she was concerned. If she didn't need his help to pull this off, she'd lobby for him to be sent away for a very long time.

Whit and Singleton were in a room one floor below with the recording equipment. She said into her microphone, "If this guy does something stupid and gets me killed, I want you to make sure he pays for it." She wasn't sure about Singleton, but she knew Whit would follow through.

Taylor had wanted the meeting to take place at the airport. Juneau had declined on "Gretchen's" behalf, citing too much hassle getting through security and her desire to meet on more neutral territory. This was better for their side. If anything happened, agents could be in the suite in a minute. They'd been posted throughout the hotel, some on the same floor disguised as housekeeping staff, others on the floor below at the stairwell.

The elevator doors opened, and only Emma and Juneau walked out. Two burly men flanked the door to Taylor's suite down the hall. They led them inside into the foyer before they checked for weapons. Juneau turned over his gun, Emma the knife in her boot. The men patted them down, anyway. Whit was right. The guards took liberties. Emma stood there trying to look bored while the one guy groped her.

"Dammit! Get your jollies on your own time," she spat irritably. Although her brooch and earrings set off the metal detector as expected, they allowed her to keep her jewelry. Dubbed "clean," Emma was taken into a living room larger than her whole apartment. Juneau was told to stay behind. Martin Charles Taylor sat near the windows in his wheelchair.

"Gretchen, my dear," he said. The electric motor hummed as he moved forward. "How good of you to come. Would you like a drink?"

"No, thanks. Let's just get on with this."

"Dear Gretchen. Always so impatient. Did you bring the Eye with you?"

"Of course not. We still have to come to an understanding."

He chuckled. "You don't trust me. Even after all these years."

"I don't trust anyone, Martin, but especially not you."

"That's what I like about you, Gretchen. Always to the point. Never afraid to speak your mind."

"I have photographs to confirm my possession of the Eye." She took them out of her bag and walked them over. Singleton had said the optimum distance for the microphone was five feet. When she reached it, she didn't move back.

Taylor looked through the stack of photos. "Excellent. And you checked the label numbers to make sure they correspond? I see them here, but my eyesight is failing me."

"Yes, the numbers are correct."

"Have I told you of the Eye's legend?" he asked. Emma shrugged, not sure how she should answer. "Hatshepsut used its power to rule Egypt, but many believe it can also restore vitality. Do you think that's possible?"

"No, I don't. But I don't really care what you do with it as long as—"

"I know—as long as you get your money. Now, what is this nonsense Mr. Juneau tells me about an increase in your fee? Six million is more than adequate."

"A girl has expenses."

"You've solicited another buyer, I understand."

"This was a difficult job. You had me kill to get information on the Eye's whereabouts. That should be worth more to you."

"Ah, yes, the unfortunate Mrs. Marshall. Killing for me never bothered you before. Why does it now?"

That threw Emma for a moment. She hadn't really thought about Gretchen having murdered others besides Marie. "Killing doesn't bother me. You know better than that, Martin. But it does increase my risk. More risk, more money."

"Very well. Eight million. I'll have the money wired to your account in the Cayman Islands, but give me until six o'clock. My assistant had a slight traffic accident this morning and will be out of touch for a few more hours."

"Make it ten million and we have a deal."

"I could order Mr. Weiss or Mr. Donner to shoot or torture you. I'm sure if we were diligent enough we would uncover where you've hidden the meteorite."

"Probably, but it might take you another ten or fifteen years to find it again if I don't talk. Do you have the time to wait and see?"

His thin lips curved into a smile. "Greedy bitch. But smart."

"Just like you, Martin. That's why we get along so well."

He liked that. The old guy threw back his head and had a good laugh.

"Where will you put the Eye, Martin? Will you stick it on a shelf somewhere to collect dust?"

He gave her a quizzical look. "Collect dust? Are you mad? Didn't you seal it upon possession?"

Emma realized she'd made a mistake, and quickly recovered. "Yes, it's protected."

"It must not be subjected to air, light or moisture. Erosion of the iron may already have damaged it."

"Don't worry. I've been careful. *You've* got a secure place for it, I hope."

"Yes, of course. I'll place it in a hermetically sealed case in my vault in San Simeon with the rest of my treasures."

With that last bit of information, Emma had gotten everything Singleton requested. Time to make her exit.

"I'll be back with the Eye," she told Taylor. Walking to the chair, she picked up her purse. "Naturally I'll check my account first to make sure the money has been transferred."

"When you return, we'll discuss a sapphire in India that I'd like you to secure for me."

"Sure, Martin," she said. She walked through the apartment, casually retrieved her knife in the foyer and left. Only when she got into the elevator alone did she sag in relief. Gretchen's personality faded and Emma's returned.

She pushed the button for the second floor. By now the agents would already be moving up the stairs to make the arrests. The elevator stopped, the doors opened and the most handsome man she knew was standing there to greet her. She flew into his arms.

"You were fabulous," Whit said. He twirled her around and around, making her laugh. "But no more intrigue for a while. Agreed? My heart can't take it."

"Agreed." She slipped her hand in his. "Take me home, Whit. The only game of cops and robbers I want to play from now on is with you."

EPILOGUE

Four months later...

I DIDN'T FEEL COMFORTABLE doing it, but Ray said I had to if I wanted to keep Abby happy. She'd planned an elaborate wedding reception for a couple getting married at six o'clock and the model for the live centerpiece had abruptly canceled. Abby wanted me to fill in.

Putting on a wedding dress, standing for two hours on top of a giant fake cake and pretending to be a bride was as close to torture as I could imagine. I'd told Abby no. She'd promptly fled in tears. Now Ray was pleading her case.

"You promised her you'd help," he said from my office doorway. "Ain't like you to go back on your word." He was in town with Jack, Lucky and the baby for a weekend visit, and he liked hanging around the restaurant with me, sticking his nose into my business. The truth is, I liked it, too.

"Yes, I promised her, but I didn't mean I'd play the *bride!*"

I don't have anything against brides, but since I was never going to be one, I was having trouble mustering enthusiasm for the role.

In the wake of the sting I'd pulled on Martin Charles Taylor, my life had taken a crazy turn. Ray,

Jack and I were celebrities—not always a good thing, I'd come to discover. Ray loved the exposure, of course. Jack and I simply tried to survive it and go about our business as usual.

Newspapers...television...magazines—they'd all carried the story about how a family of former con artists had worked with the FBI and Interpol to bring down the largest art theft ring in history. I couldn't answer the phone without someone wanting an interview. Suddenly I was colorful and interesting to the world, or at least to some of it.

I shouldn't complain. Whit had successfully negotiated with Inspector Singleton and government agencies not to prosecute me on any charges. He'd even managed to clear up my "misunderstandings" with the Internal Revenue Service, the bank and the Social Security Administration about the use of the Susan Roberts name. I was legally Emma Webster again. I had a clean slate.

Tom had decided that he too was a Webster. The court had approved the name change last week. He hadn't enlisted in the navy on his eighteenth birthday, as I'd feared. He'd applied to the U.S. Navy Academy, where he could go to college and prepare for a career as an Operations Diver.

If he didn't get accepted, he was hopeful of a Naval Reserve Officers Training Corp scholarship to the University of Central Florida in Orlando, which would accomplish the same goal.

I was on my way to college, too. Well, I hoped to take some classes later in the year. Recently I'd passed my high school equivalency exam and been awarded a diploma.

The only uncertainty in my life was Whit. I loved

him. And that was the problem. Public opinion of me wasn't all favorable. Taylor had powerful friends. To keep him from being prosecuted, they were trying to smear my name.

My past indiscretions were rising up to bite me. Because I worried that the fallout from my notoriety would damage Whit's reputation, whenever he suggested it was time to tie the knot, I hesitated. We'd gone as far as getting a marriage license, but I hadn't been able to make myself set a date.

I *wanted* to marry him. But I didn't know how to do it without ruining his life.

"Emma, don't be hardheaded," Ray said. "Help your friend out."

He brought my thoughts back to the immediate problem—Abby. How did I keep getting roped into her crazy party plans? I decided it must be a flaw in my character. One of many.

"All right," I told Ray with a sigh. "I'll do it. But this is the very last time."

A little while later, as I slipped into the wedding gown, I had to fight back tears. This was exactly the type of dress I would have bought for myself. Simple but breathtaking. The darn thing fit me perfectly.

Abby had thought of almost everything. "I want this to be as realistic as possible," she'd told me when she'd suggested the party theme a few weeks back. "I'm paying the photographer to take extra pictures we can use to promote the business."

I put on the lace garter edged in blue and tucked the new penny she'd left for good luck into my shoe. I saw no reason to point out that if I was a real bride, she'd missed giving me something old and something borrowed.

"Princess, can I come in?" Ray called from the other side of my dressing room door.

"It's open."

He walked in and stopped abruptly. "You're beautiful." His voice cracked.

"I don't feel beautiful. I feel...foolish." Reaching back, I tried unsuccessfully to do up the buttons at the rear of the dress. "I can't fasten these."

He helped me, and then fastened my train and veil. I didn't dare look at myself in the mirror. I was miserable enough. No need to make things worse.

I sniffed back tears. Ray handed me his handkerchief, and I wiped my eyes. "Thanks. I'm weepy today for some reason. Must be allergies."

"In December?"

"Mmm, it happens. Is that a new suit?" He said it was. "You look very nice. Handsome."

I tried to give the handkerchief back, but he refused it. "Why don't you borrow it for tonight? You might get weepy again."

"Thanks." I tucked it up my sleeve.

Something borrowed.

"Isn't it time to go yet?" I asked. "I want to get this over with."

Ray looked at his watch. "Almost." He reached in his pocket and drew out a piece of folded tissue paper. "I have something I wanna give you. I've been carryin' it around for twenty years or so."

Inside the paper was a cheap tarnished ring, an old fragrance ring, like I'd once wanted as a teenager. I opened the inside. The waxy perfume had long ago dried up.

"I don't understand, Ray."

"The day we pulled that last scam together, when

you was a kid, before you...left. It was Christmas. Remember? You saw these rings in a window. You acted like you didn't want one, but I knew you did."

"I remember."

"I went back the next day and got this. I bought it, too. Didn't steal it. I was gonna give it to you for a present."

"You were?"

"When you ran off, I kept it in my pocket so I'd have somethin' that made me feel close to you. Even held on to it in prison. I swore one day I'd find you and watch you put it on. Didn't figure on it takin' this long."

He threaded it through a chain and put it around my neck.

Something old.

"This is the best present I ever had." I fingered it. Back in 1979 it had probably only cost him ten dollars, but it was as precious to me as if he'd spent a million.

"It ain't much," he said, "but I hope when you look at it, you'll know what you mean to me. I love you, Princess. I always have. I ain't been a good parent. Never really knew how till I seen J.T. with little Gracie and you with Tom. But I swear to do better. I'm never gonna hurt you again. That's the God's honest truth."

Tears flowed down my cheeks. "Oh, Daddy, I love you, too." I threw my arms around his neck and hugged him.

"Girl, I've been waitin' thirty-eight years for you to call me Daddy."

"I've been waiting a long time to feel like I *could*

call you Daddy. Using the word never felt right before.''

''I know. But things is different between us from now on. I'm a new man.''

''You certainly are. I can't believe you're giving away that five-million-dollar reward from the insurance company for finding the Eye. That's your *big score,* Ray, the one you've been waiting for all your life, and you earned it honestly. Don't you want it? Now that you're no longer on parole, you're free to go anywhere, do whatever you want.''

He'd set up a family trust to fund worthy causes. The first project was a work center for non-violent offenders. A portion of their income would be used to pay restitution to their victims.

''Aw, hell, girl, I'm where I wanna be. And what would I do with that kind of money? I'm rich enough. I got you and Tom and J.T. and Lucky and Grace. I'm even sorta gettin' to like that Lewis fella. He grows on you.''

''He said the same thing about you.''

He checked his watch again. ''Well, we better quit gabbin' and go or Abby'll have her britches in a knot about somethin'. He held out his arm to help me, very much the gentleman.

Navigating the hallway and the steps in the long train took us several minutes. A very nervous Abby met us at the door to one of the private banquet rooms. She had truly outdone herself with white lattice arbors, roses and other flowers to create a Victorian garden setting. I'd never seen a more beautiful room and I told her so.

''Hurry up! Hurry up!'' she said. ''The wedding's

over and the guests are due to arrive any minute. We have to get you in place.''

She guided me toward the huge cake that dominated the room. The bottom tier would serve as the buffet table and hold the real cakes, the champagne fountain and the food. The effect was fabulous.

''How does this work?'' I asked.

''You'll see.''

She'd fixed two trap doors, one in the base of the cake and another that opened on top. I had to bend over and squeeze through the first door, then climb a short ladder to the second.

''You owe me for this, Abby,'' I told her, as I popped my head through the top hole. Somehow I forced yards and yards of satin and lace through the small opening. I'd probably never get back down again.

I stepped to the front, under the heart-shaped arbor, and tried to straighten the train so it wouldn't get wrinkled. I'd be standing beside the male model Abby had hired to pose as the groom. We would look like the decoration on top of the wedding cake.

''Abby, am I supposed to have a bouquet?'' I called across the room.

She snapped her fingers. A minute later she appeared with one. ''I'll send it up with the groom,'' she said as she disappeared around the back. A moment later, the trap door squeaked open behind me and a male hand reached around and handed me the flowers.

''Thanks.''

''My pleasure,'' said a deeply masculine and very familiar voice.

I froze. No! Abby wouldn't dare do this to me.

Holding my breath and praying I was wrong, I turned. Whit looked down at me and smiled. For one of the few times in my life, I was at a loss for words. They formed in my head, they even tried to come out, but they got stuck. I opened my mouth, but when only a hiccup bubbled out, I quickly shut it.

"You know, Emma, I think I like you best like this," he said. "Speechless. Unable to argue."

"What are you doing here? You said you couldn't get away for another visit for a couple of weeks."

"I'm the groom," he said matter-of-factly.

My gaze skimmed the black tuxedo, noting the way it hugged his rugged frame. The man could wear a potato sack and look good, but right now he was as sexy as I'd ever seen him.

But the image of the two of us, side by side and dressed in wedding garb, was too much for me to withstand. I shook my head. "You can't play the groom."

"Emma, I'm not *playing* the groom. I *am* the groom."

"I don't understand."

"The only wedding taking place tonight is *our* wedding. The catering job, the cake, the dress—everything was an elaborate ruse to get you here. You're being pigheaded about getting married, so I got your family to help me. To put it simply, sweetheart, you've been conned."

A scam? No way!

The doors to the room flew open and people started filing in. Jack, Lucky and Grace, Tom, the staff from the restaurant and Whit's business, Santiago, Tony and his family, other friends.

"You remember my mom and dad," Whit said,

indicating an older couple in the front. They smiled and waved. I'd met them one weekend when I'd flown with Whit to Pittsburgh. "Those lovely creatures with them are my sisters accompanied by their husbands and children. You've met Cassie, but the others you don't know. That's Barb," he said, pointing at the blonde. "The other one is Jan. My grandmother is the ravishing beauty with the white hair. She flew in from Nepal especially for the ceremony. She's been communing with Sherpas or looking for the Yeti or some outrageous thing." The woman blew him a kiss.

Abby came around the side of the cake accompanied by a man. "And here's the preacher."

Ray stepped forward. "Don't be mad, Princess. Whit said he was gonna marry you even if he had to trick you into it. And, well, that got me thinkin' maybe trickin' you wasn't such a bad idea. So we held a family meeting and came up with a plan."

With disbelief, I stared at each face before me and then at Whit. I couldn't imagine how he'd gotten away with it. I hadn't suspected for an instant. "You thought of everything, didn't you?" I asked.

"No," he said softly, reaching out and pulling me gently to him. "I didn't plan on you turning me down. I'm not sure what I'll do if that happens. I love you, Emma."

My hand skimmed the front of his shirt and settled on his arm. "I can't believe you engineered this scheme. What am I going to do with you?"

"How about marrying me and making me the happiest man on earth? We have the ring and the preacher. Our friends and family are here."

I asked everyone to step back a moment and allow us to talk privately.

"But Whit, we have so many problems. Where would we live? How can we run businesses in different states?"

"We'll work it out. I'll open a branch office here, if I have to. Or you can open a second restaurant in Pittsburgh and let Abby and Santiago run this one. They're getting married in the spring, you know."

"She told me. That *would* be a nice wedding gift for them, wouldn't it, giving them part-ownership in Illusions?"

"Yes, but even if you don't want to do that, remember I can fly us back and forth as often as you want."

"Whit, I—we've never talked about children. I'm almost thirty-nine. I have a grown son. I'm too old to raise any more babies. With me, you wouldn't have children."

"I'd have Tom. I've come to love him like my own son."

"Of course you have, but I'm talking about biological children. If you married someone younger, you could still have a family."

"That's not important to me, Emma. I'm content with waiting for Tom to give us grandchildren."

He took a gold band from his pocket and handed it to me. I read the inscription. *Always,* it said, along with *Emma and Whit* and the date. The names *Susan, Rachel, April* and *Jennifer* were also there in tiny letters. I laughed.

"I wasn't taking any chances," he said.

"So I see."

"I don't care what first name you use, as long as

the last name is Lewis. I'm crazy about you. Let's get married."

"But Taylor's vowed to ruin me and anyone who helps me. His friends are bigwigs in Washington. He's respected."

"Taylor's finished. He might not go to prison because of his age, but the damage to him has already been done."

"He'll still try to hurt us."

"I don't doubt that, but he's not the person standing in the way of our happiness. Another person gets the credit for that."

"Who?"

"You. Either you want this marriage or you don't. The question is really that simple."

I wanted it. Everything I'd dreamed about stood in front of me. All I had to do was reach out and grab it.

I called everyone back. "Well, should I marry him?" I asked the crowd, unable to resist teasing Whit a bit longer. "He's bossy."

"And hardheaded," Cliff yelled, making everyone laugh.

"But in his favor," I said, "he is sweet. And he's nuts about me, which should count for something."

"Go for it, Mom!" Tom yelled.

"Do it!" Tony said.

Whit's mother told me she wanted me in the family.

"Aw, get on with it," Ray grumbled. "Some of us ain't gettin' any younger."

I nodded my approval, making everyone cheer. They gathered closer as the ceremony began. "Dearly beloved..."

When it came time for the pledge of vows, I had one last attack of panic. "Are you *sure* this is what you want?" I whispered for Whit's ears only.

"As sure as I've been of anything in my life."

"But—"

"Emma, do you love me?"

"Yes, Whit, I love you desperately."

"Then quit arguing and tell the man 'I do.' You're holding up the honeymoon."